Readers love the Precious Gems series by EM LYNLEY

Rarer Than Rubies

"This book is part travelogue, romance, and hot sex between two sexy men! If any of these appeal to you, this book's for you!"

—Guilty Pleasures

"…an action-packed, suspenseful love story… Ms. Lynley went into a lot of description and I felt like I was there on the streets enjoying the amazing food."

—Mrs. Condit & Friends Read Books

Italian Ice

"…the passion they display really heats up the pages."

—Literary Nymphs

"I highly recommend this one for the suspense and… You have a very good read here."

Night Owl Reviews

Jaded

"I am impressed each time I open a Precious Gems novel to see the level of creativity this author puts forth with each story. The depth of the mystery and the entertainment value alone are fabulous."

—Joyfully Jay

By EM LYNLEY

Bound for Trouble
Dirty Dining
Hostile Takeover
Out of the Gate
Sex, Lies & Wedding Bells

THE DELECTABLE SERIES
Brand New Flavor
Gingerbread Palace
An Intoxicating Crush
With Shira Anthony: Lighting the Way Home
Spaghetti Western

PRECIOUS GEMS SERIES
Rarer Than Rubies
Italian Ice
Jaded
24-Karat Conspiracy

Published by DREAMSPINNER PRESS
http://www.dreamspinnerpress.com

24-KARAT CONSPIRACY

EM LYNLEY

Published by
DREAMSPINNER PRESS

5032 Capital Circle SW, Suite 2, PMB# 279, Tallahassee, FL 32305-7886 USA
http://www.dreamspinnerpress.com/

24-Karat Conspiracy
© 2015 EM Lynley.

Cover Art
© 2015 Anne Cain.
annecain.art@gmail.com
Cover content is for illustrative purposes only and any person depicted on the cover is a model.

ISBN: 978-1-63476-042-3
Digital ISBN: 978-1-63476-043-0
Library of Congress Control Number: 2015902184
First Edition June 2015

Printed in the United States of America
∞
This paper meets the requirements of
ANSI/NISO Z39.48-1992 (Permanence of Paper).

Love is the only gold.

—Alfred, Lord Tennyson

PREFACE

THIS BOOK is Reed Acton's story. If you've been reading the series from the first book, *Rarer than Rubies*, you'll appreciate just how much Reed has changed over the years since he met Trent Copeland. When I started the series, I hadn't thought particularly about Trent or Reed's background. *Rubies* was my second published novel, and I was still learning my way around building interesting, layered, and compelling characters. It took a while for me to get the hang of it, and as Trent and Reed have grown as individuals and as a couple, I've been growing as a writer. It's only now I felt ready to tell this story.

The germ for *24-K* started several years ago when I was writing *Italian Ice*. I colored in Reed's past for myself, and I had to decide how much to tell in that second book. I wanted to keep more revelations about Reed for a future story, but they had to be things he wasn't ready to tell Trent. Reed has never been about emotions and sharing, while Trent is all emotions and sharing. Trent has been, literally, an open book from the start, but Reed has remained more of a mystery—to Trent and to himself.

I knew this book would reveal the story of Reed's family, and I knew exactly how and where the layers would get ripped away (no easy peeling back for Reed). But after *Italian Ice*, it didn't seem right to jump into another story focused on Reed, so I wrote *Jaded*, which is more Trent's story. It's also partly my story, in that it takes place in Japan, where I lived and worked for five years. *Jaded* was a challenge for me as a writer, and a book I'm very proud of. I couldn't have written it nearly as well as when the story idea first came to me.

I can't tell you how much I wanted to write *this* book, to share Reed's history with Trent and with you! The urge to write this book was incredible. As with *Jaded*, I wanted to do the story justice, so I didn't rush it. Writing a story with mystery and suspense elements takes time and concentration, so there was a bigger gap between *Jaded* and *24-K* than I anticipated. But now it's here. I hope you'll enjoy learning Reed's story as much I did telling it.

Trent and Reed have learned from each other and grown so much over the years. Their story doesn't end here. A new one begins.

—EM Lynley, April 2015

1

8,000 Feet over Turkey

ARSLAN KADER felt the twelve-seat Cessna Grand Caravan lurch beneath him.

The passengers stopped chatting, so the only sound was that of the turboprop's engine struggling against wind and air, interrupted by the sound of a crate sliding across the rear cargo area and hitting the wall of the fuselage with a sickening clunk and another shudder. That much weight shifting in the tail of the aircraft made it even more difficult to control.

"What's going on back there?" one of the passengers shouted through the opening between the cockpit and the cabin.

"A little turbulence." Arslan checked the gauges again. The choppy air caused the small plane to fight him for control. He felt rather than heard the crates shift again. He should have weighed each item and then stowed it himself. Why had he trusted these passengers?

An envelope full of cash—American dollars—had made him throw caution to the wind, literally.

"I should—" A stronger gust of wind rocked the plane. Arslan glanced back. "It's not safe with that crate unsecured. There is still time to find a small airport before we reach the mountains."

The passenger went aft and returned to his seat. Arslan heard him talking to the other man, the one who had paid him. He felt another shift and shudder.

"I can't fly safely like this."

"How long until our destination?"

"Three hours with good weather. Four like this."

The turbulence abated, and Arslan was able to get the aircraft under control again.

"See, we're fine," the passenger said.

"For now. Over the mountains the wind can change very quickly. I suggest we put down until this weather passes. I'll radio to the next airstrip. I'm not—"

"No radio. We told you that."

No radio and no flight plan. At their first meeting, when he'd balked at their conditions, they'd nodded, then stuffed more bills in the envelope.

"We heard you're the best at this."

"This" meaning flying to remote airports where he had friends working customs and the cargo wouldn't be inspected. At least he'd given the cash to his son before they took off.

The wind continued to buffet the plane, and the instruments only confirmed what he already knew. They were losing altitude and they'd already gone off course. He kept the plane steady with one hand on the yoke and grabbed for the map with the other. Was there any place flat to land safely if he couldn't convince them to land at an airport?

They were only thirty minutes into the flight from the tiny airport outside of Istanbul, already several hundred miles away.

A deafening crash quieted the passengers again. Two men and two women. Much younger women and clearly not wives. Arslan wasn't ready to risk his life just to keep the men's behavior secret from their families.

Arslan started praying, calling his wife's name, talking to her more than to himself.

Shana, the money should keep you comfortable for at least two years.

Arslan lowered the wing angle to regain list and keep the engine from stalling. But the shifting cargo made him overshoot and he struggled to correct and avoid going into free fall. The older male passenger rushed into the cockpit only to be thrown to his knees. He grabbed at Arslan's shoulder.

"Can't you control this thing?"

Arslan gripped the controls and raked his gaze over the bad news he read in every display and warning light. "No. I can't. Not anymore. We're landing whether you like it or—"

With a final loud shudder from the aircraft the weather, the extra weight, and the shifting crate combined to send the five souls off course permanently.

2

Los Angeles, California
December

"DO YOU know yet if you'll be working over Christmas?" Trent Copeland asked. He'd been avoiding this subject, but he couldn't wait any longer.

Reed Acton glanced up from the thick case file he had been reading, his expression simmering a notch below annoyance.

"How would I know that now? It's only the first week in December. I have no idea if I'll get called away for a case."

"Well, I guess that's not really my point. I wanted to talk about Christmas. About our plans for Christmas."

"Okay. What did you want to do?"

Trent glared at him for a second, then toned it back to a mild eye roll. "Reed, you realize that holiday travel plans need to be made months in advance? Not just a week or two?" The tone implied Reed required special education on the topic.

"Not really." Reed had never made holiday travel plans—or holiday plans at all—until he met Trent. And so far Trent had been happy to handle the arrangements, knowing Reed's job was unpredictable. "Did you want to go somewhere particular?"

"It's not what I want so much as…. You really don't remember this discussion?" Trent took a deep breath and released it slowly, then gave up waiting for a reply. "My parents got their flights booked, and—"

"Your parents? Where are they going?" Reed actually sounded interested in the answer.

"Here, Reed. They're coming to LA, don't you remember? We discussed this at Thanksgiving."

"I don't remember much about Thanksgiving. I was only at your parents' house for a day."

"I know." Trent put his reaction on pause. He should have expected Reed's selective amnesia to make an appearance. But this time Trent had to let Reed know what he wanted. Trent had made plans—plans he didn't want to change. If that didn't suit Reed, they'd find a compromise. "My parents want to spend Christmas with us this year. Last year it was too soon after Italy, and I didn't want them to see me until I was feeling better. Since you didn't enjoy Thanksgiving in Oklahoma at all, I thought it would work better if they come here. Then if you have to work again…." Trent waved one hand so he wouldn't have to say what he thought about how Thanksgiving had turned out. He promised himself he wouldn't get angry with Reed, or at least not to his face.

"You could go home to Oklahoma without me."

"Reed, this is home. LA. *You.* I want to spend Christmas with you too."

"Why? What's so special about Christmas?"

"It's *Christmas*. It's a time to get together with family and the people who mean most to us."

"Why?"

"Why what?"

"Trent, you don't have a regular nine-to-five, Monday-to-Friday job, and your parents are retired. You can get together with them whenever you want. Why is everyone making such a fuss over Christmas?"

"I'm not the one making a fuss. You are. I don't understand why you hate Christmas, so would you please tell me?" Trent was banging his head against a brick wall with a question like that, but if he didn't ask, Reed would never explain.

Reed stiffened and some emotion flashed over his face before he finally replied. "I don't want to talk about it."

Just what Trent had expected. He let out the pent-up breath as quietly as possible and went into his office and sat at the desk. He'd make his own plans with his parents, and Reed could join them if he wanted. It wasn't the optimum solution, but starting an argument with Reed wouldn't fix the problem. *Reed's* problem.

Trent picked up a framed photo from his desk. It had been taken at Christmas the previous year. His older brother Robbie, sister Maggie, and their families descended on the Copelands' house outside Tulsa and all managed to stay reasonably still for the split second required to take a group shot. His dad and brother wore Santa hats, and his mom wore a hideous red-and-green sweater his sister had knitted for her back in college. It was a family tradition. Maggie had become a much more accomplished knitter, but Mom still wore that monstrosity. It just wasn't Christmas without it.

Maggie had been happily married for a decade and might have some advice for dealing with Reed. Trent pulled his cell phone out of his pocket and speed-dialed her.

"Hello?" It was Ricky, his ten-year-old nephew.

"Ricky? It's Uncle Trent. How ya doing?"

"Great, Uncle Trent. How are you? Did you write a new book yet? Mom says I can't read them till I'm thirty, but maybe you'd e-mail me one anyway?"

Trent was not about to send his nephew any of his steamy gay romance novels, but the request made him smile.

"I'll think about it, Ricky. How's school?"

"Fine. I did this science project and I only got a B+. I think I should have gotten an A, but Mrs. McGrath won't change my grade."

"I'm sure that won't keep you from getting into college, Ricky."

"I'm only ten. I hope not. Do you have to go to college to be a fireman?"

"Probably not."

"Ricky, who're you talking to?" Trent could hear Maggie's voice in the background.

"Uncle Trent."

"Let me talk to him."

"When I'm done…. Mom!" There was a short scuffle and Maggie came on the line.

"Hi, Trent, what's new?"

"Hey, Maggie. I was having a nice conversation with Ricky. What did he do for his school project?"

"Oh, he did the one where you grow seeds in the dark and different amounts of light."

"Nothing much changes, does it?" They had all done that same project years earlier.

"Nope. So to what do I owe this call?"

"Yeah, I could use some advice. About Christmas."

"I was hoping that wouldn't be an issue. What can I do to help?"

"Reed doesn't want to make plans. He thinks I should go home to Mom and Dad's again. Without him."

"Why don't you, then?"

"It's not the actual plans that worry me. It's his refusal to discuss the topic. He doesn't want to be part of any holiday activities."

"Are you sure it's the holidays?"

"What else could it be? You saw what happened at Thanksgiving. He was there one day, and when his boss called, he practically ran to the airport. Didn't even want Mom and Dad to drive him."

"That *was* really something. But I don't think it's the holidays that are a problem. I think it's something else. Did you ask?"

"Of course I asked. He won't discuss it. I don't want an argument, but I can't ignore the issue if I want a long-term relationship with Reed." It had been nearly three years. That already *was* long-term for Reed.

"Do you want a long-term relationship with him?"

Trent opened his mouth to reply, then paused. What *did* he want? He'd been operating on the assumption that his relationship with Reed would keep going, but hadn't given much consideration to *where* it was going. "Yes. I think so."

"Well, until you know for sure, don't let this family stuff get in the way. But maybe you need to consider if he has the same long-term goals for a relationship that you do."

"Gee, Maggie, I asked for one simple thing, and now you have me reexamining everything about me and Reed."

"That's not what I intended, but it sounds like there are some areas where you two don't see eye to eye. You need to decide how important they are to you."

Trent sat back in his chair. "I get your point. Let me think about this for a while. Thanks."

Trent put the phone down and stared at the photo again. He had a few framed pictures on the desk and the walls. Hardly anyone printed out photos anymore; everything was digital and online. But Trent enjoyed looking up at the photos, reliving the moments. Would there be any photos from this coming Christmas? Trent should make his own plans, though. Maggie was right about that. Reed could join in if he wanted, but if he didn't, that wouldn't stop Trent.

He picked up the phone again and dialed his parents' number.

"Hello?" said a voice that sounded like a warm hug.

"Hi, Mom."

"Trent, honey. How are you?"

"Good. I got your e-mail with your schedule, and I'm really glad you're coming to LA. I'll be there to meet you at baggage claim. I'll make some plans, get tickets for a show and whichever museum has the best exhibition. Anything else you and Dad want to do?"

"Just to see you, dear. And Reed. He'll be there, too, won't he?"

Trent hesitated before replying. "I'm not sure what his plans are. He never knows in advance about work. You saw what happened at Thanksgiving."

"Ah. Work. I see." That noncommittal, nonconfrontational tone they must teach at Mom school.

Apparently he hadn't gotten any better at lying. He didn't have any good response.

"Look, Trent, if it's going to be any trouble, we don't have to go out there to see you." The hurt in her voice came through loud and clear.

"No, Mom. It's no trouble at all. I want you and Dad to come out here for Christmas. It'll be a nice change for you. Enjoy the nice weather, eat some fresh seafood. But maybe I'm being selfish."

"Selfish? Because Reed doesn't want to spend time with us? What did we do? We tried so hard to make him feel welcome."

"I know. That's not what I mean about being selfish. If you come here, you won't get to spend the holidays with Maggie or Robbie, and their kids."

"We see them all the time. We don't get to see *you* very often. We've already got their gifts, so we'll drop them off and have a holiday dinner at Maggie's before we fly out."

"That sounds nice." Trent would like to be there for a big family holiday dinner. Was he crazy to think bringing his parents to LA would be a substitute for the kind of holiday memories he loved? "I'll send something early, too."

"I'm sure the kids will be thrilled if you do." She paused. "We can't wait to see you. Less than two weeks now." He could almost see the little crinkles at the corners of her eyes when she smiled.

"Me too. Love you and Dad."

"Bye, sweetie."

He hung up, not necessarily pleased with the conversation. He'd assuaged his own guilt about monopolizing his parents this year, but he'd let his mother know that Reed wasn't particularly thrilled with their visit. He'd book them a room at a hotel around the corner so Reed wouldn't feel they were invading his home. It would probably be more comfortable for everyone, even if Reed insisted he was looking forward to seeing them.

Trent picked up the photo from last Christmas again and hoped his mother would bring that awful sweater. The thought of it brought a smile to his lips.

"Trent?" Reed's voice startled Trent, and he dropped the picture onto the desk. "Oh, sorry, didn't mean to interrupt."

Trent didn't turn toward the door. "What?"

"I made dinner. Well, I heated up the leftover pasta and made a salad. Aren't you hungry yet?"

"Yeah." Trent wasn't quite ready to talk to Reed. "I'll be out in a minute."

"Sure." Reed's footsteps moved in the direction of the kitchen.

Trent spent another few minutes staring at the photo before he followed.

REED HAD lit a couple of candles and put them on the table while he waited for Trent, but if Trent noticed, he didn't remark. This was Trent, Reed reasoned. Of course he noticed. Little romantic details like that were his job. That he didn't mention the candles was troubling. Why had Reed expected mere candles to smooth things over?

As it was, Trent barely said ten words during the meal. He didn't bring up Christmas, and Reed wasn't about to broach the subject either. Not yet. Not until he had to. He'd have to sooner rather than later; he knew that much.

After the meal Trent went back into the office, ostensibly to do some writing, but Reed didn't hear him tapping at the keyboard. He was probably looking at that photo again. Reed wished he knew the right thing to say or do, and it pained him that he couldn't explain why he hated holidays so much. He couldn't understand it himself, much less communicate to anyone else. Not even Trent.

He lingered over cleaning the kitchen, hoping Trent would come in for tea or dessert. He didn't.

Reed got ready for bed and put the Lakers' game on the bedroom television for about ten minutes, then picked up a book. How long would Trent hide in his office? Did he expect Reed to go in and apologize?

It was past midnight when Trent finally came into the bedroom.

"Oh, you're still up."

Reed looked up from his book. "Yeah. I just couldn't put this one down."

"Dan Brown or James Patterson?" Trent's sneer indicated what he thought of Reed's reading habits. He headed into the bathroom.

"Neither. Dumas. *The Three Musketeers*. Got it at Chapter Two." Trent's favorite used bookstore.

Trent stopped in the doorway and glanced back over his shoulder. Reed raised the slightly battered book as proof. Trent nodded and shut the bathroom door behind him. Usually he left it partially open when he got ready for bed. He came out wearing only a pair of worn gray sweats, tied at the waist—a bad sign. His cock flopped under the fabric as he walked toward the bed. He stopped to grab a T-shirt from a dresser drawer and pulled it on as he covered the last few steps. Another warning.

Putting clothes on for bed was Trent's version of a Do Not Disturb sign.

Trent pulled the sheets back and slid into bed, glancing briefly at Reed as he did so.

"How was your writing tonight?" Reed asked.

"Good night." Trent rolled over so his back was to Reed.

Reed closed the book and put it on the nightstand. He scooted under the sheets and turned toward Trent.

"Forget it, Reed."

"Forget what?" Reed couldn't help asking.

"Not interested in sex of any sort. Nothing, nada, niente, nichts, I don't know any more languages."

"Who said I wanted sex?"

"You're completely naked."

"Maybe I'm just warm tonight."

"Your nipples are hard, like you're cold. Not buying that."

"If you're so uninterested in sex, why are you paying attention to my nipples?" Fair question.

"They're so damn big. I'd have to be blind not to notice. Even then I'd notice. They're like Braille."

"I have Braille nipples? Is that meant to be an insult or a compliment?"

Trent didn't reply, but the bed shook slightly. Then Trent burst out laughing. "Shut up."

"Come over here and read my Braille nipples. Tell me what they say."

"Shut up." Trent nearly choked on the words he was laughing so hard.

Reed fought off his own laughter, but he couldn't help smiling.

Trent sat up and pulled off the T-shirt. "Now *I'm* hot."

"Then come over here and warm me up a little. You can rub my nipples and see if a genie comes out."

"What, a genie in your shorts?" But Trent rolled toward Reed, grinning.

"I'm not wearing any shorts, which you also noticed." Reed slid the covers down, in case Trent had forgotten. "Now you owe my nipples an apology."

"I do?"

"Yes. And I think your genie is ready to come out too." Reed glanced at the outline of Trent's cock, thickening under the thin fabric of his sweats. "Can I help?" He reached toward the string and waited for Trent to nod before he untied them.

Trent moved closer and leaned up for a kiss, causing his sweats to slide down his hips. Reed helped slip them down and wrapped a hand around Trent's cock while they continued to kiss. He certainly hadn't expected Trent to snap out of his anger so easily, but Reed was grateful. He intended to demonstrate just how much.

Reed moved between Trent's knees and took his cock into his mouth. He teased the head with his tongue and played with Trent's balls. He slowed his movements, drawing out Trent's enjoyment. Trent tangled his fingers in Reed's short hair, and when Trent was close, Reed pushed a couple of fingers inside until he found the spot that made Trent gasp. As his moans turned to a whimper, Reed increased the pressure, and with a huge shudder, Trent came and Reed swallowed everything gladly.

Trent smiled, looking a little guilty at enjoying his orgasm so much. He closed his eyes, and Reed thought he might have fallen asleep. Well, it served Reed right. He'd upset Trent, and a mere blowjob wasn't going to fix the problem.

But a moment later Trent rolled over and slid a hand down Reed's torso while leaning in to take a nipple into his mouth.

"Mmmrry."

"What?" Reed asked.

Trent let the nipple pop out of his mouth. "Just apologizing." He grinned. "To the nipple."

Reed lay back and relaxed, glad to see Trent playful again after the tense evening. Trent apologized to the other nipple and gave both plenty of attention while he used his hands on Reed. It wasn't the best orgasm Trent had given him, but it was sincere, and Reed appreciated the effort. He got up to get a warm washcloth, even though technically it was Trent's turn, and cleaned them both before sliding back under the sheets.

This time Trent didn't turn away.

Reed sat up and looked down at Trent, who lay on his side, head on his pillow. "What did you plan for your parents' visit?"

Trent furrowed his brow. "What?" He sat up.

"I heard you talking to your mom."

"I'm sorry, Reed, but I really can't talk about my parents when you've got dried come on your chin." He smiled and wiped at Reed's chin with a thumb. "Okay. Let's start over."

"What are the plans now?"

"I thought you weren't interested."

"That's not what I said. Am I not invited now?"

"I booked a room for them at the Andaz. They won't be in your way."

"They're not in my way. They can stay here if you want."

"I didn't think you liked spending time with them. And to be honest, they think you don't like them."

Reed shook his head. How could he explain? He was sorry he'd given the Copelands that impression. "It's not that. I just feel out of place."

"Well, that's why I thought bringing them here was a good idea. It's more neutral territory—or it's your place, since you live here now."

"It wasn't their *house*, Trent. That's not what upset me at Thanksgiving."

"Upset? You were upset? I thought you couldn't wait to leave."

"I didn't plan it that way, but going home with you..." Reed paused, recalling the pangs of envy he'd felt watching the hugs and smiles as the Copelands welcomed Trent, and how he'd hated himself for feeling that way, especially when Trent's family wanted to include him. "It made me realize that I don't have a place that's home to me. I don't have a family waiting at the airport to meet me. I don't have those things, and I didn't think I wanted them...." Reed stopped because a huge lump had formed in his throat and he couldn't breathe. An invisible elephant sat on his chest, crushing his ribs and lungs as his own family memories flowed over him.

Trent reached out to stroke Reed's arm. The hand was warm, the touch firm. "You never talk about your family, Reed. But you can, if you want to. I'm here to listen."

Reed nodded, not sure if he could—or should.

Trent couldn't leave a silence alone. He had to fill it. Had to say something he thought would make Reed feel better. "My family wants to get to know you. They want to include you. If you let them, they'll love you as much as—"

"As much as they loved Marc?" Reed wished he hadn't said that. Where had that idea even come from? He'd never compared himself to Marc—Trent's last partner, who had died in a sporting accident—before. Not out loud to Trent, anyway.

Trent smiled, but Reed noticed the flash of pain in his eyes. "No. As much as they love me. They want to love you too."

"They do?"

"Why does that surprise you so much?"

Reed looked away. He wasn't ready to answer that.

"Let's go to sleep. We can talk more in the morning." Trent leaned over and gave Reed a kiss, then turned off the light and settled back under the sheets. He scooted up against Reed.

Reed lay down, and Trent put an arm across his chest. Reed smiled even though Trent couldn't see it in the dark. He was glad they hadn't ended the day not speaking to each other.

But he still wasn't sure how he'd deal with the Copelands.

3

THREE DAYS before Christmas, they took Reed's black Bureau SUV to pick up the Copelands from LAX. Trent's parents were waiting outside baggage claim with a mountain of luggage. Reed popped the back door and got out, intending to help Trent load the cases, but Mrs. Copeland came around the back of the vehicle and intercepted Reed with a hug that probably violated the Geneva Convention. He held his arms away from his body, staring at Trent, trying to breathe, not sure how to respond. But she didn't let go. Reed lowered his arms, slid them around her, and squeezed back.

"Now that's a proper greeting, Reed." She let go and kissed his cheek. "How are you?"

"Good, thanks." He stepped back a pace and congratulated himself on surviving the hug. He hadn't burst into flames and no ribs had broken. In fact, it had been kind of nice after that initial powerful squeeze. She smelled like cinnamon with a hint of woodsy smoke, like a fireplace. "It's good to see you again."

Not so good to see the head-to-toe red-and-green ensemble she had on. She wore a white shirt sporting dancing candy canes and boughs of holly over poison-green grandma pants.

"Glad to be here, out of the cold," Mr. Copeland said. He had on a matching candy-cane shirt over plain old blue jeans. He held out his hand to shake Reed's, luring him into another embrace that ended with Mr. Copeland slapping Reed on the shoulder. If Reed couldn't fight off two elderly Oklahomans, he was losing his edge. "Gotta put on my Hollywood shades." Mr. Copeland took a pair of sunglasses out of his pocket and put them on. "Do I look like a big movie star?"

"Silly man!" Trent's mom said.

"I don't know," Reed replied. "I don't see many big movie stars around."

"Don't you? Why, we were hoping we'd see someone famous. Trent? Won't we see any stars?"

Reed glanced toward Trent and realized all the cases were already in the trunk. "Oh, Trent, I was going to help with that." So much for his hug-avoidance tactics. He needed to brush up on those flagging Army Ranger skills.

"I got the bags. It was your turn to get hugged. I'm surprised they had any energy left after all the hugging they gave me." Trent grinned.

Reed smiled. That had been his plan, which was why he'd waited a few moments before getting out. But the Copelands had saved some hugs for him anyway.

"Mrs. Copeland, come sit up front with me," Reed said and opened the front passenger door for her.

"What's this Mrs. Copeland nonsense? You call me Laura."

"Laura." At least she hadn't told him to call her Mom.

THEY DROVE to the Andaz, a small but luxurious hotel a block from their apartment, got Trent's parents checked in, and had the suitcases brought up to their room. Reed hovered at the edge of the small suite as the Copelands oohed and aahed over the accommodations.

"Trent, this place is too fancy for us. We could stay at the Holiday Inn. We don't need a suite. We're not going to be spending that much time here, are we?"

That last comment brought Reed up short. Now they were here, the reality set in that for the next ten days, Rob and Laura would be a constant presence in their lives. Did they expect to be at the apartment most of the time? Having them stay here meant they wouldn't be underfoot. That was how Trent had made it sound.

Why did that instill a rising dread in Reed's gut? He could always call his boss, Tom White, if he needed an escape hatch. Besides, there was just as much chance of a real case heating up during the holidays—with all that cash and so many distracted shoppers, crime rates soared this time of year.

"We want you to be comfortable," Trent replied.

"It's more comfortable than home," Laura remarked and went into the bathroom. "Oh, lookie! Fancy shampoo and body wash!"

Now Reed knew where Trent had picked up that particular addiction.

"Really? What kind?" Trent went into the bathroom, and Rob Copeland shook his head and threw Reed a commiserating glance. They both broke out laughing. Then they stared at each other for an uncomfortable moment before Rob hoisted a suitcase onto the bed.

As blissful chatter filtered in from the bathroom, he transferred meticulously folded underwear into a drawer and had the job completed in under two minutes. Reed was impressed.

"Military?"

Rob nodded. "Joined the Corps at the tail end of Vietnam and stuck around for a while." He didn't elaborate. That alone told Reed he'd probably seen some heavy combat. Maybe they'd have something in common after all.

Reed drove home, while Trent and his parents enjoyed the fine weather by walking. He parked in their underground parking space and turned the engine off, but he didn't get out. He needed a few minutes to collect his thoughts.

The Copelands had only been here for an hour, but already Reed felt the pressure of their visit. Why hadn't he suggested a hotel farther away? Half a mile away was an even nicer hotel, and Reed would gladly have paid the difference to keep Trent's parents out of their—his—hair. But that wouldn't be fair to Trent. He hadn't spent much time with his parents since Reed had moved to LA and into Trent's condo—the one he and Marc had bought together.

Christmas with his parents meant a lot to Trent, so Reed would do his best to make sure he got it. He just hoped he wouldn't have to be a big part of it. Two weeks with Trent's parents *shouldn't* be that arduous. He'd spent months in a Burmese prison camp, but this visit threatened to be more horrific. He hadn't been meditating recently, which probably accounted for a large portion of his stress. He closed his eyes and did one of the visualization exercises that had gotten him through those months in the camp. When he finished he felt a measure of peace, so he made his way to the elevator to their top-floor apartment.

When he let himself in, he found Trent's parents taking a tour of the place. He and Trent had carefully hidden anything that might cause anyone embarrassment and had done a thorough double check again that morning.

"I'm back," Reed called as he shut the door and locked it. "How did you beat me home?"

"In here," Trent called from the kitchen, making tea or coffee based on the sounds echoing through the living room. Reed went through to the kitchen. "What took you so long? We've been home for ages."

"Ages?" Reed looked at his watch. He'd lost track of time. His meditations usually didn't take long, but he was out of practice. "Traffic?" he said, not sure why he'd lied. He sat down at the table and watched Trent.

"Did they schedule a parade down our street that I didn't notice?" Trent gave Reed a glower that should have sliced his ear off. "Do you want coffee?" Trent added in an overly cheerful tone.

Reed really wanted a beer. It was midafternoon, so that wouldn't make a very good impression. Then he realized that was a good sign, wanting to make a good impression rather than simply wanting to run screaming in the opposite direction. The problem was he'd already pissed off Trent, and that wasn't good. At least with his parents around, Trent wouldn't say anything to Reed about it. Their presence wasn't all bad after all.

"I'm reheating the leftover frittata from last night," Trent said as Reed joined Rob at the kitchen table.

"Damn airlines don't feed you anymore." Rob shook his head.

"Oh, I see you have some new art here," Laura said from the living room. "Rob, come take a look."

"Crap, I forgot to take down those X-rated woodblock prints I got in Japan." Trent slapped his forehead after his dad left. He went back to measuring coffee into the french press. "Shit, I lost count. How many tablespoons did I put in there?"

"I don't know." Reed sat at the kitchen table and tried not to laugh at Trent's nervousness. "Sorry about the pictures. I didn't even think of it."

"They'll survive. Can you go out there and entertain them so they don't start digging around in any drawers?"

One drawer in particular. The toy drawer. "I locked it. But I'll go chat with them. Start again with the coffee after I'm gone." He strode out into the living room where Rob was perusing the bookshelf.

"I see Trent's books are all here. You like reading them, Reed?"

"They're not my favorite genre, to be honest, but I have read every one of them. At least all the ones he's written since we met. Sometimes he asks me to read when he's writing, when he's stuck on something." Reed liked when Trent asked his opinion. What a change, he thought, from the first time he'd read one of Trent's books, back in that hut in Thailand. Later on, when Reed had been held hostage by the Thai mobsters, he'd found reading Trent's stories comforting somehow. Of course he'd never tell this to the Copelands.

"You into art also?"

"Yes, a little." Trent's parents didn't know Reed worked for the FBI art squad. It was probably safe enough to tell them, but he'd let Trent make that decision. Later. If they ran out of things to talk about.

"I see you haven't really changed all that much in the apartment since last time we were here, Trent," Laura said as Trent came in with coffee and frittata. Reed scooted over to make room for him on the couch.

"Oh, haven't we?"

"It looks just about the same as when you were here with Marc. Just a couple of new pictures," his father added.

Reed tried to steady his hand as he handed a cup of coffee to Laura. The mention of Marc rattled him. He stirred sugar into his coffee and concentrated on keeping his hand steady.

"Oh honey, while we're here, we want to see Leah. She sent us pictures of the twins, and we told her we'd call. They're just the cutest things!"

Trent glanced at Reed before answering. "Yes. They're cute. You told her you were coming for a visit?"

"Yes. We keep in touch, you know."

Reed sipped coffee and felt his teeth ache. He hadn't realized how much sugar he had put in there, distracted as he was by the mention of Trent's ex, Marc, and then Leah, Marc's sister. He wouldn't even analyze the sudden fear he'd felt at the way Trent's face lit up at the mention of Leah's twins. Did Trent like kids? Did he *want* kids?

He yanked his phone from his pocket. "I just got a text from my boss. Would you mind if I step out to call him back? It'll only be a few minutes." Reed set the mug down and made for the front door, heart pounding as if he were heading out on a combat mission.

What's wrong with me? He stared at the door after he shut it behind him, knowing Trent would try to cover for him but give him hell—or the cold shoulder and everything below it. But Reed needed air. He fled down the stairs, his steps echoing in the stairwell. The brisk exercise calmed his nerves. Why did everything Trent's parents said feel like some sort of judgment on him? He couldn't imagine he was coming out very well in their estimation.

Not that leaving almost as soon as they arrived was going to improve his image.

TRENT WATCHED the door shut behind Reed and stirred his coffee so vigorously he splashed his hand and his pants. Luckily he was wearing jeans, so there wouldn't be a noticeable stain.

"What was that about?" his father asked.

"Maybe we shouldn't have come, honey," his mother added. She glanced at Rob and he shrugged.

"He'll be back in a little while. I think he needed a break."

"Break? You mean he's not calling his boss?"

Trent shrugged, knowing he was opening a can of worms, but it was necessary to get the unpleasantness out of the way early.

"Why did he lie? Does he lie to you often?" His mother sounded shocked and pitying.

"I don't think so. If he does it's because he can't tell me the truth, but that's not what this is about right now."

"What *is* it about?" his mother asked.

"Mom, Reed's just under pressure from having you visit."

"See, we shouldn't have come. Let's go back to the hotel." His father stood up.

"No, Dad. It's not you. It's him. He thinks you don't like him very much."

"Well, how can we like him? How can we even get to know him when he keeps running off?" his mother asked.

"Let's forget what happened at Thanksgiving. That was work, and it was important. Let's talk about today."

"He ran off again today. Twice," Trent's dad said with a judgmental tone.

"Do you think he wanted to stay while you kept talking about Marc and Leah and Leah's kids?"

"He knows about Marc, doesn't he? He's living in Marc's apartment."

"Of course he does. But like I said, he thinks you don't like him, and then you say something to show how much you liked Marc and his family."

His mother set her cup down on the coffee table. She reached out and patted Trent's hand. "We did like Marc, and we do like his family. But I hadn't thought about how Reed might interpret the comments. I didn't mean to imply that kind of comparison."

"He's a little sensitive, isn't he?" Trent's father asked. "Maybe he lied about being in special ops too."

Trent's initial impulse was to defend Reed. His chest ached whenever someone misjudged him. It hurt twice as much when it was his own parents. It was so difficult to explain Reed without sounding like he was making excuses. Trent took a sip of coffee before responding.

"He didn't lie. He's just not used to family things. He doesn't see his family, and he feels out of place in ours. All the attention and questions overwhelm him, like at Thanksgiving. It's like going from zero to a thousand the way everyone asks him personal things."

"Where's his family?" Mom asked.

"I have no idea. He doesn't talk about them. I just know the problems started when he came out to his dad. He hasn't said much more." Trent felt a wave of guilt wash over him. "But please don't let on that I mentioned it. He had a very different childhood than I did, and he's a very different person because of it. In the Army, and now with the FBI, he's got to put aside a lot of emotion and feelings. It's hard for him to turn all that back on, especially with you. He wants you to like him, but he's afraid he's not the kind of person you would like."

"Oh. Oh, Son, I'm sorry we jumped to conclusions." Trent's dad nodded and picked up his coffee again. "What should we do?"

"Maybe avoid bringing up family, and if he decides not to join us for something, try not to take it personally. He took the week off from work for your visit, but I don't want to push him into too many family activities."

"It's nice he took time off for our visit." Trent's mom looked guilty again and quickly glanced from Trent to his father.

"Reed does want to get to know you. He just doesn't open up easily. Just stay low-key and don't bombard him with personal questions."

"We can do that, can't we?" Trent's dad glanced at his mom and she nodded.

"Of course we can. I'll be more careful about Marc. But we do want to see Leah's twins. Will that be okay?"

"Yes. I'd like to go with you." Trent glanced at his watch. Reed had been gone twenty minutes. Trent would wait another five, then call if Reed hadn't come back.

"What did he do in the Army?" Trent's dad asked.

"He was in the Rangers. Special ops, secret missions. I don't know more than that."

"Rangers?" Trent's dad nodded, lips pursed. "Wow, that's some rough stuff."

"Probably. I know some of what he's done since he joined the Bureau and…." Trent wondered if he should tell them about Reed being imprisoned in a Burmese camp. "Well, he's survived some really awful things. He's got a bunch of those little ribbons on his uniform. And a Purple Heart."

"Oh dear." His mother covered her mouth with a hand and glanced at his dad.

"Enough said, Son." His dad nodded and looked a little guilty. Maybe he was remembering some of his own horrific experiences in Vietnam. Trent was lucky he'd never had to fight, and he hadn't understood what his father might have gone through in combat until he'd met Reed.

"Let me just check and see where he is." Trent pulled his phone out of his pocket and speed-dialed Reed.

A cell phone rang just outside the apartment door.

"I'm just coming in now," Reed said, and his voice echoed over the phone and from the hallway. "Sorry about that."

"WERE YOU standing outside the door the whole time?" Trent couldn't help asking.

"No. I wasn't. I walked around the block. And I stopped to get this." He pulled a bag out from behind his back and handed it to Trent.

"What's this?"

"Some steaks. I thought we could grill them tonight. It's nice weather, and the rooftop would be a nice place for a picnic. Is that okay, or did you have other plans for dinner?"

Trent felt like a jerk for assuming the worst about Reed's escape from the apartment. He took the package from Reed and peeked inside. They were good steaks. *Really* good. Expensive. "That sounds like a fine idea to me." He glanced at his parents, who nodded in unison. "I'll put these in the fridge."

"We should have enough in the fridge for side dishes, veggies, salad, don't you think? Or I can get something else…." Reed had followed Trent into the kitchen.

"I'm sure this is fine. And when did you turn into Stepford FBI agent/boyfriend?" Trent only half smiled. Reed was overplaying the helpful partner thing.

"I felt bad for leaving, and I wanted to make up for it." Reed shrugged and glanced out the window. Trent had overreacted too, even though he'd made excuses for Reed to his parents. "Look, I'm sorry. I just felt kind of overwhelmed, and I don't do family very well."

"I know. I asked them to back off a little, too, and not smother you."

"You did? Now I feel like some sort of after-school special."

"Don't. They assume everyone likes the same things they do, including the same attention. But they hadn't realized they weren't very tactful about Marc." Trent wished he hadn't mentioned him again. So much had changed in his life since he'd met Reed. He couldn't bear to say Marc's name before, and now Trent could talk about him calmly. Odd that now it was Reed who didn't want to discuss him.

"SHIT. YOU told them I was sensitive about Marc?"

"I noticed your reaction."

Reed eased the breath out through his nose. Trent was right, and it embarrassed Reed. Until he'd met Trent, he'd never felt inadequate or worried about things like meeting mothers or giving the right impression. Usually the impression he wanted to give was to scare the living daylights out of the other guy, but that was at work, when he went undercover and had to deal with criminals to catch other criminals.

In domestic situations, Reed was a fish out of water. And Trent was so damned domestic. Reed hadn't realized how much he liked that. Which was why he cared what Trent's family thought of him.

"Well, now I feel like an insecure idiot."

"That's not what they think."

"We'll talk about this later. They'll think we're arguing in here if we don't go back out to the living room."

"Okay. But thanks for thinking of the steaks." Trent planted a kiss on Reed's cheek and wrapped his arms around him.

"Could I get some water?" Laura came into the kitchen and surprised Reed when she spoke. "Sorry to intrude."

Trent didn't unwrap his arms for a moment, which both embarrassed and pleased Reed. He liked that Trent didn't treat him differently around his parents. If it had been Reed's parents—well, that was never going to happen, but if it did, Reed wouldn't touch Trent in the same zip code. Which contributed to Reed's aversion to even discussing his parents.

"No intrusion." Reed got a glass from the cabinet. "Do you want ice? Regular water or sparkling?"

"Oh my, so many choices."

Reed opened the fridge. "We have sparkling with lemon"—he held up the bottle—"or lime, or…."

"Just plain water with ice."

"Cubes or crushed?" Reed asked.

"Reed!" Trent laughed and his mother joined in.

Reed looked at Laura.

"Cubes, please." She grinned.

"What about another glass for Rob?"

"We'll share."

Trent shook his head before turning to her. "Mom, we have a dishwasher and lots of glasses. You can have your own glass."

"We like sharing." She grinned again and turned back toward the living room.

"I like sharing too." Reed gave Trent a kiss with a little tongue and then proceeded to fill another glass with ice cubes and sparkling water. "Ready?"

"Yeah." Trent shook his head and went back into the living room with Reed.

They sat down on the couch, and for the first time since he'd met Trent's parents, Reed didn't feel pressure. He didn't need to hide who or what he was, or how he felt about Trent.

4

THE FOLLOWING evening, they had reservations at Lawry's for prime rib. Rob and Laura were excited about the prospect. Reed had never been there and didn't know what the fuss was about, and Trent had said the place was really old-fashioned, but his parents enjoyed visiting on every trip.

The Copelands were sitting in the living room having predinner drinks, and Reed felt like he'd walked into another episode of *Mad Men*. Laura had done her hair up and was wearing a double-strand pearl necklace Trent had gotten for her in Japan and what was probably her best dress—or second best since they had some big plans for Christmas Eve too, though Trent wouldn't spill the beans about them.

Reed was checking his watch to see how long they had before the taxi arrived when his cell phone buzzed in his breast pocket. He pulled it out: Tom White, his boss. He glanced at Trent and looked away. "I have to take this." He was about to head into the hallway but hovered in the bedroom doorway instead.

"Tom?"

"Evening, Reed."

Trent came up right behind him, and Reed covered the mouthpiece. "You've already cried wolf once so far, Reed. You don't get another free pass."

Like Reed had gotten a free pass the other time? Well, maybe he had. He shook his head at Trent and moved farther into the bedroom, straining to hear his boss.

"Got a job for you, Reed, if you need one," White said with a low chuckle.

"What do you mean? What's going on?"

"I figured I'd give you an out if you had enough of the family. You mentioned dinner at Lawry's tonight, and I know how much you're dreading it. So you can tell them I need you to work a case."

"What case? How long would it take?" Reed saw the curiosity in Trent's eyes morph into pre-anger. How much did he want to get out of dinner tonight? Would it be worth whatever retribution Trent would exact? He *had* been itching for a job. Almost a week off had him ready to do anything.

"About twenty-four hours? Forty-eight at the outside."

"What's the story?"

"You remember that plane crash in Turkey at the end of last month? With Shelton Matthews on board?"

"Sure."

"What *hasn't* been in the papers is that the cargo consisted of a few things that used to be on display in the Iraq National Museum."

"You're fucking kidding me. After this many years?"

"We didn't get that juicy tidbit from Interpol until last week. We've got surveillance on Matthews' home in upstate New York, and I've got two guys from the New York field office scheduled to go in as insurance appraisers, but they don't have your expertise."

This could be the case of a lifetime. Tens of thousands of objects were still unaccounted for after the looting of the museum during the US invasion back in 2003. Then again, Matthews might only have amassed a pile of junk from Saddam's vulgar palace. They wouldn't know until they did a thorough search.

Reed waited too long to reply.

"The items in the plane crash included two solid gold Babylonian goblets. Part of a set of six. I'd like you on the team to find the other four."

"You think Matthews has them?" Reed's belly tingled with excitement. The expanding frown on Trent's face meant he'd noticed. Reed moved out of Trent's range of vision.

"If not, he's been looking for them. He's not the sort to leave a set incomplete."

Reed shifted his weight from foot to foot. "Hell yeah. I'm on my way in." He turned and spotted Trent holding his mother's evening wrap. His gut twisted again as Trent glanced over. "Hang on a couple of minutes, okay?"

Reed stepped back into the living room. "It's White, my boss. There's a case he needs me for...."

"A holiday-related crime?" Trent asked, with just enough acid that Reed felt it like he'd been burned.

Laura wrung her hands and turned a worried gaze to Reed. "Oh, Reed, please be careful. I'm going to worry about you the whole time. I don't think I can go to dinner if you're about to do something dangerous." She turned to Trent. "Let's change the plans for another night." She grasped at Reed's arm, the tight grip telegraphing concern.

Reed hadn't expected that reaction from her. The fear in her eyes cut through him like a rusty blade, far more painfully than Trent's anger. He'd expected to disappoint her, but even that felt wrong right now. He was touched by her concern.

"Tom, can you manage without me? We've got plans, and unless it's absolutely necessary…."

"Do I have the right number?" White asked, though his chuckle had lost its earlier mirth.

"Yeah. But, is there any way this can wait a few days?" Reed couldn't believe the words had come out of his mouth.

"Seriously?"

Reed guessed they had. "Yeah. Till after Christmas? Don't insurance companies get Christmas off?"

It was White's turn for a long pause. Reed was tempted to recant, but White spoke before he had the chance. "Yes. That'll be fine. Come in on the twenty-sixth, and you should be back the following day. Will that suit?"

"Yeah. The twenty-sixth works better."

"I'll e-mail you the travel arrangements, and we can do the briefing on the plane."

"Thanks. And Merry Christmas."

He smiled down at Laura, who looked relieved; then he took the wrap from Trent and helped Laura into it.

Trent came up behind Reed, whispered "I love you" into his ear, and slipped a hand around his waist in a quick embrace.

Reed felt another layer of protection peel away, but this time it didn't hurt as much as he'd thought it would. He had a family now. As much as he'd resisted it, he couldn't deny it. He didn't just have a boyfriend anymore; Trent and his parents—and all the siblings and their kids—had become Reed's family too.

5

December 26
30,000 feet over Nevada

"HOW WAS Christmas?" Tom White asked as he sipped fresh-brewed coffee and stretched his legs out in the relatively spacious dimensions of business class on the United Boeing 767.

Reed and White sat aboard a commercial flight headed for Islip, New York. The seats in the rows in front and behind them remained unoccupied to give them the necessary privacy for White to brief Reed.

"Not bad." Reed nodded and turned the corners of his mouth up. "Pretty good, actually."

"I half expected for you to call and ask to fly out sooner."

"I half wanted to. But the other half of me wanted to keep living. We should never have let Trent learn martial arts or how to use firearms."

White shrugged. "But you survived."

"Barely." Reed gulped some coffee. He'd worked for Tom White for six years now, and their relationship went beyond special agent and supervisor. "I just don't do family things. Even a few days of other people's families make me long for the good old days in Iraq or Afghanistan."

"Ouch."

"So fill me in."

"Right." White pulled his laptop out of the carrier bag and fired it up. "Here are photos from the wreckage of a Cessna jet discovered in the mountains on the Turkish-Bulgarian border. The European Aviation Safety Agency, their version of the NTSB, found the victims and their cargo relatively intact after the wreckage was spotted by a flight that had gone slightly off course. Had the Cessna crashed in a more accessible area, everything would have been looted, and we might not have had any inkling of what was going on here."

"So what is going on?"

White clicked on a PowerPoint presentation, and the photo of a suntanned man in his fifties with windswept gray hair popped up. "Shelton Matthews, former hedge-fund manager and unindicted Ponzi schemer. The SEC never found enough evidence on him. His cronies from the Matthews-Pullman fund went to prison on fairly light terms. Theory is that he bought them off with his secret billions."

Reed nodded. He scribbled on a notepad. He'd wait until White was done talking before he asked any questions.

White hit the next slide. "Mitchell Granby. Another shady rich dude. Made his money in international trade thanks to big tax breaks for funding charitable work in certain African and Eastern European countries. Word is he used the IRS to subsidize arms deals, but there's no proof. Anyway, we've never seen them together before, so the crash has got a lot of heads spinning in law enforcement agencies from coast to coast as well as internationally." A smile spread across White's face. Reed could see this case had really excited his boss. This was going to be a big one. Reed's pulse sped up, and he clenched his fists in anticipation.

"The aircraft left a small airport outside of Istanbul. No flight plan was filed, or if one was, it's been destroyed. The other victims were the Turkish pilot and two unidentified women. They're not the dead men's wives or relatives since none of the relatives are missing. None of them even knew Matthews and Granby were in Turkey."

"Get to the good stuff. Why are we involved?"

"Hold your horses. Literally." White clicked and the screen filled with the image of two slightly battered golden goblets encrusted with gems around the rim and base. As he stared at the low-res image, a sense of history settled over Reed. The gold was darker in the crevices of the raised carvings. One goblet depicted a lion, jaws open wide, and the other a magnificent prancing horse. The detail was so incredible Reed could see the lion's individual teeth and the stylized tendrils of the horse's mane.

"They're magnificent."

"They were found in a pile of broken pottery. These have been cleaned up a bit, but it appears the goblets had been fired into some cheap modern pottery vases. If the plane hadn't crashed, they may never have been detected."

Reed stared at the screen, imagining a Babylonian king sipping wine from one of the goblets, then offering a sip to a concubine. He realized White had stopped talking and brought himself back to the twenty-first century.

"How were they planning to get these into the States?" Reed thought out loud, caught up in the excitement of this new mystery, awed by the momentous discovery of these exquisite artifacts.

"We've got agents in Europe working on that angle, following leads through the pilot, his known associates, and anyone Matthews and Granby met during the week they were in Turkey." White paused to finish his coffee, then raised the cup as the flight attendant walked by with a pot. "Nowadays, commercial and cargo flights, even from Turkey, are scanned multiple times before departure, for security reasons. With the continued efforts to combat antiquities smuggling, airports in certain countries—anywhere near Iraq, for example—have committed to additional customs screenings that most people don't even know or care about. And anything arriving in the US is subject to a variety of scans, whether it's private or commercial. So we're confident they were planning something out of the ordinary."

"If you've already got Interpol and their antiquities units working the Turkish side, where do I fit in?"

"Right. Matthews has an estranged wife and an adult daughter. The wife is skiing in Switzerland, but the daughter"—the image of a twenty-something woman popped up on the laptop—"Marsha Matthews, twenty-three, graduate student in social work, is the sole heir. Poor Mrs. Matthews gets cut out of the good stuff, thanks to a particularly nasty prenup. Marsha's about to get the keys to the kingdom that greed and avarice built. We've set up a team of agents out of the New York office as claims adjusters from Matthews' insurance company. Another team is working on Granby's properties in the US. We're cataloging everything that looks like it's worth more than ten bucks. Given what these two were carrying on board, we doubt these are the only items they've got from Iraq."

White flipped through a few more images of artifacts, none as spectacular as the two golden goblets. "We've found these in Granby's home, as yet unidentified, but they look like they could be Mesopotamian. I'd like you to do a thorough search of Matthews' place and make a personal connection with Marsha."

"How personal?" Reed quirked an eyebrow.

"Not that personal. Be friendly, understanding. Make sure we have continued access to his properties and his paperwork."

"I think I've got it."

AFTER THEY landed, a car from the New York field office met them at the airport in Islip. Without a winter coat, Reed shivered in his suit—a gray pinstripe he used when impersonating someone in finance or insurance. He'd been a little preoccupied that morning as Trent gave him a special good-bye fuck, and he had run out to the taxi, leaving the coat on the floor next to the bed—right where he'd dropped it.

Special Agent Tompkins drove through snow-covered residential streets on the way to a nondescript office building ten miles from Shelton Matthews' estate. After the usual introductions, White handed the op over to Reed. It was difficult showing up in another office's territory, but Reed had worked with two of the guys on previous assignments, and by now everyone who dealt with art had heard of him.

"So, how'd you feel when you knew you'd found some of the Gardner pieces?" one of the younger agents asked. The mood had turned informal while the six agents, Reed, and White gobbled sandwiches brought in from a local restaurant.

Reed glanced down at the desk and shook his head. He'd been more relieved that he and Trent were still in one piece than excited about the find, so he put his reticence aside and answered. "Fucking shocked. We hadn't expected to discover anything like that when we went in. Of course it was several weeks before the necessary confirmations...."

"What about—"

"Let's let Special Agent Acton get caught up with what you've found so far," White said, standing up next to Reed. "There will be plenty of time for war stories once we've got an idea what Matthews is hiding. Reed has to be back in LA tomorrow night."

Reed shook his head and felt his neck warming up. He didn't want to look like a hen-pecked husband in front of these guys. "No. I'll stay however long this takes."

After the summary from the most senior New York agent, Reed divided up duties among his new team members. One of the support staff had gone out to buy a new coat for Reed during the briefing, so he was ready to head out to the Matthews estate.

Estate was an understatement. Even the cast of *Downton Abbey* would have been impressed with Matthews' mock-Tudor summer home. The drive from the front gate to the house itself took several minutes, winding through a small woods before the grand house came into view. Reed and Tompkins arrived first, to be followed by two other pairs fifteen or twenty minutes later so it wouldn't look as if they'd set out in a convoy.

Reed rang the doorbell and listened to a symphony of chimes before Marsha Matthews opened the door herself. She wore a simple dusty-rose cashmere sweater with wide cables swirling up the sleeves, and dark gray wool trousers. Her shoes click-clacked across the marble entry hall as she led them into the spacious formal drawing room. While she didn't use the term, that's how Reed would describe it.

He noted their surroundings, from the ornate moldings at the ceilings to the exquisite Tabriz rug beneath their feet. Nothing even approaching the value of the goblets was on display here, but no one in the Bureau expected it would be. Trent would ask a dozen questions about the furniture, so Reed made notes on his pad as he settled onto the plush Victorian-style sofa. Tompkins chose a chair to Reed's right.

"I'm not sure what you need from us, Mr. Adams," Marsha said to Reed. She looked tiny in the plush oversized room, like a china doll in a too-large dollhouse. Her voice was soft, well educated, but toneless. She didn't look like she'd been crying, though it had been at least a week since she'd learned of her father's death. Maybe the news of her huge inheritance had served to dry whatever tears might have flowed.

Reed noticed the absence of Christmas touches around the place, probably in keeping with her recent bereavement. If there had been any, perhaps she asked the staff to remove them.

"Our purpose today is twofold. We need to make an inventory before your father's will can be executed, and his attorneys have engaged us to catalog and appraise the art collection for tax purposes as well as insurance."

She inhaled and looked Reed up and down again. He hoped she didn't notice that his coat was brand-new and was a little large on him.

"Isn't there some sort of conflict of interest there, working for the insurance company and my father's estate?"

"It seems like there might be, but there isn't. Insurance companies have been accused of undervaluing items, which is in your favor when dealing with the IRS."

"Oh. Is that so? I don't really understand all the tax stuff. My father's lawyers are handling all of that."

"There will be another independent appraisal."

"I still don't understand why this has to happen during the holidays."

There was no good reason for it, except that the Bureau wanted to make sure no one walked off with any art or evidence, especially anything that could put them on the trail of Matthews' contacts to the art black market. Reed's brain whirled to come up with an excuse.

"Ma'am," Tompkins began, "you know the IRS. Tax year ends December thirty-first. Better for you if we can get most of it done by then."

"Oh, right," she said.

Reed said a silent thanks to Tompkins even though his explanation was utter bullshit. Personal tax returns weren't due until April, even for fat cats like Matthews, and estates were given generous schedules to prepare the necessary paperwork, but she probably didn't know any of that.

The doorbell rang, allowing Reed and Tompkins to avoid any further questions. Marsha ushered the four newly arrived "insurance adjusters" into the sitting room.

"Now, Ms. Matthews, can you show us where your father displays and stores his art?" Reed pulled a clipboard out of his briefcase. "I have a listing of the items that have been insured, and we'll make sure they are all here and add anything else of value we discover."

"Sure. Some of it is on display in various rooms." She swept her hand through the air. "There is a gallery upstairs and another smaller one downstairs. We've got art in the other two properties he owns—owned."

"We'll send a team—adjusters—to visit those properties as well, with your permission?"

"I guess you can just move around the house as you need to. Let me notify the staff at the other properties to permit your adjusters in, and—"

"That would be great, Ms. Matthews." Reed followed her to the office while the rest of the agents scattered around the house with their own clipboards.

"Call me Marsha, please."

She made the necessary phone calls while Reed sat in one of the wing chairs in front of the desk. Reed slid one hand along the arm of the chair, admiring the softest leather he'd ever seen or felt. He let his gaze play across the art displayed here. A couple of paintings hung on the dark paneled walls, and a display case held a small collection of Chinese porcelain. While the office held nothing gold, or of obvious Iraqi origins, they would make a thorough search in here as well.

"All taken care of. Here's the addresses and numbers of the housekeepers. You can arrange the visits with them."

"Thank you. Now, if you know where your father keeps the provenances—documentation—of his artwork? It will help value some of the more obscure items…."

"There's a file cabinet back here, but I don't know what's in it. And another upstairs in his bedroom, I believe."

"Do you mind if I take a look?"

She shook her head. Her eyes were wide and her hands trembled a little as she tried to keep them by her sides. Clearly she was overwhelmed with the magnitude of handling her father's estate, as well as still processing his death. Reed counted on it to lower her guard.

"Are you okay?" Reed used his most conciliatory tone. "You look a little—"

She let herself fall into the chair next to Reed's. "I'm still pretty dazed over everything. I didn't even know Dad was in Turkey, and it took a couple of weeks after the crash before I got the news. Last week. Mom's coming back from Switzerland on Sunday." She started to tear up, and Reed reached out with a comforting touch to her arm. When she smiled at him, he squeezed her hand.

"I understand, Marsha." He made eye contact as he spoke her name. "We will try to be as unobtrusive as possible." He filed away the information about her mother. They needed to find something suspicious in order to get the properties sealed off before she arrived. She wouldn't be the pushover her daughter was turning out to be, and she might walk off with something priceless that didn't rightfully belong to Shelton Matthews or his heirs.

"Thank you." Marsha gave him a shy little smile that told Reed he'd connected with her as more than just the insurance guy. He was a man she wanted to trust, and he just needed to drive it home, that he could take all this hassle away and handle everything for her. Sometimes he felt like an asshole doing this, but he knew Matthews had been involved in at least one illegal antiquities transaction. As long as Marsha didn't know anything about what they'd found on the plane, she'd be fine. "I better let you get to the paperwork." She stood up and Reed got out of his chair. Marsha glanced at him as if waiting for him to ask her to stay, or kiss her, or something equally unlikely. That was a good thing.

He gave her a kindly nod, and she walked out of the room.

Reed rushed to shut the door and headed for the file cabinet. He squatted down and pulled on the bottom drawer. No one ever put illegal documents at the top of their file cabinet. The drawer was locked, and he began a systematic search for a hidden key in the carved teak desk—probably on the long list of illegal items in this house. He looked through the drawers to no avail, then pulled each out and slid his hand along the bottom, side, and back panels.

Under the middle drawer, his fingers encountered resistance, and he discovered a key taped beneath the drawer. If it didn't open the file cabinet, it would open something Matthews hadn't wanted anyone else to access. Reed grinned and went back to the cabinet.

Sure enough, the key fit. With a twist, the lock clicked open.

6

THE FIRST set of files had nothing to do with art. At least not on the surface. They were itineraries and receipts from Matthews' travels during the past five years. Several trips to Turkey, Italy, Thailand, Hong Kong, and Japan, all countries where Matthews had been known to purchase legal art. Chances were he'd also made transactions he wanted to keep private.

Reed flipped through the rest of the contents of the drawer, but nothing appeared worth hiding the key. Then his hand came up against the back panel of the drawer and his heart rate accelerated as the wood shifted beneath his fingers.

Another compartment, concealed behind a partition.

He forced himself to slow down and carefully remove the divider, but he couldn't help smiling as he retrieved a notebook no larger than a standard business card. Reed squinted at the cramped handwriting, then pulled a magnifier from his pocket.

Reed had hit the jackpot, or was well on the way. The tiny ledger was written in code, and all he could recognize were dates. He flipped back to the travel receipts and found the dates corresponded to those in the coded book.

Could this be a ledger containing Matthews' art purchases?

Matthews had been considered a reasonably scrupulous businessman, so the book probably didn't contain illegal business or banking transactions. It was much more likely he'd recorded private acquisitions here. Reed would task another agent with matching travel dates against art auctions and unsolved art-related crimes in the areas Matthews had visited.

Thrilled with the discovery, Reed was startled when a text message announced itself. He pulled the phone from his inner pocket as he stood up and stretched out his achy knees.

The text was from one of the agents upstairs. "Found something promising. Third floor."

Reed locked the file cabinet, slipped the key into his jacket pocket, and raced for the stairs, taking them two and three at a time. On the third-floor landing, he met up with Tompkins and Jones—at least Jones was his name for the day. They usually chose easy-to-remember surnames.

"Come see this." Jones motioned for him to follow. At the far end of a long hallway, Reed opened a door and found himself in a beautifully appointed room that had the feel of a library, containing glass cases rather than built-in bookcases. Each case held a small work of art: a bowl, a vase, a sculpture. Along the far wall, the cases were larger. Reed recognized the origins of most of the items in the room, but he couldn't say when or by whom any of them had been made. He'd been in museums that didn't have such comprehensive collections.

"Anything in particular catch your attention? Anything on the lists of missing art?"

Tompkins gave a cryptic grin and motioned for Reed to follow him through a door in the back of the room. It led to another room, darker and smaller but full of even more incredible items. Only half of the shelves held display cases, each of which was spotlighted from fixtures built into the ceiling. The purpose-built room was Matthews' private museum.

"Was that door locked?"

"Y-no." Jones grinned but didn't elaborate. Technically, without a warrant, they were limited to items in plain sight. Marsha either wouldn't know the door might have been locked or she wouldn't admit to knowing about this room. They weren't likely to be found out. Reed didn't like skirting the law, but sometimes it had to be done, and this was one of them. He'd take the flack later, if necessary.

For a few moments, Reed took in the contents of the room. The lighting served to enhance the beauty of the objects, almost all of which were made of gold or precious gems. Some contained both.

"Jesus Christ." Reed let out a long, loud breath. His pulse spiked. This was turning out perfectly. They could eventually cross off dozens of items from the lists.

"He gave us a Christmas present for real," Tompkins added.

"This is incredible, but is any of it illegal?"

Jones pointed to an item shelved at eye level to the right of the door: a golden goblet with the image of an antelope curving around the bowl. It had to be a companion piece to the goblets found in the plane wreck.

"Yahtzee!" Reed said and speed-dialed White.

THE AGENTS catalogued every item while Tom White arranged for search warrants and started the necessary paperwork for the US Marshals to take possession of the house. They had authority to seize any property connected to illegal activities. They would handle security while the Bureau continued their search for artifacts and incriminating documents.

Two hours later the doorbell rang, followed by pounding on the door. "Federal agents!"

Reed was back in Matthews' office and stood up and dusted himself off as Marsha's heels clattered across the entryway, then came back in his direction.

"Mr. Adams, what's going on?" She wrung her hands and looked over her shoulder as the pounding on the door continued.

"I'd open the door before they knock it off the hinges."

"Wh-what?"

Reed stepped around her and opened the door. White greeted him, and a dozen men filed inside and milled in the foyer.

"What's going on?"

"Ms. Matthews, I'm Thomas White from the FBI." He handed her the warrant and seizure paperwork, then glanced at Reed as if they'd never met.

"Adams, insurance adjuster for—"

"I don't understand." Marsha glanced at Reed, looking even more like a deer in the headlights than before. "Mr. Adams?"

"Marsha, one of my colleagues discovered an item that's on an international watch list of stolen antiquities."

"There must be some mistake. My father's a collector, but he wo—"

Reed pulled out his phone and showed her a photo of the goblet. White handed her the Interpol announcement showing the exact item marked as missing from the Iraqi museum.

"I need to sit down." She walked into the drawing room, not bothering to invite them along with her.

White took charge. "Marshals, do what you need to here. Acton and I will deal with Ms. Matthews."

The marshals filed out of the entrance hall. White and Reed found Marsha huddled at one end of the couch. "Ms. Matthews, I'm afraid the marshals have sent agents to take possession of the other two properties until everything can be searched and inventoried."

Marsha glared at Reed. "Mr. Adams? Did you do this?"

Reed glanced at White, who shook his head and motioned for Reed to sit on the couch with Marsha while he took a chair.

Then White replied for him. "Mr. Adams here is obligated to report when his team discovers any item believed to be on any list of stolen items. That goblet is one of a set of six that an Interpol task force is searching for. Two other items from the set were discovered with your father, in the wreckage of the plane."

Marsha blinked at Reed and scooted a little closer to him on the couch. Reed put his hand on hers and gave her another reassuring smile. When he glanced back at Tom, he spotted a glint of amusement in his eyes. *Bastard.*

"How do you know Dad even knew the items were stolen? Maybe he bought them in good faith."

"Yes, Mr. White?" Reed asked, trying not to smile.

"Legally, that's irrelevant. However, while I can't go into details, the items in question were concealed in a way that led the authorities to believe he attempted to avoid discovery by customs agents."

"Oh." Marsha blinked a few times, and tears slid down her cheeks. She kept wringing her hands and twisting the ring on her right hand.

"May I see that ring, Marsha?" Reed held out his hand.

She sniffed and nodded, then handed it to him. He pulled a jeweler's loupe out of a pocket and held it to his eye in order to examine the ring. It was beautiful. Pure gold and heavy, it was gorgeous even if the workmanship wasn't as detailed or delicate as anything created in the past thousand years. While he couldn't be certain, the stylized image of a winged lion looked remarkably like the style of the three goblets. He'd need to bone up on his Babylonian art.

"Did your father give this to you?"

She snatched it back. "Yes. It was a present when I graduated from college. Bryn Mawr."

Bryn Mawr, of course.

"It's beautiful."

"I'm a Leo, so Dad used to buy me lions." She sniffed again. "He said he had something special for me for Christmas." Now the sobs shook her body, and Reed glanced at White with an unwelcome weight of guilt. At least they knew who was supposed to be getting the lion goblet that had been found in the wreckage.

"Miss, we're going to need to examine that too. We'll give you a receipt," White said.

"I don't care about your fucking receipts!" She pulled her knees up to her chin and wrapped her arms around them.

Reed slid closer and laid a gentle hand on her shoulder, then smoothed it across her back. "Marsha?"

"I don't want him to have it. I'll never get it back."

"Maybe it's not illegal. There are many Babylonian items on the legitimate market." He kept his voice soft and soothing.

"Really?" She sniffed again. "I don't want him to check. You do it." She pulled the ring off and thrust it at Reed. He put it in a small envelope and into his inner pocket. Then Marsha flung herself at him and caught him in an iron embrace.

Reed stared at White over her shoulder and mouthed, "You fucker." He added a smile because Tom White was his boss and Reed liked his job. Just not this part of it.

7

TRENT HAD just finished dinner with his parents and was walking back to the apartment when his cell phone rang.

"It's Reed," he told them and stopped to answer. He hated walking and talking, especially on the phone with Reed. "Hi, babe. How's it going?"

"I finally got back to my hotel room and I'm waiting for room service. How're you and your parents?"

"We just finished dinner. You've had a long day."

"Really long day."

"Let me walk Mom and Dad to their hotel and then call you when I get home."

"Sure."

Trent felt guilty for rushing them the last three blocks and leaving with just a quick hug and kiss before racing around the corner to his apartment. Reed had barely been gone eighteen hours, but Trent already missed him. He pushed speed dial as soon as he got out of the elevator on the top floor of the building.

"Hey," Reed said. His voice was all thick and gravelly, kind of like right after sex. Trent's chest hurt a little to hear it and know he wasn't the one who made Reed sound that way.

"Hey. You sound so sexy right now."

"Really?" Reed made a noise that sounded like he was sucking on something.

"Uh, yeah. Well, you did. What are you doing?" Trent paused. "Or is that who are you doing?"

This time there were swallowing sounds.

"Reed!"

"Sorry, I'm just stuffing down a burger. I haven't eaten since lunch, which was about a hundred hours ago."

"Oh. Sorry." Heat bloomed at the nape of his neck and he ran his hand up along the back of his head. "I like those sounds, when you make them on me."

Reed laughed. "I will soon. Promise."

"You up for some phone sex?"

"I guess your parents aren't around?"

"Sure they are. They want me to put you on speakerphone."

Reed made a strangled sound, then started coughing. "Jesus, Trent, I almost choked to death here."

"Is that a no?"

"Yes, that's a no. Even if your parents aren't listening."

"Fine. I can wait till tomorrow."

"I'm going to have to stay another day. We found some incredible things today and…. Well, I'll tell you about it when I get back, okay?"

"Really?" Trent sat up. "You'll tell me?" Reed rarely gave him details about his cases. What made this one different?

"Yes. We'll all go to dinner on Monday, okay?"

"Sure." Trent didn't want to sound too excited, but he was. "Uh, you still want to go to that New Year's Eve party I mentioned?"

"The one on someone's boat?"

"That's it. Beth did some work on one of Wes Tremayne's films, and he invited her to bring some friends."

"Who's Wes Tremayne?"

"The actor? The one who got outed last year and there was that big fuss with his network?"

"I remember now, vaguely. Are you sure Beth can bring us *and* your parents?"

"It's all taken care of, as long as you'll be back by then."

"I promise."

"I'll still love you anyway. But I am going to spend New Year's Eve with Wes Tremayne, even if you aren't there."

"Uh-oh. I don't like the sound of that." Clicking noises came across the miles into Trent's ear. "Oh, hey, no. Uh-uh," Reed said.

"Uh-uh what?"

"I just googled Wes Tremayne, and you are not going to that party without me."

Trent nodded and smiled to himself. "Yeah, he's pretty hot, isn't he? Afraid you can't trust me?"

"No. I'm afraid I can't trust him around you." Reed made a kissing sound and hung up.

Trent lay back on the bed and stared at the ceiling, smiling until his face hurt.

This was too good to be true.

TRUE TO his word, Reed arrived home late on Sunday night, and Trent stayed up to give him an appropriate welcome and was still sleeping when Reed slipped out of bed and went to work.

Later, Trent and his parents walked down to the LMNO Gallery that he co-owned with Leah, the sister of his former partner, Marc.

Reed even managed to arrive on time at the restaurant he chose—and Trent approved—for dinner. In fact, he was early because Trent had told him they were eating at six thirty when the reservation was for seven.

"You look familiar, but I think I'd remember if you were ever *early*," Trent teased.

Reed ignored him and bent to give Laura a hug and kiss, then shook Rob's hand before finally kissing Trent.

They let Trent order for everyone, because he seemed to be the only one who really cared that much.

"I'm sure everything here is delicious, dear," Laura said. "You know what I like."

"Ditto," Reed said.

"What he said," Rob joked as he sipped one of the trademark gimlets.

"Fine." Trent ordered a mix of dishes. They could share or fight over things when the food arrived, and he'd take whatever was left. He loved this place and had been thrilled when Reed suggested they come here.

"Do you have to work a lot of weekends?" Rob asked Reed.

"I don't have a lot of say in when things happen at the Bureau. My division requires a lot of travel and weekend work. Sometimes I have to be gone for weeks at a time." He threw Trent an apologetic glance, and Trent's pulse sped up. How could he still be so head over heels for Reed after three years? Just a glance from him, the way his gray-blue eyes could flash like lightning in the summer sky, and Trent would follow him to the ends of the earth, forgive him for missing events and being so secretive about work. Two days with Reed were worth two weeks with anyone Trent had been with before.

"Trent?" his mother shook his arm.

"Yeah?"

"You okay?"

"Perfect." He gave Reed a sappy grin, and Reed returned it. *What happened to my real boyfriend?*

"Reed, you haven't told us much about the kind of cases you work on. Now I'm even more curious." Rob reached for a piece of flaky crispbread from the napkin-lined wire basket in the middle of the table.

"Usually I don't have that luxury, but since it's interfered with your visit, I owe you some explanation."

Now Trent was all ears. He put his crispbread down on a plate. It was too crunchy to hear properly, and he wanted to hear every word of whatever Reed was about to tell his parents.

Reed lowered his voice and leaned down over the table. "This isn't for public knowledge. You heard about the plane that crashed in Turkey with a couple of American businessmen on board?"

"Yes," the others replied.

"Authorities investigating the crash found they had been taking some antiquities out of the country. Items that were stolen from the national museum in Iraq back during the initial US invasion."

"Really?" Laura's eyes widened.

Trent raised an eyebrow. Reed never shared this stuff with him. Why now? Was Reed changing, or was it some lie for Trent's parents' sake?

"What did they find?"

"All I can say is that the pieces were gold. Beautiful examples dating back almost three thousand years."

"Wow." A tingle of excitement shot up Trent's spine. "Come on, tell us what they found."

"I can't just yet, because we're still waiting for expert authentication. But we found more items in one victim's house. I've been helping to catalog the items and looking for leads as to how he acquired them."

"That's so exciting," Laura said.

At that point their entrées came, allowing little opportunity for talking as everyone dug into the delicious food and shared pieces with everyone else.

"Will you have to go back?" Trent asked. He wished it didn't come out sounding like the prospect upset him.

"Not back to New York. But I will need to travel again in January." Reed turned to Laura. "My boss is handling the travel arrangements, but I won't be leaving until your visit here is over."

"Oh, Reed, you don't have to schedule your work around us." Laura put a hand on his arm and gave him a lipsticky kiss.

Trent concentrated on his short ribs so he wouldn't wonder why Reed was so nice all of a sudden. Then he reminded himself that he *wanted* Reed to be like this, so what was he upset about?

"Arranging international travel takes time, so it's not a problem. Besides, I have a lot of information to study before the trip."

"International?" Trent hated the little pang of jealousy creeping through his belly.

"That sounds exciting," Rob said as he raised a fork full of roasted brussels sprouts to his mouth. "Where?" He plunged the sprouts in and chewed happily.

"Turkey."

Trent scooped up some cinnamon-scented couscous dotted with currants on his spoon and avoided Reed's eye.

"And Trent's coming along too."

Some idiot dropped a piece of silverware, and it clattered as it first hit a plate, then the edge of the table, before finally settling on the floor, attracting the attention of everyone in a three-table radius. Then Trent realized he'd been that idiot and had scattered couscous all over his lap and the floor.

Three staff members raced toward their table. When they'd finished cleaning up, Trent felt like he'd had his tires changed during a Formula One pit stop.

"Me?" Trent finally managed to choke out.

"If you want to come along."

Trent shrugged and made a pretense at acting nonchalant. He failed miserably and leaned over to kiss Reed. "Thank you."

After that announcement, for the first time in his life, Trent didn't even care what they ordered for dessert.

8

ON NEW Year's Day, Trent and Reed slept in.

"Wow, Reed, that was some midnight kiss, and I think you fucked me a few years into the future when we got back here." Trent scooted up against Reed and pulled him close.

"I hope that's a good thing."

Trent beamed.

Reed wouldn't admit that seeing Trent dancing with Wes Tremayne sent waves of red-hot jealously through every fiber in his body. The intensity startled Reed, even though Wes's partner, another movie-star gorgeous guy, was there too.

Of course he trusted Trent completely, but now Reed wondered what Trent did while he was left alone in LA for weeks at a time. What if Trent got tired of waiting for Reed to come home?

The possibility terrified Reed.

"Let's pretend it's midnight again." Trent's voice was low, honey-thick.

But the love shining in Trent's eyes meant so much more than the way his cock dug into Reed's hip.

"Let's."

LATER, LAURA and Rob came over for homemade waffles, courtesy of Trent. The four of them spent the day relaxing, though Rob insisted on watching the New Year's Day college bowl games.

"Both Oklahoma and OK State are in bowls today!" He settled himself into the comfortable chair with Trent on the couch. Based on Trent's heretofore unstated interest in college football, Reed suspected this was a family tradition.

"Rob and the kids would spend the whole day watching games when they all lived at home, and our house is still the gathering place," Laura explained.

"Don't you like football, Reed?" Rob asked as he and Trent grabbed beers Laura had brought from the kitchen.

Reed took the last bottle from Laura. "Got nothing against football, but I don't really watch it."

"Did you play growing up, high school or college?" Laura asked.

"Shhh," Rob said. "The commercials are over."

Laura rolled her eyes toward the ceiling, and Reed concentrated on his beer.

"No, I didn't get a chance," Reed answered.

"Why's that?" Rob asked, though he kept his gaze on the television. "Damn, just another pregame show full of chatter and hard-luck stories of the players."

"I like those stories," Trent said. "Reed grew up on Army bases around the world."

Rob glanced over at him, and Reed nodded. "We lived abroad, and there wasn't a league. By the time I got to West Point, I wasn't good enough to make the team even if I'd wanted to."

"West Point, huh?" Rob asked.

Trent beamed, and Reed felt an odd warmth in his chest. Trent was proud enough to announce Reed's accomplishments to his family, and that was a new feeling for Reed.

"My, your mother must have been thrilled for you to get accepted there!" Laura said, sipping her iced tea.

"His mother?" Rob said. "How about his father? That would sure make a dad proud."

Trent looked at his feet. Had Rob's comment been some kind of insult to him?

"I suppose." Reed didn't exactly want to discuss what his dad thought of anything he did. "Proud" was probably the last emotion his father had felt toward Reed. No matter what Reed did—including applying to West Point and graduating near the top of his class—he'd never earned his father's approval.

"I'd be thrilled," Laura said.

"Me too." Rob raised his bottle toward Reed for a clink. "Good job, Reed."

"Thanks." Reed glanced toward Trent to see if his father's comments had upset him at all, but Trent was smiling. He reached up for a clink against Reed's bottle too.

Rob lowered the volume on the television and turned toward Reed. "What'd you do in the Army after that?"

"Rangers, then Special Forces." It was all he would say unless Rob asked something specific. He didn't care for talking about Army days, or his past. Trent wanted to know, but Reed always put him off the topic.

"So, who looks good for the Rose Bowl?" Reed asked, adept at steering conversations away from prickly topics.

"Stanford is looking particularly good this year."

Reed nodded and let the conversation go through him. But Trent joined in, and soon he and his father were batting around team records, players' health, and a variety of topics Reed hadn't known Trent even cared about.

Laura caught Reed's eye and smiled. "I could use some help in the kitchen, if you're already footballed out?"

Reed smiled and Rob snorted. "We haven't even gotten one bowl game under our belts today!"

"Sure, I'd love to." Reed stood and followed Laura into the kitchen.

"I think you've got everything we need to make some bread. It takes a while, so it's a good thing to bake when I don't want to sit around in the living room all day."

"Not a big fan of football?" Reed sat at the table, not sure what she needed him to do.

"I like going to the games, but not watching it. And it's nice to give Trent some time with his dad." Laura opened cabinets, searching for ingredients, then placing the ones she wanted on the counter.

Reed nodded. "They seem to have a lot of fun together."

"They do now. There were years when things weren't so smooth. I guess it's that way with all kids."

"I remember more rough than smooth."

Laura sat down next to Reed. "I'm sorry to hear that. Sounds like you and your dad never managed to reach that friend stage that comes after high school."

"Friend stage?"

She fixed her gaze on him. "Sure. Up to a certain age, I think boys find everything their fathers do is wonderful—in a happy home, at least. Then when puberty hits, they can't agree on a single thing. During high school and college, Trent and his brother seemed to disagree with just about everything Rob or I even suggested. Never in an unpleasant way, but they started to form their own ideas about things. Before then, they agreed with Rob. And once they finished college and had established their individuality, things became much more equal. Not father/son as much as two guys hanging out. At least that's how it's seemed in our household."

Reed inhaled slowly and thought about her comments. "I sure remember that hero-worship stage," he admitted. "My dad rose quickly in the Army, and that meant moving around a lot. I wanted to be just like him when I grew up."

"And are you?"

Reed knew exactly when things had gone off the rails with his dad. He shook his head. "I very much doubt we have anything at all in common."

"So where are your parents? You haven't said a thing about them, except mentioning your mom a few times."

"I talk with my mother now and then, but I haven't seen my father since I was about twenty."

"Oh dear. That's a long time."

"I'm not *that* old." Reed tried to make a joke out of it.

"You know that's not what I meant. Wasn't he there for your West Point graduation?"

"Supposedly. I spent time with my mom, but he didn't join us. I haven't even mentioned this much to Trent." Reed glanced toward the kitchen door for a moment before he stood up and grabbed the bag of flour. "How do we turn all this stuff into bread?"

Laura joined him at the counter and put an arm around his waist and gave him a motherly squeeze. "If you'd rather make bread than talk about your family, it says a hell of a lot. Now where are the measuring cups and spoons?"

Reed opened the drawer with the cooking utensils and watched Laura organize the ingredients. He appreciated how adroitly she changed topics. She and Rob were leaving in a few days, and Reed would actually miss them, especially Laura. He already felt the strength of her love warming his life.

He missed his own mother more than ever.

9

TRENT FELT guilty, but he almost couldn't wait for his parents to leave. As much as he had enjoyed their visit, he wanted to concentrate on the upcoming trip to Turkey. White had asked Reed to go out a few days early to scope out some of the contacts they'd identified.

"So, when will you be leaving?" Trent asked when Reed got back from a pretravel briefing at the LA field office.

"On Thursday, with you."

"Not early?"

Reed shook his head. "I won't make any significant progress in a couple of days, and I know you can't manage to pack without me."

Trent pressed his lips together to avoid a response that might make their trip less enjoyable.

"You're going to have a great time," Laura said as the four of them sat down for breakfast at the street-side cafe a couple of blocks from their apartment. "I'm kind of jealous."

"Me too," Rob added as he poured half the container of syrup on his waffles.

"Honey, that's more than enough."

"We don't have wild blueberry syrup at home. Plus, it's a special occasion."

Trent shook his head and leaned in close to Reed. "I don't sound like that, do I?"

Reed looked directly at Trent. "No, of course not."

The tone had Trent doubting Reed's veracity, and he was extra careful not to put more than a reasonable amount of syrup on his waffles.

"Make sure to take a lot of photos," Laura said, cutting into her fluffy, veggie-filled omelet with her fork. "Especially at the markets."

Trent nodded. He'd stopped to buy guidebooks a few days earlier. Then, the night before, they'd gone out for Turkish food, and afterward he'd encouraged everyone to watch *Topkapi*. Not "forced," which had been Reed's word. Reed had no sense of fun sometimes.

"I don't think it's going to look at all like the film. It's fifty years old. Istanbul's changed a lot since then. Much more modern, even in the more traditional areas."

"Whatever." Trent preferred to think of it as some Arabian Nights adventure. "You can't tell me they've modernized the old harem and Topkapi Palace, or the Blue Mosque."

"It's not that difficult to imagine big changes. Remember the Aya Sophia Mosque used to be a church until the fifteenth century," Reed said as he picked up a glass of blood-orange juice.

"You take all the fun out of everything." Trent yanked his napkin out from under the silverware, which went clattering onto the sidewalk, causing a waiter to rush to his side with replacements.

Reed frowned. "Not everything." He gave Trent a wink, and Laura made an overstated gesture of looking in the opposite direction as Reed kissed Trent's cheek.

"Okay, not everything."

"Look, you don't have to come along if you don't want...."

"I do want to. I really do, but I want us to have some fun too. It's not going to be like Rome again, is it?" Trent hadn't enjoyed being left in Rome while Reed took off on an unexpected Interpol case.

"God, I hope not." Reed's expression grew serious.

"No, I don't mean *that*," Trent responded and put his hand on top of Reed's.

"Don't mean what?" Laura asked. Rob was busy attacking his waffles and hadn't even tried to join the conversation.

"Nothing, Mom. So, how's your omelet? What've you got in there?"

"Trent?" Her voice rose as she turned one syllable into four.

He stuffed waffle into his mouth so he wouldn't have to answer. He'd never told her what had happened during that harrowing boat chase. If it hadn't been for Reed and another agent's quick thinking... well, Trent didn't want to consider what could have happened.

When Trent didn't reply, Laura started in on Reed. "What happened in Italy?"

"We went down to those islands off Sicily. Did Trent tell you we hiked up a volcano at sunset and watched it erupting?"

"What? An active volcano?" Laura's eyebrows shot up so far, Trent expected them to leap off her face.

"An active volcano?" Rob asked. "That sounds really cool."

Trent nodded, glad Reed had moved the discussion away from something even worse. "It was incredible. It only coughed up some glowing rocks. No lava, and it wasn't very dangerous."

Reed nodded and made sure his mouth was full too.

"Somehow I don't think I'm getting the whole story," Laura said and turned her attention back to the omelet. "Don't think I won't find out. Sooner or later."

LATER THAT afternoon Reed dropped Rob, Laura, and Trent off at the LAX departures level and drove around the airport once. He wanted to give them a little time to say good-bye, and Trent loved going to the airport, even if he wasn't traveling. Reed was used to his little quirks and found them charming. At least he did now that he knew what to expect.

For the first year or so, they'd had some growing pains, learning to navigate their way around each other. Reed wasn't perfect by a long shot. He never expected to feel guilty about leaving Trent at home when he had to travel so much, but as time went by, he found it more difficult, not less. Maybe that said something important about their relationship. What, exactly, he wasn't sure.

On the second circuit, he spotted Trent waving from near the American Airlines departure hall. Reed stopped to pick him up.

"That was fun, Trent. I'm glad your parents came for the holidays."

"Seriously, what happened to you, Reed? It's almost no fun if we don't disagree about things."

Reed shot Trent a glance, but with the traffic, he couldn't risk trying to figure out what Trent was talking about.

The next two days raced by as they finished preparing for the trip. Tom White insisted Trent come in for a pretrip briefing, and Reed sat quietly in the chair next to him while White told Trent exactly what he could and couldn't do on the trip. The "couldn't" list was much longer, and as the discussion went on, Trent's face got longer too.

But White was a master at dealing with people—one of the key requirements for his job. He waited until he'd given Trent all the bad news before handing him the passport he would use.

Trent glanced over at Reed as he took the little blue booklet from White. "Is this an official passport?"

"If you mean are you going under the auspices of the US government, no." White sat back in his chair as Trent flipped it open.

"Trent *Carpenter*?" Trent's face brightened and he appeared to let go of any residual disappointment as soon as he learned he was going to travel under an alias. "I'm Trent Carpenter. *Trent* Carpenter. Tr—"

"We know." Reed shook his head, but he enjoyed Trent's reactions to little things like getting even half of a fake name.

"But why? And who is Reed?"

"I'll be Richard Applegate. And it's just in case I hit the jackpot with any of the contacts I'll be making. They're likely to check me out, and I can't have any ties to my life here and to Trent Copeland. It could be dangerous if anything goes wrong."

"What could go wrong?"

"Trent, you really have to stop saying that." Reed worked hard to keep the smirk off his face.

"Sure, *Dick*, I'll try."

"I go by Richard, thank you."

"Dick."

"Ahem." White paused until he had their attention before continuing. "We need to go over some contingency plans, Trent. Specifically, who you'll contact and what you'll say if anything happens to Dick." White could match smirks with the best of them.

"Okay." Trent pulled the little notebook out of his pocket and turned his attention to White.

Reed felt an odd swelling in his chest at how Trent could focus when necessary. It hadn't been Reed's idea to bring Trent along. For some reason Tom White wanted it, and he hadn't yet explained his reasoning to Reed's satisfaction.

Trent took notes and confirmed anything he wasn't sure about. It dawned on Reed that this might actually work out well. He hated having a partner on missions—after what happened with Peter Isett in Myanmar, he'd done his best to avoid teaming up permanently, but the Bureau and Interpol didn't like to leave agents on their own in another country.

On the drive home, Reed expected Trent to go back to his usually chatty self, excited about the trip and talking about what clothes he'd pack and what they should eat. But he remained uncharacteristically subdued.

"What's up, Carpenter?" Reed flashed him a quick smile as he navigated the 170.

Trent exhaled and looked out the passenger window for a moment before answering. "I just hope like hell I don't have to call the embassy and ask for Mr. Black."

Those were the instructions if Reed went missing for forty-eight hours—or was found dead.

10

THE FLIGHT from LA to Istanbul took sixteen hours. They had a layover in Zurich, and Trent was disappointed they didn't have enough time to leave the airport. Instead, he bought some chocolate, and a stack of postcards to send his parents, nieces, and nephews. Reed had to remind him that international security rules made a Swiss Army knife out of the question.

"But they have like fifty different tools on here! I've never seen one like it. Who knows when you'll need some of these things?"

"It's for me?"

"Yeah." Trent nodded vigorously, but Reed didn't believe him.

"Half of those fifty would make excellent weapons for hijackers. I'd hate to have to report that Mr. Carpenter was detained in Switzerland and won't be joining me in Turkey."

"What color is that?" Trent frowned, trying to remember.

"Red."

"There's no Mr. Red on the list."

"That's what color Tom will be seeing if your knife causes us to get extra scrutiny. And he won't be as likely to include you in any future plans."

"Fair enough." Trent put the knife back on the counter and thanked the woman in the airport shop.

It was too bad, because in Reed's opinion, Trent could use something like the knife. They went to their gate to wait for the last leg of the journey.

"I understand about the scrutiny, Ree-Richard. I do."

Reed raised an eyebrow.

"We can't draw any attention to ourselves as anything but what we are. A rich guy who likes antiques and his *friend*."

Reed nodded.

"But wouldn't a rich guy like you expect you could take whatever you wanted on board, expecting special treatment?"

"Do you think I'd get special treatment?"

Trent pressed his lips together as he considered the question. "Probably not. And then we'd probably have to leave the knife here."

"You can get one back in the States, even with fifty different tools."

"It's not the same as buying it in Switzerland."

"Maybe we'll have time on the way back to get one and mail it home."

"Thanks... Dick." Trent winked and gave Reed a noisy smooch on the cheek.

Trent's arm was just sliding around Reed's waist when the announcement to board came over the loudspeakers. They were traveling first class—as part of their cover—so they were boarding first.

"To be continued," Trent said and gave Reed's hand a squeeze.

11

IN ISTANBUL, a chauffeur-driven car dropped them in front of the Hotel Sultania, and a bellman brought their luggage inside to the registration desk.

"Richard Applegate. I have a booking for seven nights."

Reed slid their passports and a credit card across the counter, and the clerk opened both passports, then started typing away at the computer.

"Welcome, Mr. Applegate and Mr. Carpenter. We are very glad for you to be staying here." He squinted at the screen, then turned his gaze back to Reed. "There's a package waiting for your arrival. Would you like me to send it up with your baggage, or will you take it now?"

"I'll take it now."

"Certainly." The clerk finished the registration process, made three keys, which he handed to Reed, then proceeded to explain some of the hotel's amenities. "Now, let me fetch that package for you."

Reed collected a brown-paper-wrapped package the size of a shoebox from the clerk, and they headed for the elevator. In the spacious room, Trent discovered their luggage had already been brought up, and both suitcases were set up on luggage racks.

"Wow, check this place out!"

Reed sat on the bed and examined the package. Without looking up, he replied, "Trent, you read every single thing about this hotel online already and showed me four thousand photos. How can you still be so excited?"

Trent shrugged and pressed his lips together before answering. "It's different in person. And why don't you ever get excited about hotels and exotic destinations?"

"Because I'm working. This isn't my vacation."

Trent's mood plummeted, and he sat next to Reed on the burgundy-and-gold brocade bedspread. "I forgot. Don't you at least have today off?"

Reed looked up from unwrapping the package. "Not really. I need to identify and attempt to make contact with the dealers who worked with

Matthews and Granby. If they sell their inventory to someone else, we may never catch them."

"I get it. So what's in that package?" Trent had watched Reed examine it from all sides before untaping one end and carefully peeling back the brown paper. "Who's it from?"

"A friend at the tourist office."

"Oh." Trent's eyebrows rose of their own accord. "Tourist office" was their code word for the US consulate here in Istanbul. Reed was worried any room could be bugged, so he'd schooled Trent on a whole list of code words. Trent had added a few of his own, including "It's hot in here" for "I love you" in case whoever was listening might be offended.

"Trent, if someone bugs our room, I doubt our relationship is going to make any difference to them or whatever they're planning. Besides, that phrase might be necessary for its original meaning."

"It's January. It's cold even in Istanbul."

"Fine." Reed had relented. "We'll use that one too." He shook his head and pulled Trent in for a soft kiss.

Now, in their room in Istanbul, all Reed's preparation suddenly felt surreal to Trent. He watched Reed open the box and pull out two slightly used smartphones and two folded notes on pale green paper.

"Here's your phone." Reed handed one over to Trent. "It should already be set up for speed-dialing the other."

"Wow, that's some kind of service from the tourist office."

"They're good like that. Remember, these aren't for your usual web surfing and e-mails."

Trent nodded. Reed had drilled that into him too. They couldn't let themselves be connected to anyone back home. If Trent wanted to check his personal e-mail, he was supposed to go to an Internet café. But the most important thing was to act the way their cover personas would act. Reed was a businessman here to arrange a deal, and Trent was his boyfriend, who had time for playing tourist. Later, Reed would do some shopping once he'd located the suspected fences that Matthews and Granby had been buying from.

"Trent, you'll be on your own for the morning and probably the afternoon. I have some meetings about the financing." Reed fluttered one of the notes that had been in the package.

"Already?"

"Yes."

Trent took the note from Reed and read it. "Mr. Applegate. We would be delighted to discuss the options for financing your construction project upon your arrival. Please meet us on the 8th, at 9:00 a.m."

"But it's already p—"

Reed put a finger to his lips; then Trent recalled the code for meetings. Subtract the date from the time and reverse a.m. and p.m. This meeting was really at 1:00 p.m. Reed had forty minutes to get there.

"I'll call you when we're done, sweetheart." Reed winked.

"Do you know how long you'll be?"

"No. Just entertain yourself."

"Okay. But what things do you want me to save to see with you? And what about dinner?"

"I don't know when I'll have free time. If there's something you really want to see or do while we're here, then go ahead and do it. Don't wait for me."

"But—" Trent stopped when he saw the pinched look around Reed's eyes. The only way to let Reed concentrate on work was for Trent to act as if he wasn't disappointed. He should be good at that by now.

"Okay. Well, I've got a whole list of things I want to see." Trent held up his little notebook and pasted on a smile as Reed collected his fancy-looking faux-alligator-skin laptop bag and turned toward the door. "Remember, Dick, it's hot in here."

"Wh—" Reed grinned. "I think it's hot in here too." He blew Trent a kiss and left.

12

TRENT CHANGED into a pair of jeans and a black leather jacket and headed down to the lobby. The place was immaculate, and the staff smiled and nodded as he passed.

"Do you need a taxi?" a doorman asked as Trent neared the door to the street.

"Not yet. Maybe later."

The man nodded and opened the door. Before he'd even stepped outside, the incredible noise and bustle of the street assaulted his eardrums. Up above in their hotel room, the soundproof windows had insulated him from the real Istanbul.

He turned right out of the hotel and wandered down the street. The smell of car exhaust and dust pervaded his senses, and the chill in the air surprised him. He'd barely noticed the temperature when they'd gotten out of the limo because he'd been so excited to arrive—and more than a little sleep deprived. Now, he was wide-awake, and the energy of being in a new place took hold.

In some ways Istanbul reminded him of Thailand. The crowds, the mix of old and new buildings, and the aromas of delicious food snaking their way through the streets. His stomach growled. He had no clue what time it was back home, but it was lunchtime here, so food would be the first thing on his agenda.

As with any city, the best place to eat was the one full of locals, so Trent peered through shop and restaurant windows looking for somewhere packed with Turks. He was so focused on the street-level view, when he finally glanced up and spotted the hazy outline of a quintessentially Turkish-style mosque and its towering minarets, he felt the first electricity zinging through his body.

I'm in Istanbul! Not Constantinople.... He fought off the urge to sing the catchy tune. He suspected Turks didn't find it as amusing as Americans.

Eyes still on the beautiful building on a hill on the other side of the river, he nearly ran over several people. Time enough to look around later.

He found a little café that had a few tables scattered on the sidewalk, where several people bundled up in wool coats and colorful scarves sat taking in the view and enjoying the delicious-smelling food.

A waiter seated him outside with a great view and handed him a menu with only a smattering of English.

"Do you speak English?" Trent asked.

"Yes, a little," the waiter replied.

"Can you help me with the menu?"

The waiter smiled. "Come with me." He led Trent inside to the display cases full of food. "What do you like?"

As far as Trent remembered from reading about Turkish food—and that one visit to a Turkish restaurant with Reed and his parents—there wasn't anything he wouldn't want to eat. So he pointed to two or three items that looked good. The waiter nodded and shouted to someone behind the counter.

Trent went back to his table to wait for lunch.

When it arrived, everything had been heated and the plate smelled like heaven. Cinnamon and allspice mixed with garlic, eggplant, beef, tomatoes, and other scrumptious smells. One item resembled a small ground-meat-covered pizza, another a roasted eggplant smothered in a rich tomato sauce, and the third was a grilled chicken in a tomato-based sauce redolent of basil, thyme, and oregano. He tasted one bite from each item, thrilled with his choices. He'd make sure to find out what everything was called so he could try them again.

At this rate, he wouldn't have room for baklava or the other luscious desserts he'd seen piled up in the case inside. He couldn't wait to taste Turkish delight too. He'd have to do a hell of a lot of walking to burn off everything he intended to sample during this visit.

Before he'd finished eating, the sound of the prayer call—amplified through loudspeakers—flowed over the city. He was nowhere near a mosque, but he heard it loud and clear. Despite the eerie sound, no one around him reacted. Trent had put his fork down out of respect, but around him no one stopped eating or walking or talking or driving cars and buses. The traffic continued as if the prayer call had happened on another planet.

While there were many Muslims in Turkey, it was by and large a secular country. Just another contradiction from what he'd expected.

ACROSS TOWN, Reed entered a nondescript office building, rode an elevator to a nondescript office staffed by a dozen nondescript Turks and assorted Westerners typing, talking, and, for all intents and purposes, running an import-export financing firm, and entered a nondescript conference room with framed prints of Turkish sites and scenery on nondescript beige walls.

"Good to see you, Applegate." The woman shook Reed's hand, and they settled into chairs on opposite sides of the brown faux-woodgrain table.

"Same here, Clifford. Looks like you've got a nice posting in Istanbul."

"Too much paperwork, but the food's amazing."

"That's what everyone says when they're posted abroad." Reed grinned. He'd gone through initial training at Quantico with Clifford—or Walker, as she'd been called once upon a time.

"I hear Asia'll never be the same after your time there."

"That's only half the story." Reed glanced around the room, always vigilant in new places for bugs, cameras, exits.

"I hope to hear the rest. After we get our work done." She cocked her head and let her gaze play over his face, but he kept his on the corners and ceiling. "Nothing to worry about here. Swept daily. There really was a Western Asia Trade Finance Group years ago. No way to trace anything here to any of the agencies or alphabet soup that runs the show now."

"Good to hear."

"Your driver is a Turk working with Europol and seconded to our unit for as long as we can keep him. You can trust him completely. He can translate for you as well as get you to and from anywhere you need. He's also the go-to guy for restaurant recommendations." She cracked a smile. "Seriously. He's a good guy."

"I trust you." Reed flipped through the briefing folder Clifford had handed him. "Let's work through this."

"Sure." She opened her folder. "We knew Matthews was here. Because he had been under suspicion of trading in illegal antiquities, he was under surveillance for most of the time he was in Istanbul. We lost track of him when he left the city, but I've compiled a list of everyone he spoke to and everywhere he went on our watch."

"How did he manage to acquire the items, and load them onto a plane?"

"Probably because he didn't. I suspect the purchase and the flight must have been arranged by his travel companion, Mitchell Granby, who wasn't on our radar. We noted that they met several times in Istanbul, but our focus was on Matthews, and we dropped the ball on Granby."

Reed didn't have to belabor the point. He respected Clifford even more for not making excuses for the team's oversight.

"My local analysts compiled dossiers on everyone Matthews met, with special attention to contacts in the black market, particularly in art. I've prioritized the likelihood they are connected to anyone supplying items taken from Iraq. Only three look promising. The others are involved in drugs, weapons, or money laundering."

"Not my problem for this trip."

"Understood. They aren't going anywhere. If they don't get killed by a rival or someone they trust, they'll be here next time someone wants to come to clean up that mess."

"Have you got any advice for me?"

She looked up from her folder. "Sure. Make sure to visit a *hamam* while you're here, take your traveling companion on an evening cruise up the Bosporus, and don't drink Turkish coffee after dinner."

He let out a pent-up breath with a burst of laughter. Her unspoken advice was not to take everything so damn seriously. Clifford had been the prankster in his class, while Reed had been the uptight, rule-following prick—her words. They'd butted heads until they kicked the snot out of each other during a hand-to-hand training session. Anyone who could hold their own against a former Special Forces operator had his utmost respect. She liked the fact that he never stared at her tits. They'd become fast friends after a few weeks of intense animosity.

"I'll keep that in mind. There might even be a chance for you to meet Trent."

"I'd like that. It wouldn't be out of place for us to arrange a dinner meeting while you're here seeking *financing*, would it?"

"Probably not. Let's see how much progress I make over the next few days." Reed closed the folder and put it in his laptop bag. "The groundwork your team has done will save me a lot of time."

They spent another thirty minutes on details of the men most likely to be involved with Iraqi and other antiquities smuggling. Then Reed went back down to his car for the ride across town in traffic that rivaled that of Bangkok—far worse than LA.

13

REED HAD Deniz, their driver/Europol agent, take him over to the Grand Bazaar. While the Bazaar remained one of Istanbul's biggest tourist attractions, it was also filled with shops where locals could purchase items required for daily life, whether it was a lamp, tea, or spare lightbulbs.

The largest single shopping area in the world, the Grand Bazaar consisted of sixty streets and alleys under covered walkways, a maze of tiny shops unchanged for decades or even centuries; and larger, more modern shops with electrical goods, computers, cameras, and things the fifteenth-century builders could scarcely imagine.

In one part of the market was a section of even narrower walkways where one could find jewelry and all manner of art and possibly even artifacts looted from archaeological digs in what used to be Mesopotamia—including Iraq.

Deniz stopped near the southern entrance. Reed opened the door but didn't get out at once.

"Call me if you need anything—or preferably text. I'll park as close as I can and catch up with you, but I can't say how long it will take me to find you."

"I'm just looking around this time, not making contact. We'll do that together next time."

"Fine. I'll still park and—"

"Could you do me a huge favor? You can say no."

"What?"

"Can you pick Trent up from the hotel and bring him here? I know it's not work...."

"Forget what's work. I'm part of your cover, as well as backup. It will make you look more authentic while shopping if he's with you."

Cars behind them honked incessantly.

"Here's an idea. Stay in the car, and we'll get Trent together, then I'll drop you both off. Otherwise you'll never find each other. Even locals get lost in there, never to be seen again." Deniz grinned and chuckled.

"If you're sure." Reed slammed the door shut.

"Don't mention it." Deniz pulled away from the curb, but the honking behind them didn't abate.

Reed dialed Trent, who picked up on the second ring.

"Trent, it's Richard."

"Hi, honey."

"Where are you?"

"Hanging out near the Spice Market."

"Spice Market," Reed said to Deniz.

"Who are you talking to, Rick?"

"Our driver, Deniz. We're on our way to pick you up, then we can wander around the Grand Bazaar together. How does that sound?"

"Perfect."

Reed relayed the location of the best meeting point, and within minutes they stopped around the corner from the southern entrance and Deniz opened the door to let Trent inside, then closed the door behind him.

"Thanks," Trent said, then slid over to give Reed a kiss. "Is that okay?" he asked in a whisper.

"It's fine." Reed met Deniz's gaze in the rearview mirror and spotted nothing to worry about. "I want to hear all about your day, but first I need to tell you what we'll be doing at the Bazaar."

"Not shopping?"

"Yes, shopping. But I'm also checking out a few of the shops where my old friend might have purchased items." Code for Matthews.

"What do you want me to do?" Trent buzzed with visible excitement, probably over being part of Reed's recon work.

Maybe this wasn't such a great idea after all. He should have briefed Trent carefully before bringing him into the market. "Nothing special. We're just going to look at things. You let me know if you see something you like, though. We can buy whatever you want."

"We can?"

"Deniz gave me all the tips on negotiating. Let's have some fun too."

Trent beamed. They pulled up at the southern entrance again and this time they both got out. Reed leaned in the passenger side window. "Deniz, we'll just take a taxi back to the hotel."

"Don't worry, Mr. Applegate, I won't be far away. Please call me when you're ready to get picked up."

Reed shook his head.

Deniz held up a hand. "At least for your first few days here, it's best for you to rely on me."

"Okay. We'll call when we're ready. Then we'll want to have dinner."

"Should I make reservations for you somewhere?"

"Where would I want to have dinner?" Reed grinned, recalling Clifford's comment about Deniz's knowledge of restaurants.

"I'll take care of the right place for you, Mr. Applegate. Enjoy your shopping."

The honking behind their car increased, and Deniz pulled away with a screech of tires.

ENTERING FROM the south led them through a maze of shops and stalls selling carpets, leather clothing, and other leather items as they headed toward the heart of the market and the jewelry and antiques stalls.

Trent found a leather jacket he insisted Reed try on, then spotted a gorgeous leather briefcase. Reed soon found himself overwhelmed by the close quarters with the seemingly thousands of other people making their way from shop to shop. The ceilings were fifteen feet high, and the air circulating above them was the only thing that made the space bearable. It took all of his concentration to remain aware of his surroundings. Getting distracted could be deadly if he made contact with the wrong people.

"This certainly isn't the place for anyone who's claustrophobic," he commented. The Bazaar reminded him of the huge covered market in Thailand, where you could buy anything from saffron monk's robes to magical amulets to plastic microwave egg cookware. Everything and anything all piled under one roof, though each shop had a specialty.

"The Spice Market is a lot like this, only everything smells really good. Nuts, spices, a hundred kinds of olives, another hundred kinds of pickled vegetables, and beautiful squares of about a hundred varieties of Turkish delight, all glowing like gems."

"You're reminding me I never got lunch."

"Do they have food in here?" Trent glanced around them.

"Who knows? Let's take a look at that map."

A fast-moving crowd of people brushed past them and nearly knocked Reed into a display of hand-tooled wallets. The leader was carrying a small Japanese flag, and the group behind him rushed ahead, then stopped to take photographs, further clogging the narrow walkways.

They ducked into the nearest shop while the Japanese group snapped away at the shops, each other, and the inevitable selfies. Trent dug into the inner pocket of his jacket and produced the map he'd grabbed near the entrance.

"There's a café around the next corner," Reed said. "Let's grab a snack to tide us over until dinner."

"Dinner?"

"Deniz is going to surprise us." Reed smiled and hooked his arm through Trent's elbow. Connected against any new onslaught, they made their way to the café and shared an order of fresh warm pita and smooth, smoky baba ganouj.

Reed smiled as he polished off the last piece. "Is this a lot better than what we can get at home, or is it just the excitement of being here?"

"Both, probably." Trent ran a napkin across his mouth. "Are you excited, Reed?"

"About this trip? Yeah. Why would you ask?"

"I don't think you ever really seem to enjoy anywhere we've visited together." Trent's face didn't exhibit any particular emotion.

Reed opened his mouth to protest but shut it again. Trent was right. Traveling wasn't the adventure for Reed that it was for Trent. Had that attitude dampened Trent's enjoyment of their previous trips?

"I just don't express it the same way you do," Reed said, but he avoided Trent's gaze.

Trent raised his eyebrows and pressed his lips together. He hadn't bought that excuse.

"I've enjoyed being with you… and I'm having fun now."

"We've been together twenty minutes." Trent shrugged. "I'm not asking you to spend more time with me than you can, just saying that I wish you did enjoy this more. I feel a little guilty, and more than a little sad that you can't enjoy the trip much."

It was Reed's turn to feel guilty. Trent could entertain himself, and he'd clearly enjoyed the time he'd spent on his own, but Reed vowed to set aside time for doing things together on this trip if at all possible.

"Well, let's go look at some antiques." Reed reached a hand out to Trent and they both stood up.

THEY TOOK their time moving past shops. Now and then Reed pulled Trent into one and they examined the goods in more detail. Reed appeared to be making an effort to have fun, but after a while, Trent thought he actually was enjoying himself. They tried on Turkish caps, a couple of jackets, and Reed asked Trent if he liked specific items.

It seemed they would never get to the center of the bazaar. There really were hundreds or even thousands of shops. The shopkeepers were friendly, though some loudly hawked their goods or tugged at an elbow to encourage tourists to examine their wares.

Several of the shops they stopped in had high-end items. Nothing looked like the museum-quality gold pieces Reed was searching for, but he looked at price tags on dozens of items, although he didn't inquire about anything in particular.

"Did you see something you liked?" Trent asked when they had left what must have been the thousandth shop they'd visited.

"Actually, I saw several nice things."

"Things Richard would like?"

"Yes, and some other things too." Reed grinned. He looked at his watch. "Still plenty of time before dinner, unless you're ready to eat again."

"I'm always ready to eat." Trent's appetite invariably amused Reed, but lately Trent had been watching what he ate. He needed to start working out more. "I had a really delicious lunch. I'm definitely going to enjoy the culinary aspects of this trip."

"Good. Would you mind if we split up for an hour or so?"

Getting lost concerned Trent more than the idea of wandering on his own again, but he wouldn't get in the way of Reed's recon mission here tonight. "Sure. Where and when should we meet up?"

"Remember the shop with the ugly chairs?"

"I think so."

"Meet me there in an hour?"

"Okay."

Reed held on to Trent's arm and went up on his toes to plant a kiss on Trent's lips. "See you in a bit. Text me or call if you get lost."

"Have fun," Trent added in an ironic tone that Reed probably didn't even notice. Before Trent could take another breath, Reed was gone, lost in the sea of tourists all ready to shell out their cash on an unforgettable souvenir of their visit to Istanbul.

It wasn't the worst thing to be on his own. And this was a good chance to pick up a few gifts. He'd spotted some nice rings and bracelets at a shop about ten meters back along the main row.

Half an hour later, he had selected items for his mother, sister Maggie, his best friend, Beth, and a few extras he'd allocate later. He got an even bigger discount from the shopkeeper because he'd purchased more than one item. He put the parcel into his inner pocket so he wouldn't run the risk of someone taking it out of his messenger bag in the throng.

A glance at his watch told Trent he still had plenty of time before he needed to find Reed. He recalled a few items Reed had paid extra attention to in the shops, and one of those would make a good gift. Trent wove his way back to a shop selling nice antiques of various prices. Reed had eyed a ceramic lion in the back corner of this shop. It was about two feet tall and completely unlike anything else he'd seen so far. The quality wasn't great, not very detailed and clearly not an antique at all. Trent reached for the price tag taped to one ear.

A quick calculation told him it was about US$1000. Ridiculous. Even with bargaining, it cost more than it appeared to be worth. Why had this interested Reed? It slightly resembled some of the pieces he'd shown Trent from the list of missing items from the museum in Baghdad, but it couldn't possibly have been on that list.

"Do you like lion?" The shopkeeper came up behind him, and Trent nearly leapt out of his skin.

"It's okay," he said, not managing to lie politely after being so thoroughly surprised. "Is it Turkish?"

"No. You want Turkish ceramic?"

"Not particularly. Just looking, really."

"I have other item, like the lion, but older. Beautifuler."

"Really?" Trent glanced around the shop.

"Not here. In the back room. Come have some tea, and I show you." The man smiled and a little gold chip in one tooth glittered in the dimly lit shop.

"Why not?" Maybe the man had something in back Reed would like as a gift.

"Follow." The man waved a hand as he turned away.

Trent followed him deeper into the shop.

REED HAD put out feelers in three shops, careful not to overdo his interest on the first visit. He didn't get what he'd consider a promising bite from any shopkeeper who might have the quality of the items Matthews and Granby had purchased. It was a rather disappointing result, but he'd try again the following day. Any really shady dealer wouldn't jump at the first overture from a total stranger.

He'd spotted some nice men's rings in the last shop and considered selecting one as a gift for Trent. Jewelry wasn't one of Trent's passions, but he'd pointed out several rings and pendants while they'd been window-shopping. But what significance would Trent place on a ring from Reed? Would he get the wrong idea and think it was a proposal?

Reed stared at one particular ring: an oval-shaped emerald set in a band of reddish gold comprised of a series of openwork leaves. Despite the delicate work, the ring wasn't at all feminine. It wasn't hit-you-over-the-head masculine either. It suited Trent's taste perfectly. Going by the price, the emerald was most likely real, though not of top quality, even taking into account the usual prebargaining markup. He didn't have to decide right away, but he might not get another chance to come back here for casual shopping, especially if he made contact with one of the antiquities fences on a subsequent visit.

"How much is this one?"

"Very good price for you. Would you like some tea while we discuss?"

"Thank you."

The shopkeeper motioned toward a small table near the back of the shop, and Reed perched on one of the rickety wooden chairs. He took only a tiny sip of tea so as not to appear inhospitable, still taking care not to get drugged. It was a common ploy in order to rob customers, at least in some shops.

After five minutes and some casual chitchat, Reed left with the ring. He'd paid far less than he'd expected, so maybe the gem wasn't real after all. But it was pretty, and Trent would love it. He could already picture Trent wearing it and trying to find the right angle to make the emerald's deep green fire dance on his finger.

On the way back to meet Trent, Reed paused to check out another suspicious shop. He'd seen an intriguing sculpture of a lion tucked away near the back. Its stylized head and body screamed ancient Mesopotamia—nothing like the Ottoman or earlier Turkish style.

He hadn't done more than glance at it on the first visit. This time he'd pay more obvious attention. One tactic was to see if the shopkeeper offered to show him something similar but of much higher quality that wasn't on display. That was a sure signal of something illegal.

After a few twists and turns in the crowded indoor street, Reed came upon the shop with the lion. He stepped inside and spotted the shopkeeper in the back of the shop. Then a familiar shape came into view. Trent.

And he was stepping through a doorway in the back corner of the shop. The shopkeeper followed and shut the door before Reed could reach them.

Oh, shit.

"Trent!" Reed shouted and grabbed for the door, hidden so well behind some Turkish carpets hanging on the wall that Reed couldn't easily find it.

"Can I help you?" Another shopkeeper, an elderly bearded man wearing a green cap, black-and-yellow striped vest, and the traditional loose pants, appeared at Reed's side.

"My friend went in back. Let me back there, please."

"Certainly." The man slipped a hand under a rug and swung open the door.

Reed raced inside.

"Trent!" Reed saw he was about to sip a cup of tea and smacked the cup out of Trent's hand. Hot tea splashed as the cup hit the floor and rolled away.

Trent leapt to his feet. "Reed? What's wrong?"

Reed grabbed Trent's hand and pulled him back into the shop and then into the street. "You okay?"

"Yes, Reed. Richard. Shit. Sorry!" Trent gave Reed a nervous smile and hunched his shoulders in a shrug that made Reed feel like a jerk.

"What were you doing in there?"

"Looking at—"

"You know not to drink the tea."

"Yes. I know. I hadn't drunk any. Just holding the cup. I remember what you told me." Trent pressed his lips together in a frown. "Don't you trust me? I'm not a five-year-old."

Reed pressed Trent's hand to his lips and kissed it. "I know you're not. I was just scared. Worried." He pulled Trent close, hoping he wouldn't notice the tears stinging Reed's eyes. He'd die if something happened to Trent.

Reed tightened his grip around Trent and they stood like that, Reed holding Trent and Trent not hugging back. A few people gave them odd looks and walked pointedly around them. Finally Reed let go and stepped back. "I'm sorry. I panicked and all sorts of scary images flashed through my brain."

"I get it. But we did go over all these things several times. I listened to all the precautions. I love that you want to keep me safe, but please stop worrying." Trent put an arm around Reed and kissed him.

Finally, tension drained out of Reed's body, replaced by dizziness and hunger. "Let's go have dinner."

"Good idea."

Reed phoned Deniz, and he picked them up at the southern entrance ten minutes later. As they drove through the dark streets and passed a brightly spotlighted bridge that looked remarkably like the Golden Gate Bridge, Reed finally felt safe.

"Trent, I do trust you. I *know* you know what to do and what not to do. But no matter what, I'll never stop worrying. As long as I love you, I'll always worry. Because I wouldn't know how to go on without you."

They held hands in the back of the car and Reed thought he saw Deniz smiling in the rearview mirror.

14

THEY SAT across from each other at a window table in the Maiden's Tower, perhaps the most ideally situated restaurant in all of Istanbul. Deniz sat a few tables away, in sight, but not in earshot. To anyone looking on, he was simply a bodyguard/driver for a couple of wealthy American tourists.

A waiter brought them a bottle of wine made from a Turkish grape variety even Trent had never heard of, while they nibbled on Turkish bread and olives.

"This place is incredible," Trent said as he stared out the window.

"Deniz said it's the most romantic place in town, but the food's not great." Reed popped a salty black olive into his mouth. He loved the way Trent's eyes had lit up when they'd parked the car near the water and taken the little boat out to the restaurant.

"It's romantic. Right in the middle of the river between Europe and Asia. I don't even care what we eat."

"I'm glad." Reed reached out to hold on to Trent's hand. The ring was in his pocket. This was the perfect place to give Trent a gift. Reed slipped his hand into his jacket. "Trent, I've got—"

"Reed, I have some information for you." He grimaced. "Richard. Damn, I'm sorry."

"It can wait. Let me just—"

"No. It can't." Trent was smiling. "This is important. You'll like it."

Reed took his hand off the little box and out of his pocket. "Go ahead. I'm all ears."

Trent leaned closer and lowered his voice. "The shop… the one with the lion?"

"Yeah?" Reed hated the way Trent dragged everything out for maximum drama, but he took a breath and waited. In his own time, Trent would get to the point. Still, Reed's stomach leapt at Trent's mention of the lion sculpture.

"I had noticed you looking at it." Trent paused. "The shopkeeper noticed *me* looking at it. And he asked if I was interested. It was really expensive and not all that impressive." He ate an olive.

Reed sipped wine and waited.

"I said I wasn't particularly interested, so he asked if I might want to see something else, in the back."

Reed sat up and stared. Maybe it was a good thing he showed up when he had. What had Trent gone and done? If he blew their cover.... Best not to think about it.

"Well, you saw me go in the back. He mentioned he had some other lions, and I said I was interested in gold."

"Trent, that's not your job...."

"He didn't have any, but he suggested I go see this guy." Trent pulled a shop business card out of his pocket and handed it to Reed.

The card was pale blue with gold foil filigree around the edges. The name Mehmet Ozan was printed in a delicate Oriental font along with a phone number. "I'll check this out tomorrow. Alone."

"But—"

"Thank you for this. But there's no way you can talk me into bringing you along."

"I was thinking...."

"Trent, just think about being a tourist. Do some research for a book. Shop."

The waiter brought their main dishes, and for a few moments, the subject was forgotten, at least by Reed.

"How's your dinner?" he asked Trent.

"It's okay. I hope you won't think this is rude, but the lunch I had at a little café near our hotel was better."

Reed put his fork down. His beef and lamb dish wasn't particularly tasty. The best that could be said about it was that it was hot. "I guess we're paying for the view."

"You're a millionaire, Richard, you can afford it."

Reed pushed his half-eaten dinner to the side and grabbed Trent's hand. "God, I love you."

"If I say 'I love you, Richard,' I kind of feel like I'm cheating on Reed." Trent gave a charmingly shy shrug, and Reed wanted to take him right back to the hotel that instant. "But, I do love you." Trent pushed his own plate away and reached into his jacket. "I got something for you, R-Richard. I hope you like it." He put a little box on the table in front of Reed, then looked into Reed's eyes.

Reed's hand went to his chest and he felt his own little box through his jacket. He frowned as he reached for the box Trent had given him. "What is it?"

"We have this wonderful American tradition where you open it up to find out."

"How quaint." Reed flipped the box open, and there on dark blue velvet sat a silver ring dotted with a flat disk of brilliant blue lapis lazuli. "Wow, this is beautiful."

Trent beamed. "Really? You can't see in this candlelight, but it's got veins of gold running through it. That's how you know the lapis is real."

"Is that what the shopkeeper told you?"

"No. I read it on a gemological web site before we left LA." Trent shook his head. "Put it on. If it doesn't fit, we can get it resized pretty easily."

Reed slipped the ring on his right hand. It was a little loose, but not so much it might slip off. "I love it. Thank you." He gave Trent a PG-rated kiss. "This feels so anticlimactic now, but you stopped me earlier when…." Reed pulled the box out of his pocket and put it in front of Trent.

"Is this what you wanted to say?"

Reed nodded.

Trent flipped the box open and stared. His eyes went wide and glittered even more in the low light. "This is gorgeous! Wow. Thank you." Trent blinked a few times and Reed felt all warm and tingly. He took the ring from the box and slipped it onto Trent's finger.

They stared into each other's eyes for a few moments, and then Trent yawned, breaking the magical spell that had enveloped them.

Reed looked at his watch and realized they'd had only a few hours' sleep on the plane. "Let's get you to bed before you turn into a pumpkin."

"Hurry up, or you'll have to carry me to the boat."

"God forbid."

BACK IN the hotel, they washed up, then slid into bed, and Reed fell asleep as soon as Trent wrapped his arms around Reed's waist. Sometime in the middle of the night, Trent woke to Reed kissing his neck and shoulders. Trent pulled him close and covered Reed's mouth in a rough, needy kiss. Reed returned the kiss, ramping up the heat and the urgency.

With smooth, practiced moves, Reed slicked Trent up and plunged inside. For the first few minutes, desire controlled their movements, but once that initial need ebbed away, they continued, making love slowly and comfortably. Reed came first, then finished Trent with a languorous, loving blowjob.

Afterward, as Reed snored softly against his chest, Trent gazed out the windows into the hazy moonlit night, wondering what he would be doing if he'd never met Reed. Would he be in LA drinking cocktails with Beth and Mick? Or would he be sitting at home in his boxers, watching movies and talking to Godiva, his queenly, demanding Siamese?

Trent brushed damp, dark hair off Reed's temple, then combed his fingers through the thick strands. The brand-new ring on Trent's finger glinted in the light coming in the window. He loved the gesture because impromptu gifts from Reed were few and far between. Even the Christmas presents Reed had gotten him felt planned. Reed had likely agonized over what to give Trent for Christmas and lost sight of the joy of giving. It shouldn't be about getting the perfect gift, only about getting something Trent wouldn't think to buy himself.

In the morning, Reed would call the number on the blue-and-gold business card and meet some total stranger, who might be dangerous, with little or no thought to whether he was walking into peril or ambush. Sure, Reed would be careful, but he wouldn't put his own safety ahead of stopping someone breaking laws. It was part of what Trent loved about Reed, and exactly what sometimes kept Trent up at night wondering if that would be the last time they would lie together, whether Reed might not come home in one piece the next time he walked out the door.

"REED?"

It wasn't even light outside when Trent nudged Reed awake. "What? What's wrong?" Reed's heart thudded at the fear he thought he heard in Trent's voice.

"Nothing. Not really."

Reed sat up and looked at Trent, noticing the puffiness around his eyes and the exhaustion visible around his mouth. "Didn't you sleep?"

"Not much. No."

"Just jetlag. Come back to sleep."

Trent shook his head. "I'm fine." His voice wavered and Reed forced himself to wake up.

"Trent, you're scaring me."

"Reed, would you marry me?"

Reed blinked a few times as the oddly phrased question sank in. Usually it was *will* you marry me. "You want to get married?" They'd never discussed it, even after Prop 8 went down for good.

"No. Not exactly."

Reed waited, knowing Trent would explain whatever he was thinking, even though Trent's response was vaguely insulting.

"I mean, we don't actually have to get married, but would you want to, someday?" Trent paused. "I love you, Reed, and.... Well, I just need to know."

"Yes, Trent, I'd marry you, if you asked. Are you asking?"

Trent shook his head, but he seemed calmer now.

"Did you want me to ask *you*?"

"No. I'm good. Thanks." Trent gave Reed about the most unromantic kiss imaginable after that strange conversation and lay down on the pillow and closed his eyes.

Now Reed couldn't sleep, wondering what the hell had prompted Trent's sudden concern about his marriageability. It couldn't have been the rings. Trent had given him a ring, too, and hadn't made a big fuss about it at dinner or after.

Beside Reed on the bed, Trent kicked the bedsheet away, exposing all of his smooth, tanned skin, all the places Reed liked to touch and kiss, and all the parts that made Reed feel good. As easy as it was to figure out how Trent's body worked—though Reed would never tire of exploring it—figuring out what Trent was thinking would take the rest of Reed's life, and he still wouldn't be sure he understood.

In his sleep, Trent let out a sigh. One thing sank into Reed's consciousness: he had all the time in the world to spend understanding Trent Copeland.

Maybe that was all Trent needed to know when he'd asked Reed about getting married.

He ran a finger along Trent's chin and throat to his collarbone, noticing again the ring Trent had given him circling the ring finger of his right hand.

"Yes, Trent, I'd be proud to be your husband." He slid the silver band off and put it on his left hand.

15

REED HAD showered and was dressing when a knock sounded at the door.

"Room service."

"I'll get it," Trent said. He was only wearing a towel, but he was closer to the door.

A waiter wheeled a silver cart inside. "Breakfast, sirs. Traditional Turkish breakfast. You want on the veranda?"

"Yes, please," Reed answered, and the waiter rolled the cart near the window and proceeded to set the food down on the small white wrought-iron table on their private balcony.

Trent slipped the hotel robe on and sat down while Reed finished buttoning his shirt.

"Here is *ekmek*—bread, *beyaz peynir*—Turkish white cheese, plus olives, honey, and yogurt. Also, coffee. You need anything else?"

Reed looked at the feast set out and shook his head, then glanced at Trent, who said, "No, thanks."

"Enjoy, please." The waiter turned on his heel and left.

"Wow," Trent said, licking his lips.

The sight made Reed forget about breakfast for a moment, until his stomach growled. He recalled they hadn't had a very satisfying dinner, despite the elegant and impressive restaurant.

Even though the meal was simple, everything was delicious and filling. "I wonder if we can get this cheese back home," Reed said, popping another cube of the semisoft cheese into his mouth.

"It's kind of like feta, but a little less salty."

"Who knew olives were a breakfast food?" Reed picked one up and fed it to Trent.

Trent chewed, then kissed Reed's hand. "Hey." He pulled Reed's hand from his face and stared at it. "You switched your ring?"

Reed had forgotten that early-morning discussion until then. "Is that okay?"

Trent beamed, and Reed wondered how that smile managed to make the morning even brighter. How wonderful it would be to see Trent this happy every single day.

"It's okay. More than okay." Trent took Reed's hand again and kissed the palm.

"You know how much that turns me on, Trent."

"Yes, I do." Trent kissed Reed's palm again, then brushed his lips across it.

Reed's body responded instantly, nipples tightening and cock swelling. He tried to catch his breath.

"Come here." Trent tugged at Reed's hand until Reed stood next to Trent's chair.

Trent undid Reed's belt, unfastened his pants, and pulled the zipper down. He slid Reed's pants and shorts down enough so he could free Reed's erection and balls, then took Reed into his mouth.

"Uh, mmm. Trent." Reed gave up even thinking about protesting and let Trent do what he wanted. Plenty of worse ways to start the day. When he came several pleasant minutes later, he expected to find tufts of hair in his fists, but he hadn't pulled any out.

What he did notice was the way Trent's cock pushed its way up and out of the hotel robe and pointed toward the sky.

"I think I need to attend to that," Reed said.

Trent grinned. "Since you've got your pants down already...." He motioned toward the railing. "You can enjoy the view at the same time." He winked.

Reed nodded and leaned against the railing, then slid his pants the rest of the way down. Trent stood behind him and pulled the lube out of his robe pocket.

"Why do I get the feeling you planned this?"

THE SHRILL ring of a cellphone cut through the sound of traffic below. Trent reached out and handed Reed his phone.

"Applegate."

"Deniz here. I'm downstairs."

"Give me about fifteen minutes."

"I may have to drive around the block if they're giving tickets."

"Then I'll wait till you come past again." Reed hung up and turned to Trent, who was sitting at the table gulping water, the hotel robe open and showing off his beautiful body in the morning sun.

"You leaving?"

Reed nodded. "How fast can you get dressed? You're coming along this morning."

"I am?"

"Sure. You have ten minutes."

Trent was heading for the bathroom before Reed finished the sentence. While Trent showered, Reed freshened up at the sink, then changed his shirt and pants. He called down to the front desk to have someone pick up the laundry while Trent dried himself off and dressed.

"Why did you decide to take me along?" Trent asked in the elevator on the way down.

"I want to buy you something shiny, baby," Reed replied in a sleazy-sounding voice. He blew Trent a kiss.

"Thanks, Richard. Glad you know how to reward a guy for sucking your cock."

Even though Trent was joking around, the comment hit a little too close to home. Was that why he'd wanted to bring Trent along? For the Applegate cover, it made sense to bring his lover along. It would set whomever they were meeting at ease. Cops and law enforcement didn't bring boyfriends along.

"Sorry," Trent said, clearly reading Reed's thoughts.

"I know." Reed squeezed Trent's hand as they walked through the lobby. What worried him now was whether Trent had read Reed's mood from his expression or just knew Reed well enough. He hoped it was the latter, because if Reed couldn't conceal his thoughts, he could be sending both of them into danger.

TRENT BIT his lip as he walked through the lobby with Reed. Why had he said something stupid like that? Reed had just been making an offhand remark as Richard. A heavy mass formed in his gut, and even Reed's reassuring smile didn't ease it away.

When they stepped onto the sidewalk, Deniz got out of the car and opened the back door for them to slide inside. Then he shut the door and got back into the driver's seat.

"Good morning, sirs."

"I want to call the man recommended by the shopkeeper at the Grand Bazaar last night," Reed said. He handed the card to Deniz. "You know this man?"

"I'm familiar with the name, but I've never dealt with him. How do you want to proceed?"

"I'll call and see whether he has anything I'm interested in. Does he speak English?"

"If he's been dealing with the American collectors, probably."

Reed dialed the number and gave Trent a reassuring eyebrow raise as he waited for the call to connect.

"Good morning. I'd like to speak with Mehmet Ozan please." Reed paused. "I don't speak Turkish." He handed the phone to Deniz.

They waited while he started up a conversation, then paused every now and then to translate. "Mr. Applegate, he would like to meet you at a tea house over on the Asian side of the city to discuss your interests."

Reed nodded. After some back and forth, he arranged an appointment for an hour later. Reed put the phone away, and Deniz set off for their destination.

They drove past the teahouse the first time around so Reed and Deniz could get a feel for the neighborhood and plan any necessary escape routes. They were still ten minutes early.

"What do you want me to do?" Trent asked.

"Just go along with my lead. If he mentions any items, just react as if we are only here to buy something. You saw photos of the items found in the plane and at Matthews' house. I think you can handle yourself."

Trent gulped and nodded. That niggle in his belly had turned into a black hole threatening to pull him inside out. What if he messed up and Reed got hurt trying to keep Trent safe?

"Are you armed?" Reed asked Deniz.

"Yes. Armed driver/bodyguards don't raise eyebrows, but if *you're* carrying, you're more likely to blow cover than if you go in unarmed."

"Right." Reed removed his ankle holster and shoved the handgun under the front seat. "You're coming in with us, though."

"Of course. You need me to translate."

"At least that's how he's playing it," Reed said. He squeezed Trent's hand. "Trent, I need your ring back."

Trent put a protective hand over his new ring. "Why?"

"If I'm as rich as I'm supposed to be, I'd have bought you something much more expensive. We can't have that giving me away." The sadness behind Reed's eyes tore at Trent's heart, an unmistakable disappointment that Reed couldn't give Trent more.

Trent nodded and took a last glance at the dancing green stone before he handed the ring to Deniz, who stowed it carefully in the glove compartment.

"Let's go." Reed waited for Deniz to get out and open the door for them. They followed Deniz to the door and let him speak to the man who greeted them inside.

"He's taking us to the back room," Deniz explained.

They were led through several rooms and out the back of the house, which looked out onto the river far below. The sound of boats' horns drifted up. The teahouse owner seated Reed and Trent at a table while Deniz stood behind Reed, and then the man left.

Several uncomfortable moments passed before another man entered. He was in his forties, sported a jet-black, neatly trimmed, pointed beard and thin mustache. He wore an immaculately tailored dusk-gray suit that almost hid the few extra pounds he carried around his waist.

He spoke Turkish even though he addressed his words to Reed. Deniz translated.

"Thank you for going out of your way, Mr. Applegate. Pleased to make your acquaintance." He shook hands with Reed, and then Trent was introduced as Richard Applegate's friend. Once Mehmet sat down, the man who seated them came back to the table.

Reed let Mehmet order. They were guests here, and from what Trent understood, this duty fell to the host.

While they waited for the tea, Mehmet inquired about their impressions of Istanbul so far. Reed gave a terse comment about not having time for sightseeing, so Mehmet asked Trent.

"I'm enjoying the city very much. I wandered through the Spice Market, and even strolling down the streets is so fascinating. I think after Istanbul, Los Angeles will feel boring."

That seemed to please Mehmet. He grinned and chuckled after Trent's response had been translated. He asked a few more questions, and Trent mentioned some of the dishes he'd enjoyed at lunch.

"Mr. Applegate would do well to follow you instead of the other way around. He might enjoy himself a bit more," Deniz translated.

Reed frowned and shifted on the cushions.

"How do you Americans say, 'all work and no play'? We have a similar admonishment. It's one reason our tea and coffee shops don't rush the orders out. We like to take time to enjoy the little things in life. Time enough for working, but a rest should be a true rest."

At that point, the tea arrived, along with some pastries and dried fruit.

Deniz explained to Trent and Reed how to hold the small tulip-shaped glasses full of deep reddish brown liquid.

"Pick it up with the fingertips, so as not to burn your fingers on the hot glass." He demonstrated. "Help yourself to sugar from the tray. If the tea is too strong, let me know. Mehmet ordered it rather stronger than foreigners may be used to. But it will give him a good impression of you to take tea the Turkish way."

"Thank you," Trent said. The day before he'd been served only a half glass of tea, so it had been easy not to burn his fingers. Now they had been given glasses full nearly to the top. He added one lump of sugar and stirred it into the glass, adorned with a thick gold band at the rim and another gold band at the "waist" of the glass.

"I was surprised how popular tea seems to be here," Trent said. He glanced over at Reed, who was blowing on the hot tea before taking tiny sips. "I've heard of Turkish coffee, but not Turkish tea."

"You are very observant, Trent. In fact, coffee is a tradition here since the sixteenth century, as it was in much of the Arab world. Tea caught on here only in the 1800s as Turks tried to adopt more European habits." Mehmet smiled and nodded as he waited for his words to be translated.

Trent threw a cautious glance toward Reed, fully expecting a frown or admonishment, but Reed seemed to approve of his attempts at conversation.

They sipped tea and nibbled on pastries. Trent bit into a cookie with a crisp crust and bursting with almond flavor. It was so good, he grabbed another from the platter. Reed took one cookie, but didn't eat until Deniz tilted his head slightly and pressed his lips together. Apparently not eating would be an insult to Mehmet, who served Trent more delicacies. The baked rings covered in crispy sesame seeds reminded him of small bagels. He took smaller bites to prolong the pleasure of these treats.

Mehmet spoke. "The sesame pastries are called *simit*. They are popular street food. And these rolled pastries are from my hometown in Eastern Turkey. The string pastry is stuffed with nuts and apricots. Please try it." Then Mehmet sat up and his smile faded away to a more serious expression. "So, Richard, why don't you tell me what I can do for you?"

Reed nodded. "I was given your name when I inquired about the availability of certain items I like to collect."

"And who gave you my name?"

"A shopkeeper in the Bazaar.... Who was it?" Reed glanced to Deniz, who supplied the name of the shop.

"Ah, yes." He glanced over to Trent. "Would you care to try out the nargileh? I believe you may know it as a hookah—water pipe"

"I-uh. No, I don't smoke."

"It's quite different from puffing on a cigarette or cigar. You should take the opportunity while you are here. It is another relaxing local custom." He spoke in Turkish, and the server returned, bringing the pipes, including one for Trent.

Mehmet explained how to use it, then began puffing away as he turned back to Reed. "And what did you have in mind, Richard?"

"I collect gold. The older and more intricate the better."

"Very nice, but very expensive."

"Not an issue. I'm used to paying for what I want—and what something is worth."

Mehmet glanced at Trent, and a heated flush came across his face. Did Mehmet think he was just bought and paid for? Reed didn't seem offended, and that annoyed Trent more than it should have. *We're here playing roles. It has nothing to do with what Reed thinks about me.* Trent reminded himself what Reed had said in the middle of the night and the way Reed had put his new ring on his left hand.

"I might be able to find something for you. Anything in particular you'd like?"

"Something along the lines of what you obtained for Shelton Matthews."

Mehmet put the nargileh down at mention of the name. He rubbed his thumb along his beard and waited for a few moments. Trent suspected he was watching to see how Reed reacted, and the best reaction was none. Trent sipped tea as if he had all the time in world.

"You're friends with Shelton?"

"We never met, but we had mutual friends. Friends who can provide certain things."

"And how is Shelton lately?"

Reed began to stand up. "Let's go, Trent."

The movement stirred Mehmet from his relaxed state, and he waved Reed back to his seat.

"I'm done here." Reed stood. "Either you're testing me or you don't know Matthews, and I have no time to waste on pretenders." He waited for Deniz to translate, then turned toward the door.

"Wait," Mehmet said in English. "Richard, please wait."

Reed turned slowly. If he was as surprised as Trent was that Mehmet spoke English, he wasn't letting on. "Tell me why?"

"I had to make sure you were who you said."

"I haven't lied to *you*, Mehmet."

It frightened Trent a little to see how easily the untruth slipped off Reed's tongue. All they'd done since they arrived here was lie.

"Fair enough. But someone in my position can't be too careful. There are cops and Interpol agents all over. I'm not about to get myself into hot water for a total stranger."

"So let's cut to the chase. Can you get me any of the remaining goblets in the Babylonian set?"

"You don't mess around, do you?"

"No. That's what I want. If you can't get it, I'll be on my way."

"Give me a day or two. I know who can find them, but items like those cannot be rushed."

"If I don't hear back in three days, I'll assume you can't produce."

"I'll know by then, but I can't guarantee to have the item that quickly."

Reed nodded. "I understand. Three days." He stood up again and nodded to Trent, then headed for the door.

Trent rose and turned to Mehmet. "Thank you for the tea."

Mehmet smiled. "I enjoyed our chat, Trent. I hope I can find what Richard wants, and we can talk again. Enjoy your stay in Istanbul."

"I—we will." Trent followed after Reed, with Deniz a few steps behind.

Reed was standing near the car when they exited the tiny teahouse.

Deniz opened the door and took off once everyone was inside.

"It's almost lunchtime. While we're here on the Asian side, might I suggest somewhere for lunch? I think it's time you had some real Turkish food."

"Sounds good." Reed's mood seemed positively ecstatic compared to his demeanor back at the teahouse. Trent couldn't wait to find out what he was thinking.

As they approached the water, Deniz navigated the increasingly narrow streets, then found a place to park. They walked along a sunny street and into a tiny restaurant Trent would never have noticed had he been on his own.

A waiter brought them to a seat near the window, and Deniz ordered for them. While they waited for the food, Deniz brought up the meeting with Mehmet.

"Richard, I think you could have handled that a little more diplomatically."

"I'm not here to make friends."

"I understand, but this is still Turkey, and we have certain expectations in business transactions. You may get more cooperation if you take our customs into consideration."

Reed nodded. "What do you suggest?"

Trent let out a pent-up breath. He thought Reed might snap at Deniz.

"Chitchat never hurts, and thanking someone for his hospitality is expected."

Reed nodded again. "Thankfully Trent handled both of those well." He gave Trent a grateful smile, and Trent's spirits rose. He'd never expected to earn Reed's praise while working a case—or at least not to have it pointed out this way. That heavy mass in his stomach floated away, replaced by a warmth that made him want to wrap his arms around Reed. Probably not a good idea at all just now.

"I don't think we're any worse off than if I'd been more polite," Reed continued. "He either knows how to get the item or he doesn't. He's hardly going to stand on ceremony where a sale is concerned. He is a businessman."

Deniz nodded. "Agreed, in general. If you were actually buying something, I'd suspect he'll jack the price up."

"I'm willing to pay whatever he asks." Reed grinned.

At that point, the waiter came over with their food on a red plastic tray. He set the items down in the center of the table, then left them alone to enjoy their lunch.

16

AFTER LUNCH, Reed took the afternoon off to do some sightseeing with Trent. They visited the most famous mosques, the Blue Mosque and the Aya Sophia, both of which Deniz said shouldn't be missed. Then Trent talked Reed into a tour of the Sultan's palace and harem. Reed had never seen so many mosaic tiles in his life. He fully expected Trent to want to redo their bathroom and kitchen with Turkish style tiles as soon as they got home.

Ready for a rest after traipsing around, they had Deniz drop them back at the hotel for a few hours. They didn't get much resting done, but Deniz didn't need to know that when he called around to pick them up for another visit to the Grand Bazaar, where Reed approached several more shop owners, trying to connect with anyone else who might have links to dealers who could supply items not on public display.

Just like the previous evening, they had limited success, but Reed found another jeweler who offered to put him in touch with someone specializing in more expensive items than those he sold in the Grand Bazaar. He wrote his friend's name on the back of his own shop card.

Reed thanked the shopkeeper by buying something from his shop, a silver bracelet inlaid with cabochons of bright lapis lazuli.

"Who's that for?" Trent asked as they made their way out of the tiny overcrowded shop.

"I don't know. If you want to keep it, go ahead."

Trent opened the small box and admired the bracelet. It was far too delicate for him to wear and wouldn't fit his wrist in any case. "I already got things for Beth, Cassandra, Mom, and Maggie. Let's hold on to it. You never know when you'll need a gift for someone. Maybe for Leah or Tom's wife?"

"Good idea. I hadn't even thought about getting gifts for anyone. I'm glad you reminded me."

Deniz drove them back to the hotel and parked outside. "What's on the agenda for tomorrow?"

"Let's call this other shopkeeper now and arrange a meeting," Reed said.

Deniz made the call, then informed them they had a late-morning appointment. "After that, I'd suggest you pay a visit to a traditional hamam—Turkish bathhouse—while you wait to hear back from Mehmet."

"I'd like that," Trent said. Reed probably wouldn't want to, but that wouldn't stop Trent. He wanted to experience as many new things as possible, even if he had to do everything on his own.

Deniz smiled. "I'll pick you up at ten tomorrow morning for the appointment with the shopkeeper."

"Sounds good." Reed put his hand on the door to get out.

"Hang on," Deniz said. "Let me get the door. If Mehmet is watching you, we can't have him suspect you're not what you say you are."

Reed frowned. "I hate having you waiting on me like this."

"That's how we keep you and Trent safe, right?"

"Right." Reed pursed his lips and nodded, then waited for Deniz to open the car. Out on the sidewalk, he slid his arm around Trent's waist.

Trent fought the urge to wave good-bye to Deniz, who had proven to be helpful in so many ways. As he and Reed walked toward the restaurant, he smiled at Reed's response to Deniz wanting to keep Trent safe. He slipped a hand into his pocket and pulled out the emerald ring Deniz had returned to him. He slipped it onto his left hand this time, then put an arm around Reed, enjoying the warmth of his body in the evening chill.

17

THE FOLLOWING morning Reed answered his cell phone as he sipped the last of his coffee on the balcony.

"Mr. Applegate, this is Deniz. I'm downstairs."

Five minutes later Trent, Reed, and Deniz were on their way to meet the second lead at his antiques shop in the shadow of the Blue Mosque. It was a popular area for tourists, with more foot traffic than vehicular traffic, so Deniz easily found a spot to park, and he followed Trent and Reed to the address.

They hadn't taken the usual precaution of checking the area out first simply because there were so many people around. Deniz had assured Reed the shop was clean and the owner was completely unknown to Europol, Interpol, and the Turkish authorities. He'd discovered nothing untoward connected with the man or the location.

As soon as Reed put a hand on the doorknob, a sixth sense he'd developed over years of exposure to danger sent warnings through his body. But the shades in the windows were up, and nothing looked out of place from the street. Reed pulled the door open but signaled for Trent to enter behind him. The place was deserted, and no one responded when he called out a greeting.

Like yesterday, Reed had left his weapon in the car, and now he wished he hadn't.

"Wait here, Trent."

"What—"

Reed put a finger to his lips and made a hand signal that he was going to check behind the counter. Deniz busied himself with a wall hanging, and Trent glanced down into a lit glass display case as Reed eased behind the counter. An unpleasant scent tickled his nostrils a split second before he saw the splash of red on the floor.

In two quick steps, he was in the back room when the back door slammed shut ahead of him. Then he spotted the body of an elderly man propped up against the wall. Blood dripped from a wound in his chest. The fact that it wasn't spurting told him the man was dead.

Reed calculated the options for racing out the door and decided against it. The door opened out, and he'd be vulnerable if anyone was waiting for him on the other side. He could send Deniz outside, but that would indicate he was either law enforcement or that Mr. Applegate wasn't worried about the authorities showing up, and Reed didn't want to look law-abiding. He wanted the opposite.

When he got back to the front of the shop, Trent gave him a questioning glance.

"Don't go back there."

"Why not?"

"Yilmaz's dead. Stabbed."

Deniz whipped his head around. "What? Did you see who?"

"No."

"What do we do now?" Trent asked.

"Let me search back there, and when I'm done, Trent, you'll start screaming."

"Why?"

"Why should you scream?"

"Yeah." Trent looked offended. Why did he choose now to show how unafraid he was? Part of Reed was proud of Trent, but another part felt guilty that dead guys didn't bother Trent anymore.

"Because that's what normal people do, Trent. Remember normal?"

Trent nodded. "When?"

"Keep acting like customers till I come back." Reed gave the storage and office areas a quick but thorough search. The safe had been opened. A pile of cash remained. Clearly if the killer had removed something from the safe, it wasn't money. Had Reed arrived too late to ask about some Babylonian gold?

"Deniz, can you come back here?"

"What do you need?"

"Check the papers in the safe and on the desk. Let me know if anything looks promising about who did this or what they were looking for. Do you see anything that would indicate Yilmaz was dealing in the kind of goods we're looking for?"

Deniz flipped through papers. They both wore latex gloves so they wouldn't leave prints. He hoped Trent hadn't touched anything. While his prints shouldn't be on file anywhere, Reed didn't want them taken and possibly matched up at some point in the future.

"Nothing here."

"Fine. Can you go back and wait with Trent?"

"Sure." Deniz gave Reed a questioning glance, then left the office.

When Reed was sure he'd gone, he grabbed the papers from the desk, pushed aside a ceiling tile, and deposited all the paperwork up there. Then he stopped in the bathroom, pulled his gloves off, and flushed them before returning to the front of the shop.

"Okay, Trent, listen up. After you start screaming, run outside and into the next shop and tell them to call the police. Deniz and I will go back to the car. As soon as you can, get out of the shop and head for a crowd of people, then get back to the car. Got it?"

Trent nodded. "Now?"

"Now."

"Help! Oh my Goooooooooooooooood!"

As Trent shouted, Reed and Deniz rushed out of the shop yelling "call the police" in English, then disappeared into the crowd of gawking tourists. They raced to the car while Trent attracted all the attention to the front of the shop.

Two minutes later Trent came around the corner and got into the backseat with Reed. Approaching sirens wailed as he opened the door, then cut off when he slammed it shut.

"How'd it go?"

"Fine. They wanted me to wait till the cops got here, but I told them I was feeling sick and they could find me at the guest house around the corner."

"There's a guest house around the corner?" Reed asked.

"Lots of them. It should keep them busy trying to find which one I'm at." Trent grinned.

Reed glanced toward Deniz, who nodded with a look of respect at Trent. Reed felt a little more pride than usual bubble up in his chest. "Good. Let's get the hell out of Dodge. Deniz, can you take us back to the hotel, then check in with Clifford about this?"

"Yes, Mr. Applegate."

TWENTY MINUTES later Trent and Reed sat at a sidewalk café two streets over from their hotel. Reed took a seat that let him see everyone passing in both directions.

"Why'd you get rid of Deniz?"

Reed sipped hot tea. Even in the sunshine, the day was cool and breezy, and he shivered slightly. He'd stopped to purchase a scarf two shops away, rather than go back to the hotel immediately. "Everything was a little too much of a coincidence this morning."

"You think Deniz had something to do with the dead guy?"

"He made the appointment for us, and he didn't take the proper precautions before we went inside. Just because it's a crowded tourist area doesn't mean it's safe to skip a thorough recon of the surroundings. Either he's lazy, or he's involved."

"Is that why we didn't wait for the cops?"

"Yes and no. I don't know how robust our covers are here in Turkey. If Deniz is compromised, we might not be safe enough to get involved with the local cops. I didn't want to risk either of us getting detained even for routine questioning."

"Who killed him? And what did they take?"

"I don't know. I suspect I know who does." Reed finished his tea and signaled the waiter for more.

Trent folded his arms across his chest and tucked his hands under his arms.

"Take my scarf, Trent. I'm warm enough now."

Trent nodded gratefully, then accepted more tea from the waiter. They spent twenty more minutes before going back to the hotel. They had made it only halfway across the lobby when a man stood up and blocked their way.

"Mehmet?" Trent said and glanced to Reed.

"Right on time," Reed said.

Mehmet smiled calmly. "Just what I was thinking. Let's take some tea and chat, shall we?"

"I've had enough tea," Trent said. Fear pinched the muscles around his eyes.

"Let Trent go up to the room."

Mehmet nodded. "As you wish."

"No, I'll wait with you, Richard." Trent put on his brave smile and Reed loved him even more.

"It will be a short discussion, Trent," Mehmet said. "Nothing to worry about. Richard will be up before you know it."

"It's fine, Trent."

Trent gave a parting glare at Mehmet that should have singed the man's beard right off, then headed for the elevator.

Inside the hotel's restaurant, Reed and Mehmet played at being polite as the waiter brought tea.

"There's only one reason you'd be here now, Mehmet."

"I don't like competition."

"Fair enough. I noticed the safe was empty in Yilmaz' office. Do you have what I'm looking for?"

Mehmet shook his head, but he smiled. "Empty? There was enough cash to support several Turkish families for a year. Or did your driver make off with that?"

"I don't need to steal. The dead man's family could use that money, I suppose."

"Unless the police are already spending it." Mehmet sipped tea. "But no, I didn't find what you're looking for. My contacts are still hunting."

"By hunting, do you mean killing other dealers?"

"No. That's not how I do business. But it might become necessary to keep my network in line. I'll contact you tomorrow with an update. Assuming you're still here."

"Why do you say that?" Reed's sixth sense shouted another warning. "Will I be connected to this morning's developments?"

"No." Mehmet stroked his beard. "But I find it interesting how unruffled you are about what happened. A little suspicious, in fact."

"It's not how I prefer to do business, but I'm no stranger to violence."

"I'd be willing to bet you're not at all what you appear. It's only that I saw real fear on Trent's face that makes me give you another chance. You're a lucky man to be with someone so ingenuous and genuinely kind. However, if I change my mind about you, he'll be the one who gets a special visit from me next time."

Reed rose and had to stop himself from putting his hands around Mehmet's throat. "Don't even think about touching him. Sometimes I do enjoy a spot of violence."

Mehmet pressed his lips together. "So there is something you care about as much as gold?"

"Just one." Reed didn't even have to pretend he meant it.

"Until tomorrow." Mehmet put cash down on the table, then got up and walked out of the restaurant.

Reed closed his eyes and counted to ten to calm his racing heart. He didn't doubt a word of Mehmet's threats against Trent.

Trent had been alone upstairs while Mehmet detained Reed.

Reed ran for the elevator as if the devil himself were on his tail.

18

REED HURRIED silently to the door of their hotel room, then slid the plastic keycard in, dreading the loud click it would make. Still, if anyone was in there with Trent, he wouldn't have much warning before Reed was on top of him.

But Trent was alone, holding a towel around his waist and looking out at the view from the balcony.

"Hey," Trent said, turning toward Reed.

"Everything okay?" Reed kept fear out of his voice. Best not to upset Trent just yet.

"Considering what happened this morning? Yes."

Reed let out a sigh of relief that Trent hadn't said precisely what had happened. Then he chastised himself for still expecting Trent to do or say the wrong thing. "You still want to go to the hamam this afternoon?"

Trent's face lit up. "Of course."

"Then get dressed. I'll just call and see when they have an opening."

Trent tossed the towel on the bed and stood in front of Reed, tall and naked and such a temptation. There was time for that later.

"Are you in that much of a hurry, Richard?" Trent gave Reed an inviting smile.

Reed wiped his hand across his mouth and nodded, frowning. *Focus!* As Trent dressed, Reed scribbled a note on the pad from the hotel desk.

We're not coming back to this hotel. No suitcases.

Trent read the note and asked a thousand questions with his eyes, but Reed pointed toward the street and mouthed "Later." Then he grabbed his cell phone, punched in a number he'd memorized, and a woman answered in Turkish.

"Is this the Clifftop Baths?"

"Yes, how can I help you?" Clifford asked with no trace of an accent.

"I'd like a booking for two. What's the next available time?"

"We can take you whenever you arrive."

"Great. We'll be there in about twenty minutes. Name's Applegate."

"Thank you, sir."

Trent pulled a small package from the dresser and stuffed it into the inner pocket of his coat, which he draped over his arm. "I'm ready. I can't wait for that Turkish bath. I kind of thought you didn't want to go."

"I definitely want to." Reed pulled the SIM card from his phone and stomped it underfoot, then tossed the rest of the phone off the balcony.

Trent stared at him, then handed over his own phone for Reed to do the same. He followed Reed out of the room to the elevator, and they rode in silence to the lobby. Then Reed led them two blocks away before hailing a cab. He handed the driver a piece of paper.

"We're not going to the hamam, are we?"

Reed shook his head. "We've got another kind of appointment. Let me have your jacket."

Trent handed it over, and Reed checked the pockets and lining for bugs, RFID chips, or anything else that would give away their location or their plans. Then he went through the bag of gifts Trent had purchased. Everything was clean. He would have hated to toss Trent's gifts out the window, but he was prepared to do so.

Twenty minutes later the cab pulled into a small industrial complex at the outskirts of town. Reed paid the driver and, after he drove away, buzzed the security gate.

Trent glanced around. "This definitely doesn't look like a hamam."

"That's what I call perfect timing." Clifford greeted him at the entrance with an ironic grin and hands crossed over her chest.

"Clifford, this is Trent. Trent, Clifford."

"Hi." Trent nodded, a smile forming.

"Mr. Red wants you to call ASAP." Clifford handed Reed a phone. "Speed-dial four." She poured mugs of coffee for Trent and Reed, then left the room.

"Richard, how's your trip?" a familiar voice said once the call had connected.

"Unexpectedly messy. Miss us?"

"More than you know. Cliff is arranging a ride home."

"Uh-oh. Did we make such big waves already?" It wasn't like Tom White to pull Reed out without a debriefing first.

"Quite the opposite. We've hit pay dirt here at home, and I need you to follow up on a more promising line of inquiry."

"I'm still working my contact here. I should—"

"Unless your guy has gold to sell you today, I want you on the next plane. Understand?"

"Yes. See you tomorrow."

White hung up. Trent looked at Reed with tired eyes.

"That was Tom. We're going home as soon as we get transport out."

"Because of… this morning?"

"It's safe to talk here. Clifford is with the Bureau, working with a Europol joint task force."

"Because of the dead guy?"

"I'm sure that's part of it. There's nothing to be gained by staying here any longer. Mehmet doesn't have what we want, or he doesn't know how to find it. White wants me to work the case from another angle back home."

Clifford came back into the room. "You're booked on a private flight to Athens, where you'll transfer to a commercial flight on to Los Angeles. You'll be leaving in two hours. Any luggage?"

"No."

"I'll arrange for some." She sat down at the table across from Trent. "Deniz was picked up by the police."

Trent's eyes went wide, and he bit his bottom lip and avoided eye contact with Reed and Clifford.

"What happened?"

"Someone might have caught the plate leaving the scene. There are more and more security cameras on the street. There have been an increasing number of political demonstrations and riots the past few years, and Turkey is finally catching up with technology. He's got an arrest record that's part of his cover, and sometimes those backfire."

"Is he in trouble?" Trent asked.

"They can't tie him to the crime unless someone fabricates evidence. He runs a greater risk of getting beaten until he gives up the names of the foreigners he drove to the shop. I'll send word to our guy in the local police force to let Deniz know he can give them your names, now that you'll be leaving."

Trent stared into his coffee mug, then pushed it away and looked like he was going to be sick.

"Trent, it's not our fault." Reed hated himself for even saying it.

"Yes it is. Don't you care what happens to him?"

"Or course I care. Cliff, make that call right away?"

She nodded and left the room.

"Reed, I'm sorry, but I don't feel okay making excuses."

Reed sat down next to Trent and reached for his hand, but Trent pulled it away. "You're right. I'm glad you won't get used to this kind of work. But remember that Deniz, Clifford, and I all know what the risks are when we take the job and every morning when we walk out the door putting ourselves into these kind of situations. Even when we do everything right, we all still run the chance of getting hurt, arrested, or much worse. Sometimes telling the truth is even more dangerous than lying."

Trent wouldn't meet Reed's gaze. Whether it was because he understood the truth or because he wanted to pretend he didn't, Reed didn't know. But Trent couldn't have it both ways. He either had to accept the risks to being part of Reed's work, or he had to keep his distance.

If he knows what's good for him, Trent will keep his distance from me too. It was a truth Reed didn't care to admit.

Trent was still giving Reed the silent treatment when Clifford returned. "They've released Deniz. He's a little battered, but there's no major injury. The national police are looking for Applegate and Carpenter."

"Who are we traveling home as?"

"Mr. and Mr. Clifford. You were on your honeymoon."

Reed chuckled, but Trent wasn't amused. He twisted the ring on his finger and looked like he might be toying with the idea of taking it off, if not completely throwing it away.

"A taxi will be here in twenty minutes to take you to the airport. Your luggage should be ready now."

"Why do we need luggage?" Trent asked.

Clifford glanced at Reed, then answered. "You'll trigger all sorts of alarms at security and US immigration checkpoints if you show up with no luggage after several days abroad. It doesn't work to lie that it went missing because now everything's X-rayed and tracked digitally."

Trent nodded.

"Did Reed tell you we went through New Agent Training together at Quantico?"

Trent looked at her with a little less animosity and a glimmer of curiosity. "No."

"'Strue. We got to be friends after he lost a bet that I could beat him at hand-to-hand combat."

Trent glanced at Reed. "She beat you up?"

"That's not *quite* how it happened."

"Sure it was." She sat at the edge of the table near Trent. "Army wusses refuse to admit the superiority of the Corps."

"You were a Marine?" Trent asked.

"Stop sounding like you're impressed," Reed said.

A glimmer of a smile played at the corners of Trent's mouth. "But I am."

"I let her win. I was taught never to hit a woman."

Clifford smirked. "And that's why you didn't graduate at the top of our class."

"Which I'm perfectly fine with. I'd rather beat up female bad guys than female cadets."

"You barely wanted to look at female cadets, much less touch us— even for beating up. Not so with a few particularly hunky male cadets...." She winked at Reed.

Clifford's cell phone buzzed. "The taxi is here. Safe trip." She shook Reed's hand and then Trent's before taking them back to the security gate, where one of her team was waiting with suitcases and packets containing their new passports and travel papers.

Reed waved, then opened the back door of the taxi for Trent while the driver put their suitcases—battered enough not to look brand-new— into the trunk.

19

THE FLIGHTS home were uneventful unless you counted Trent's disappointment that all he saw of Greece was the airport in Athens. He added it to his list of places to visit when they weren't working on one of Reed's cases.

By the time the plane left Athens, Trent had decided not to hold Reed responsible for Deniz getting arrested and beaten in police custody. Trent still felt guilty, but he'd come to terms with what Reed had told him about agents accepting the risks that went along with their jobs.

They slept most of the last leg of the flight from London to LA. The effects of jetlag, the stress of the short visit, and the long flights combined so that by the time they landed in LA, Trent could barely remember his name, much less why he was disappointed with Reed.

Back in their apartment, they fell into bed and slept until the alarm woke them up the next morning at eight.

Reed rolled over and kissed Trent. "I'm heading in to see Tom this morning. Are you okay?"

"Yeah."

"Are we okay?" Reed sounded as if Trent's answer might upset him.

"Yeah. Yes." Trent pulled Reed in for another kiss. "How long do you have?"

"Not enough time to do anything right."

"So, do it quick. You can do it right later." Trent smiled. He should make it up to Reed after giving him the cold shoulder before they left Istanbul.

"Save that thought. I'll meet you right back here when I'm done at the field office."

"I like that idea."

After Reed showered and left, Trent fought the urge to go back to sleep. He needed a shower in the worst way. Reed would appreciate coming home a lot more if Trent didn't smell like the back of a taxi when he got into bed.

He treated himself to a nice long shower with plenty of bodywash. He'd left a small bottle in their hotel bathroom when they'd made their unexpected escape. Nice and clean-smelling again, Trent went back into the bedroom to wait for Reed.

REED KNOCKED on Tom White's door.

"Come in." Tom looked more serious than usual, which immediately told Reed that this wasn't going to be the most pleasant meeting they'd had. "Have a seat."

Reed sat. "I'll get working on my report when we're done here."

"That can wait. I've got Clifford's report. You can elaborate on the details later. First I want to fill you in on the new developments."

This might have been the first time any manager at the Bureau had told an agent not to get started on a report, especially on returning from a trip to another office. Whatever had transpired while Reed was in Turkey had to be big.

"While you were trying to contact Matthews' dealer in Turkey, we had another set of agents going over Granby's properties and offices with a fine-tooth comb."

"And?"

"And what they found sends the investigation in a whole different direction."

"Somewhere besides Turkey, I take it?"

"It brings everything right back home again."

"Home to LA?"

"No. Granby's files had a contact number that was also found at Matthews' house in New York."

Several questions crossed Reed's mind, but he would get answers more quickly if he let Tom finish explaining.

"The number was out of service, but it once belonged to an office on a US Army base. We cross-referenced that number with the discovery of another item recovered from the list of missing artifacts from Baghdad." Tom smiled for the first time since Reed had entered his office that morning. "Together, that points to the source of the smuggled items being connected with the Army."

Reed waited through three breaths, but Tom didn't add to what he had already said. "Which base, and who was the phone number registered to?"

"Let's just step back a minute." Tom looked a little shifty again. There was something he wasn't telling Reed just yet. "First, the number hadn't been in service for three years."

"That's interesting. When did Granby or Matthews call it?"

"Never. We went through their phone records—home, office, cell, every number registered to them or a member of their family—and not a single call could be traced to the number. Who the number was assigned to is going to be a dead end. But I'm still trying to get my head around why we didn't see any new Iraqi items surface for years, and then in the space of two months, we find several in addition to the ones on the plane that crashed in western Turkey."

"Whoever brought them in must have been sitting on them until they thought the coast was clear. Or it's someone who only recently returned stateside."

"That makes sense. Reed, you were in Iraq. What's your take on how a soldier could bring in items that Interpol is watching for?"

"I can think of—" Reed stopped. Tom had asked the question so casually, Reed hadn't even noticed he'd been played. He sat back in his chair and ran a thumb across his chin. He could see where this discussion was heading, and he didn't like the smell of it one bit. "I don't think it's possible."

"Bullshit."

Yeah, it wasn't going to be that easy. Reed shrugged, but he kept quiet until Tom asked him an outright question. He should have learned his lesson back in the Army: Never volunteer any information. Make them drag it out of you. How had he forgotten his SERE training so easily?

Tom interlaced his fingers and stared across the wide expanse of desk at Reed. "Care to try again?"

"Not particularly."

"You've got exactly the right background to go undercover on the base to investigate."

"I can't be the only agent who's ex-Army."

"No. But you're the best. Usually you're begging me to give you cases with this high profile. What's the problem now?" Tom's gaze bore into Reed, but he didn't flinch.

"I'm done with the Army. If I still wanted to run around in green, I wouldn't have quit to join the FBI." Reed stopped while he was behind. That wasn't why he'd left the Army. He'd gotten out when DADT threatened to ruin his life. No, that wasn't it either. He'd left when he'd fallen for another guy in his special ops unit. If DADT hadn't run him out, then lusting after his buddy would have gotten in the way of doing his job. That kind of emotional attachment could only spell trouble. One wrong move, a wrong word, and everyone would know. And fear of making the wrong move threatened to paralyze him when he could least afford to perform at less than 100 percent. That kind of thing got men killed. It was safer for his team if Reed and his buddy-crush weren't fucking up their chances of coming home in one piece.

But Tom didn't need to know all of that.

And it still had almost nothing to do with why Reed wouldn't set foot on another Army base if he had any say in the matter.

From the look on Tom's face, Reed had absolutely no say in the matter.

Fuck.

20

TRENT WAS just crawling back under the sheets when the phone rang, so he let it go to voice mail. The only person he had any intention of calling back today was his mother. She'd want to know how the trip to Turkey went.

"Trent, pick up."

Reed! Trent dove for the phone. "Reed?"

"Hey."

"What's wrong?"

"Nothing." A pause. "Not really. Can you come downtown to the field office? Tom wants to talk with you this morning."

Trent sat up on the edge of the bed. "Now?"

"Yes, please."

"On my way." He hung up and dove into a clean pair of jeans, a nice button-down shirt, and some shiny black low-cut boots. Or should he wear a tie? What had Reed been wearing when he left? Trent had barely opened his eyes. Well, if Reed or White expected something better than jeans, they should have told him.

Ten minutes later he hailed a cab and headed for the LA Field Office.

In nothing flat he signed in, received a visitor badge, and went up to Tom White's office. Reed sat with his hands in his lap and barely looked up when Trent walked in.

"Morning, Trent," Tom said with more cheer than his usual demeanor. "Thanks for coming in on short notice."

"Okay." Trent dragged the word out as he looked to Reed for a signal to what this was about. Were they in trouble? Had things blown up in Turkey after they left? Reed threw Trent a neutral look. Even Trent knew that when it came to Bureau business, never answer a question that hadn't been asked.

He sat down next to Reed and waited. White didn't say anything. The man was a master at letting the tension ramp up until someone felt the need to break the silence. Trent twisted the ring on his left hand and took slow, deep breaths the way Reed had taught him.

White lifted one corner of his mouth and glanced from Trent to Reed and then back to Trent. His gaze zeroed in on Trent's restless fingers and the glittering emerald. Trent let go and put his hands on his thighs.

"You've learned far too much from Reed, haven't you?" White grinned. If he expected Trent to take the bait, he was wrong. "Fine."

Reed rubbed a hand across his chin, scraping against the stubble. The office was so quiet, the sound practically echoed off the walls.

"Just to update you, Trent," White started, "we've got a new set of leads on the smuggled artifacts. We now believe someone in the US military was involved, probably Army. One lead is connected with an Army base, and I've asked Reed to go undercover there to investigate."

Trent glanced over; Reed's mouth had settled into a frown.

"The easiest way to bring contraband onto a base is through the logistics team. That's my first choice for your cover, Reed. Unless you have another suggestion?"

"No."

"I'm sending you in as enlisted. An officer won't be able to get close enough to the other enlisted soldiers. You'll be an outsider at first, so I honestly don't know how long it will take for you to insinuate yourself into the unit and base life. I think you'll attract less attention if you're married. You'll be able to move easily among both the single and the married soldiers."

Reed nodded. This was why White had brought Trent in, to ease him into the idea that Reed would be "married" to some female agent and clearly wasn't going to be coming home on weekends. While he appreciated it, Trent couldn't quite understand why White was suddenly including him in the planning stage of a case.

"Tom. *Sir*." Reed emphasized the word. "I don't need a wife to be able to get close to the people I need to."

"I'm not sure about that."

"I'm a good actor. I've been in plenty of assignments on my own."

"I think this will make it easier for you. And your spouse will also be able to ask a lot of questions you wouldn't be able to get away with. Don't Army wives like to gossip?"

"That's a generalization I wouldn't care to mention in front of any Army wives."

Trent couldn't help laughing. It was fun watching Reed and Tom dance around this issue. Tom was going to get his way in the end, but Reed was not giving up without a fight.

"You really want to do this on your own, don't you?" Tom paused. "Because I was ready to send Trent in as your spouse. But if you'd rather have a female agent...."

Reed coughed and sputtered. Was that some sort of insult? Trent stared at Reed, then at Tom, then back at Reed.

"Sorry, Tom. I don't get why you think I'd help." Trent shrugged.

"You're already a couple, so you won't raise any red flags the way a Bureau married couple might. Try as they might, a fake couple can't fool most real married couples. If you're there it will be easier on Reed in case the mission takes longer than we expect. And you'll be a hit among the base wives. You'll end up invited to everything. You put people at ease, making someone likely to say something incriminating. Plus, as much as I hate saying this, the suspects probably won't expect a gay soldier to be an undercover agent."

Reed shook his head, and the start of a smile played across his lips. "I hate to admit it, but I agree. And the guys won't think I'm hitting on their wives."

Everyone laughed, breaking the tension in the room.

"I take it this plan is acceptable to both of you?"

Trent nodded and looked over at Reed.

"It's better than some of the alternatives, so yes. Assuming Trent can spare the time away from his writing."

"Why can't I write at the base?"

"That's settled," White said. "Now for the details. You should take some notes."

Reed pulled a small pad out of his shirt pocket. Luckily Trent always carried his own little notebook, which he flipped open.

"You'll be leaving in five days for San Antonio."

"San Antonio?" Reed asked.

"Oh, San Antonio!" Trent was really getting excited now. He could have some fun exploring while Reed was busy hunting down gold smugglers.

"Yes, you'll be stationed at Fort Sam Houston."

"Fort Sam?" Reed shook his head so hard Trent thought it would pop off his neck. "Send someone else." He got up and walked out without another word.

Trent glanced to Tom for a clue to what had happened. *He* didn't work for Tom and didn't owe him anything. And if Trent wanted an explanation, Tom probably wouldn't supply one, so he ran after Reed.

"What's wrong, Reed? Reed. Wait, please. Don't run off." He felt like an idiot shouting down the hall and attracting attention. Reed didn't stop, which made the situation more embarrassing.

Trent caught up to him at the elevator. For once the crappy old elevators in the Federal Building came in handy.

"I don't want to discuss it." Reed took one step into the elevator when the doors opened, but Trent grabbed his elbow and pulled him back out.

"I do. I deserve to know why this bothers you so much. Is it because we're supposed to be married?"

Reed frowned, but the hard set of his chin relaxed. "Of course not. It has nothing to do with that."

"I guess it's all right, then." Trent laid on the irony.

"It doesn't concern you." Reed pulled out of Trent's grasp and went into the stairwell.

Trent watched him go. Should he go back to White's office or just head home? Reed was dealing with something upsetting, but he didn't want to share the problem. Best to wait and give him space.

From inside the stairwell, Reed's phone gave its familiar jingle, then the door opened up again, and Reed almost ran into Trent. "White wants to see us." Reed practically stalked back to Tom's office and hovered in the doorway while Trent stepped inside.

Tom set his gaze on Reed. "You'd prefer I assign this to another agent?"

"Yes."

"Would you care to explain to Trent and me why you can't—or won't—take this assignment."

Reed glared at Tom, then visibly reined in his anger. He looked at Trent, then back at Tom. "Fine. I'll go. The sooner I can wrap this investigation up the better."

"I couldn't ask for more than that," Tom said. "Now, let's go over the logistics."

Reed nodded and sat back down.

Trent took his seat again and started writing, not daring to even mention Reed's odd behavior.

21

OVER THE next few days, both Trent and Reed were so busy getting ready to move to San Antonio—PCSing as Trent learned it was called—that there wasn't any good time to ask Reed why he'd been so adamant about not wanting to go to Fort Sam. While Reed was out being fitted for Army uniforms and getting an awful haircut, Trent busied himself with learning about Army life and memorizing his legend—his fake life according to the FBI.

Instead of being a published romance novelist, he was an aspiring author. That way no one could connect "Troy Atwater" with any of Trent Copeland's real life. He'd never mentioned Reed by name or even by profession on his web site or promotional material, but best not to risk it.

Reed would become Rex Atwater. "Troy" liked the name Rex. It meant king in Latin, which contributed to Reed not caring much for it. They started using their new names right away.

Trent asked Reed to model his uniform when he arrived home, and glanced up and down at this new vision of Reed in the fitted dark blue jacket and shiny new shoes. He looked like a completely different person with the close-cropped hair and uniform accentuating his broad shoulders. How hot must he have looked wearing desert camouflage?

"I like it, except for that hat." Trent pulled the black beret from Reed's head and skimmed his fingers across the spiky shadow of hair left on Reed's scalp.

Reed skimmed his own fingers across his skull and twisted his mouth. "I sure didn't miss this part of the Army. And you'll discover there's a special word for everything. It's not a hat; it's generally called a cover, but this one is actually called a beret."

"Should I be taking notes?" Trent cocked his head and raised one eyebrow.

"It couldn't hurt."

THEY MADE an uncomfortable shopping trip in order to buy wedding rings. Reed—Rex—just wanted the plainest, simplest option, while "Troy" wanted to pick something special. Given Reed's sour mood since the morning in Tom White's office, Trent considered not even going along. Let Reed do the investigation on his own, but when he mentioned it, Reed got angry.

If this was marriage, Trent didn't want any part of it. Would this faux marriage ruin things between them? They'd gotten so much closer while they were in Turkey, but they'd gone a hundred steps backward since they returned.

"Which set did you decide on?" the man in the jeweler's asked.

Trent looked at Reed. The ugliest ring was preferable to any discord between them.

"You liked this set best, Troy?" Reed pointed to the ones Trent had suggested.

"It's up to you, honey."

"We'll take these." Reed slid Trent's favorites across the glass counter. "Can we get them sized today?"

"Certainly." The man fitted the gold bands, then rang up the purchases. Reed put the rings in his pocket and took Trent's hand as they walked out of the shop.

"Let's stop for lunch," Reed said when they were out on the sidewalk. "Isn't there a place you like around here?"

"Mellie's, around the corner. I like their salads."

"It might be the last salad you get for a while. It's not a food group in Texas." Reed grinned as they walked to the restaurant.

While they waited for their food to arrive, Reed pulled the rings out of his pocket. "I know this isn't the official way, but…." He reached for Trent's hand and slid the ring on his finger. Then he pulled off the lapis ring Trent had given him and put it into the box that held the wedding rings, before putting on his new ring. "This isn't as pretty as the one you gave me."

He took Trent's hand in his and brought it to his mouth and kissed the new ring.

"I'm not the pope."

"Thank God." Reed chuckled. "Literally." He kissed Trent's hand again. "I'm sorry for being a prick."

Kisses and a wedding ring weren't enough to erase the memory, but it wouldn't help to mention it. "You *were* a prick."

"I can see our marriage is off to a nice start."

"It might be nicer if you didn't give me the impression you don't want to be married to me—even for show."

"That's not true. I told you in Istanbul I'd marry you. And my bad mood has nothing to do with you. I'm sorry if you think it does."

"What's it about, then?"

"Will you give me a little while before we talk about it?"

"Okay, but I want to help you through it, so whatever it is won't upset you."

"I know. I love you... Troy." Reed kissed his hand until the waiter showed up and ruined the moment.

22

THREE DAYS later they arrived in San Antonio, driving a used Honda with California plates registered to Troy Carpenter because he hadn't changed the registration since they'd gotten married. In fact, they'd flown into Amarillo, where they'd picked up the car and driven south so they'd be suitably wrinkled and fed up by the time they hit the base, just in case anyone was paying attention.

Rex showed his papers at the gate and received a map to their temporary housing. The neighbors watched them unload suitcases from the car. Troy waved but only got a few bewildered—but curious—stares in return.

"The weather's cooler than LA. I expected Texas to be hotter." Trent dug a sweater out of his suitcase.

"It's the middle of January. They have winter in Texas too."

"Clearly they have more winter here than LA."

"Be glad we're not in Afghanistan."

"Is it hotter or colder there?"

"Colder."

"It's also colder in New York, and I'd love to be in Manhattan. I'm not sure I get your point."

"I don't remember what point I was making. I'm exhausted."

"I guess it's a good thing you're not in Afghanistan. If you're the best the Army has to offer, I'm kind of scared for national security."

"I'm not the best." Reed frowned.

"Right. You're the best to me." Trent smiled, glad he hadn't said anything he shouldn't have. Rex wasn't a Ranger. Rex was a sergeant in logistics, which might be as far as his career would go if he couldn't drive six hours without wimping out.

"You're going to be better at marriage than I am, Troy, I can tell."

Was that Reed talking, or Rex? This was going to drive Trent crazy if he kept wondering what to believe. How did Reed do this over and over? Maybe it was easier when the other person on the case wasn't your real-life partner.

They had been assigned base housing in a section reserved for married soldiers without kids. The condos were smaller and the area was quieter. The place was clean but looked like something from an old sitcom.

"I guess you can't complain when it's free, can you?" Trent remarked.

"Exactly. Let's just get the stuff out of the car, then we'll figure out dinner."

Trent had wandered into the kitchen to scope out the appliances. Not bad. He liked the gas range. On the kitchen table, he spotted a blue binder with the words "Army Spouse Handbook" printed on a white adhesive label. He burst out laughing and brought the binder into the living room to show Reed.

"Look at this!"

Reed chuckled too. "I never had need for such a book back in *my* Army days. What's in there?"

Trent flipped through the pages. "Mostly where to find information… oh, look at this!"

"Does it have instructions for blowjobs or something?"

"It does!"

"Really?" Reed reached for the book, and Trent whirled out of his grasp.

"It says 'A soldier should only expect a blowjob after giving his spouse oral sex first.' Who knew the Army was so progressive after the end of DADT? I might not hate it here as much as I expected."

"Clearly that book is full of shit," Reed replied and grabbed it out of Trent's hand. Without even looking, he tossed it onto the living room table, then pulled Trent into his arms.

He kissed him until Trent's toes curled and it was too hot.

"Let's take a break, Troy. We can flip a coin to see who gets to be the soldier and who's the spouse."

"You can be the soldier if you promise to wear those sexy green boxer briefs."

"Where the hell did I find you?" Reed asked as Trent unzipped him.

"I'm nonreturnable, you know?"

"I know. But I'm finally used to you, so I might as well keep you."

THEY HAD the weekend to settle in before "Rex" had to report for duty Monday morning. Since he couldn't start snooping right away, this investigation could take a lot longer than Trent had realized. Tom White was pretty smart sending Trent along so Reed could take his time and not risk blowing his cover just to take shortcuts.

"Whoever is running this ring is in it for the long haul," Reed had said before they left LA. "They've been sitting on the gold items for years before starting to move them again. They're not in a huge hurry, and I'll have to bide my time and observe without tipping anyone off."

"This won't take years, will it?" Trent asked.

"No. It takes a while for people to trust you when you move to a new unit, but then everything gels, unless you're a dick. Once someone else new shows up I'll be part of the crowd. White's having someone else transfer to the same unit in two weeks. That will help me."

The process was eye-opening and fascinating for Trent to witness first-hand how an investigation worked. He was looking forward to seeing Reed as a soldier, but understood as an enlisted man, his duties would be vastly different from his work as a Ranger doing special ops.

On Monday, Trent kissed Reed and waved as he left their little house to report to work.

It took less than a week for Trent to see that Army life—at least life as a supply unit grunt—didn't suit Reed at all. He came home in the evenings frustrated, but they couldn't risk talking openly about it. Instead they went for walks around the neighborhood when they needed to talk.

"I had forgotten how damn stupid most of the Army is."

"Stupid how?"

"Don't get me started. Sometimes it seems we're supposed to move things around just for the sake of moving them and for no real purpose."

"It's not your real job. Don't let it get to you so much."

"I can't help it."

"If the job's that easy, then you should have plenty of time to use looking at things that are out of place."

"It's harder than it sounds, because nothing makes a lick of sense. I can't tell what's wrong and what's just fucked up the Army way."

"You've only been there three days. Give it some time."

"I may kill someone before the end of the week."

"I guess it's not a good time to mention that at some point I'll have to host some of the spouses for coffee."

"As long as I'm not home when it happens, I don't care."

"They're very curious about you." Trent grinned at Reed's discomfort at the thought of being the center of attention of a bunch of Army wives.

"Well make something up so they aren't curious."

"I'll tell them you're gay."

"Good idea."

"THE LADIES told me that there's a welcome barbecue on Sunday, and we can't miss it."

Reed frowned. "Do I have to go?"

"Of course. We'll meet the other new families. It's supposed to be a fun social thing, and it will be a good way for both of us to get to know some people besides our neighbors and your coworkers."

"Fine. If you want to be the social butterfly, that's great. As long as I don't have to do more than smile and drink beer."

"Is that what soldiers do on Sunday afternoons?"

"During the playoffs, sure. In Texas, definitely."

"What playoffs?"

Reed shook his head, but he was smiling. "Football. NFL. The Super Bowl is in a couple of weeks…. Tre-Troy, even if you're gay, you're male. And I know you like college football. I saw you watch with your dad."

"Outside of Oklahoma college teams, I don't know anything about football."

"You don't need to."

"I don't want to hang out making iced tea and serving cookies to children."

"Not loving the life of an Army wife?"

"They call us spouses now. We're not all wives."

"Could have fooled me."

"You want to sleep on the couch?"

"Sorry, honey." Reed gave a silly grin and ducked out of Trent's reach. "I'll give you some pointers on pro football before Sunday."

"Sounds good."

JUST BEFORE noon on Sunday, Trent reminded Reed of the barbecue. "We can't be late. That wouldn't look good."

"Who cares if we're late? No one's ever on time for social events unless they might run out of beer."

"Really? Well, I'll leave that up to you. But the party starts at twelve thirty."

It was closer to one when they got in the car, and Trent gave Reed directions as he read the map.

"Just go to the end of this street and it should be on the left."

They parked and made their way through the line of trees surrounding the property.

Even from down the street, the aroma of grilling meat made Trent's stomach rumble. As they got closer, he spotted couples standing around the yard and children racing about between the groups of adults. It was nice and sunny and warm enough for an afternoon picnic.

"Looks like we're the last to arrive."

Trent hurried toward the house, with Reed bringing up the rear. At the front door, a woman waited for them, holding her hand up to shade her eyes from the midday sun. She was in her sixties, slim, and wearing a loose denim skirt and a long-sleeve sweater. She shouted to someone inside and moved out of the doorway.

"Hurry up, Rex."

When they were ten feet from the door, a man with short-cropped dark gray hair came to the doorway and looked Trent up and down.

"Welcome to Fort Sam."

"Hi. I'm Troy Atwater."

"I'm Colonel Atkinson. Nice to meet you."

Trent held out his hand to the colonel and shook. Behind Trent, Reed stopped. "This is my husband, Rex. I'm sorry we're late. I didn't know it was a formal event."

"Come right in, Sergeant Atwater." The colonel stared past Trent.

Trent turned to Reed, who was gazing at the welcome mat. "Rex, hurry up?"

"Atwater? Come inside so I can close the door."

Reed hurried past the colonel without stopping to shake his hand. Trent was embarrassed. He'd never been invited to a colonel's house for a welcome party. What was Reed doing?

"Sergeant, don't run off just yet."

Reed spun on his heel and glared at Atkinson.

"Rex?" The silver-haired woman reappeared. "I didn't believe it."

"Hi, Mom."

Trent spun around, knocking over a little table in the entry hall and sending something crashing to the floor. "Oh, no. I'm sorry… I-uh."

"Could you both come into my office?" Atkinson said and started walking down the hall without waiting for a response. "R-Rex… please?"

Reed followed, then Trent, while Mrs. Atkinson trailed.

Trent stared from Reed to the colonel to his wife.

"Mom?" Trent finally said.

"Troy? I'm so glad to meet you. I'm Maya Atkinson. Reed's mom."

"And I'm Reed's father. Nice to meet you."

"Reed?" Trent said. His head was spinning. Reed had barely mentioned his family. He'd only said that he hadn't seen them for years. Trent had the impression Reed's father might be dead. "I'm sorry, but I'm totally lost. What's going on?"

The colonel sat in the chair behind the desk. Maya waved Trent and Reed to chairs while she leaned against the edge of the desk.

"Blair, did you know Reed was coming to Fort Sam? And why are you calling him Rex?"

"Reed's here for an investigation. He's undercover as Sergeant Rex Atwater. Troy—no it's Trent, isn't it? Trent is posing as his husband."

Reed's strange aversion to Fort Sam was starting to make sense. He must not have wanted to see his family.

"Reed, I'm so glad to see you." Maya threw her arms around Reed and hugged him so hard Trent expected to hear bones breaking. "You look fantastic, honey. You know how much I've missed you."

"It's good to see you, Mom." Reed sounded like he meant it.

"Trent, are you with the FBI too?"

"Ah, no, ma'am." Trent glanced at Reed, not sure what to say.

"Trent's my partner, Mom. We're not married. Yet." From the glare Reed gave his father, Trent filled in a lot more of the missing pieces to this puzzle.

"So nice to meet you, Trent." Maya gave him a hug.

"You look good, Son. I was surprised not to hear from you directly after I was informed of your mission."

"Really? Why's that?"

"Reed." Maya's tone of warning was universally understood.

"Look, Mom, I'm here for work, not because I want to be. I'll do what I must to keep my cover, but this isn't going to be a joyful family reunion—no matter how much Mom might like it to be." Reed directed the last venomous words at his father. "Trent, let's go."

"Hang on. I have no idea what's going on here."

"It doesn't matter. We won't be socializing with the colonel while we're here." Reed took Trent's elbow and steered him toward the door.

"Reed, honey. I'd like to talk with you while you're here."

"I don't think that's a good idea, Mom, at least until the investigation is over."

"Hang on a minute, Sergeant." Reed's father sounded every bit the authoritative base commander. "We do have some business to discuss in regard to that investigation. Right now no one else on this base knows why you're here or what you're looking for."

"Fine. If I need any assistance, I'll make contact. Otherwise, not." Reed headed to the door and opened it. He couldn't seem to get out of the office fast enough.

Trent stared at Maya and then at the colonel. "I'm sorry not to meet you under better circumstances. Maybe later—"

"Troy?" Reed said impatiently from outside the office.

Trent frowned and went into the hallway. He had to sprint to catch up to Reed, then waited until they were nearly to the car to speak.

"Reed, what the hell is going on?"

"Not here."

Once they were in the car, Reed drove off base and kept going until he found a sports bar several miles away. Inside it was so loud Trent couldn't hear himself think. They found seats across the room from the enormous television. It was only slightly quieter, but at least no one would overhear them.

"Rex, this is no place for a serious discussion."

"I know. I just want a beer."

Trent wrinkled his nose and shook his head. There was nothing to be gained when Reed was in this mood. "I could use one too."

They drank their beers and watched the game, then ordered some food. Trent was starving. He'd been looking forward to some good barbecue at the colonel's party, and the undercooked greasy burger didn't come close to replacing it. "You owe me a nice dinner after this."

Reed bit into his burger and put it down. "You're right. Let's find some real food."

Halfway between the bar and the base, they passed a barbecue joint with cars overflowing the parking lot. They parked down the street and got on the end of a long line to get in.

"If the food tastes one tenth as good as it smells, this must be the best restaurant in town."

A woman standing in front of them turned and grinned. "Pretty close. You two don't sound like you're from these parts."

"Just moved here from LA," Trent said.

"Stationed at Fort Sam," Reed added, but his glance to Trent warned not to get too chatty about themselves.

"My husband's stationed there too. He's watching the kids while I pick up dinner. Name's Molly Miller. My husband's Ronny Miller, who runs the supply unit."

"Troy Atwater, and this is my husband, Rex."

"Nice to meet you." She shook their hands and smiled like she meant it.

"I'm in supply too, but I don't think I've met a Ronny Miller."

"He's Master Sergeant Miller, and he manages all the enlisted soldiers in that section."

"That explains it. Guess he's my boss's boss."

They made chitchat as the line crept forward. A restaurant employee came by to take their orders. Molly squinted at the chalkboard menu and selected about seven items. Trent chose three.

"That's a lot for just one person," the guy said.

"That's for two."

"Then it's about right. First time here?"

Trent nodded. "Did I do something wrong?"

"Nope. You stayin' or goin'?"

"Staying," Reed replied. "Add some coleslaw too."

"Got it. It'll be about ten minutes. Have a seat and put this number on the pole at your table." He handed Reed a plastic disc with the number 39 on it.

Molly exchanged phone numbers with Trent and hurried to the counter to pay and pick up her order.

When the food came, Reed dug in immediately, clearly before Trent could ask him anything about his father. The food smelled and tasted so good, Trent was willing to let it slide. But when Reed sat back and took a break, Trent jumped right in. He moved the platter of brisket out of Reed's reach.

"If you want another bite you'll start talking."

Reed let out a long sigh. "Fine. Ask away."

"No. I'm not letting you off that easily. You start. From the beginning."

Reed frowned but looked resigned to his fate. "How far back?"

"As far as you need to go to explain the way you treated me and your parents today."

Reed nodded. "You're right. I'm sorry I didn't tell you everything before. Here goes."

IF REED could have run out the back door, he might have. Reed's silence had hurt Trent, and now he deserved answers. Typical Trent; he thought every problem had a solution. The thing with Reed's parents wasn't a problem—not anymore. It had stopped hurting years ago. Only an empty hole remained where his heart had long ago stopped aching.

"My dad and I don't talk. We haven't since about five minutes after I came out to my mom. I talk to her now and then, but since then I've only seen her a few times. I know where they are, and until now I've been able to avoid my father." The words rolled off Reed's tongue, completely disconnected from emotion.

Trent stared at him for what felt like an hour. "I hope you don't think you're done. That's barely even a beginning."

"What do you want to know?"

"Where do I start? Reed, there's so much to ask."

The pain in Trent's eyes made Reed's heart heavy. "Go ahead. I'll answer your questions. Tell you anything you want to know."

"I'm sorry about your family—about your dad's issues. I don't understand why you didn't tell me the situation sooner, that we were coming to the base where your dad is commander. Looking back I see Tom White knew. But why wouldn't you share that with me?" The pain glowed bright in Trent's gaze and Reed looked away for a moment until he could collect his thoughts. Telling Trent was harder than he'd expected.

"Trent, your family is close. It's not perfect—I know that—but when I see how much your parents care about you and your happiness, it makes it more difficult to accept how fucked up my family is." Reed shrugged. "It's embarrassing."

"Don't be embarrassed. I'm not judging you by your father. But I'd like to be here for you when you have a problem. I want to help you."

That was so Trent. He didn't get it. Reed reached to squeeze Trent's hand. "I love you for that. But you can't fix everything, even if you want to. And talking about my problems doesn't do me any good."

"You don't know that. You never really try, so what makes you so sure?"

Reed smiled. "That's fair. But…. Talking won't change the situation. I already understand the problem, and it can't be fixed. I'm okay with it. It doesn't bother me anymore. So don't let it bother you."

"I don't agree, but I won't argue. It never does any good with you." Trent finally cracked a smile. He'd at least learned one thing about Reed.

"Anything else?"

"Yes." Trent sipped iced tea. "What's your dad's problem? He seemed really nice today. He didn't give me the evil eye or call us names or anything."

Reed hadn't noticed. He'd given up paying attention to anything his father did or said. But Trent was right. "I can only guess it was because my mom was there. Or for some crazy reason he didn't want to offend you."

"We were in the office with the door shut, so it wasn't even part of maintaining our cover. It felt normal to me."

"Then I don't know."

"Tell me more about what happened when you came out to your parents."

Now Trent was treading on more painful territory. It was one of the few things that still hurt. "My mom saw me holding hands with another guy when I was thirteen, fourteen. Dad was just starting to move up and we were posted to Brussels, an important tour for him. I was walking around the Rue Nueve, a pedestrian shopping area, with Paulus. He was a local guy whose dad worked on the base." Reed smiled—he had some nice memories of Paulus.

"She came to my room and asked me about him. We'd talked about girls before—birds and bees stuff—and she knew I wasn't interested in them. That day she asked if I liked that boy the way some boys like girls. She asked in such a nonjudgmental way I didn't even think there was any problem in telling her the truth."

"So she was okay with that?"

"Yeah. I thought so. She went downstairs, and a few minutes later I heard my dad yelling at her. I found out later he'd overheard part of our discussion and he was mad. He ran upstairs and gave me some sermon about it being wrong. How his son was not gay, couldn't ever be gay, and I'd better get over this phase already and move on." Reed stared at a spot on the far wall. He could hear his dad's voice booming, echoing around the little bedroom. He felt hot air and spittle flying out of his dad's mouth. Remembered how he'd raised his fist.

But he hadn't hit Reed. He'd never struck him.

It might have been easier to accept if he had. A bruise or broken bone would heal. But the accusation is his father's eyes had never gone away. The silent repudiation haunted Reed's days and nights for years. Odd that he hadn't noticed it that afternoon at Fort Sam, but then again, Reed hadn't looked long enough to see it.

"What happened after that?"

"We never discussed what happened again. Not with my dad or my mom. Maybe they talked about it, but no one said anything to me. But from that day, I saw something change in my dad. In the way he treated me. Always watching me. I wasn't sure if he expected me to sprout rainbow-colored wings and fly away, or whether he thought he'd change me through the force of his stare."

"That sounds awful." Trent gripped Reed's hand.

Reed found himself blinking, eyes stinging. "It was. I just didn't understand." The pain rushed back at him like a freight train about to run him down. "I hated that look, that displeasure, antipathy, knowing I'd let him down. I—I started playing every sport, trying out for every team, doing tough, manly things." A bitter laugh escaped Reed's lips, and Trent starting blinking too. But Reed went on. He'd never told anyone all of this, but he'd gone too far to stop. "I pretended not to be gay to make my parents happy. I hated myself a little more each day, just as my dad seemed to believe I had 'reformed.' I applied to West Point. Boy, he was really proud of me. Then the night before I left for college, my dad saw me get out of a guy's car down the street from our house. I didn't see him again for two years."

"What about your mom?"

"She came to visit me at West Point, but I stayed with friends over school breaks or went on training during the summers. I did every training program I could, then went directly to Ranger School. She tried to make excuses for my dad's actions, but I wouldn't listen to her if she even mentioned him."

"I'm sorry it was as bad as that. He wasn't proud of any of your Army accomplishments?"

"Not as far as I know. I doubt he heard about any of them."

"Did your mom ever mention them to you?"

"Yes."

"Then your dad knew. How else would your mom have heard about them?"

Reed stared at Trent. It had never occurred to him. But the fact that his dad knew what he'd been up to, the awards, medals, etc., and still never apologized or tried to contact him? Then again, Dad would have known Reed wouldn't listen.

Trent pushed the platter of food toward Reed.

"Oh, God, I can't eat anything else, Tre-Troy."

"Let's take it home. It will make a nice breakfast." He asked a passing waiter to bring a box for their leftovers.

"You're not going to cook me breakfast in the morning? What the hell kind of Army wife are you?"

"Exactly." Trent stood up, grabbing the bag of food. He smiled and reached for Reed's hand.

THEY DIDN'T talk in the car on the way back to the base. Reed didn't have anything to say and Trent didn't attempt to break the silence. Back home, Trent ran a bath and forced Reed to get in, then proceeded to wash him and give him a nice foot massage until the water cooled off. In the bedroom, Trent massaged his way up the rest of Reed's body and they made love, long and slow and lovingly.

After, they lay together trying to describe the water stains on the ceiling.

"It's an elephant."

Reed shook his head. "Water buffalo."

"How's that different from a land buffalo?"

"Land buffalo? Who calls them that?"

"I do." Trent shrugged off Reed's mock insult.

"Water buffalo don't have that big fluffy head like the 'land buffalo' do."

"Got it." Trent reached up and stretched, then pulled Reed in close. "This is nice. I can't remember the last time we didn't have somewhere to go or something to pack."

"I know. The last time was probably before your parents visited."

"Right, because after that...." Trent smiled.

Reed shook his head, hoping Trent wouldn't mention Turkey, at least by name. "That was a nice time on that balcony, wasn't it?"

"Oh yeah. The balcony." Trent's tone and smile sent heat through the lower half of Reed's body.

"Maybe we'll get a chance to go back there on a future vacation."

"I'd like that, Rex."

"Me too." Reed kissed Trent's throat, feeling the pulse under the skin. "Thanks."

"For what?" Trent hooked a finger under Reed's chin. "For the... massage?"

"No. For listening. For making me talk to you and then really making me feel better."

"Are you saying I was right about something for a change?" Trent's tone was teasing, playful.

"No. I'm saying you were right again. You were certainly right about this. I forget how lucky I am."

"Don't worry, I'll keep reminding you."

23

MONDAY MORNING, Reed went to work while Trent planned another spouse activity with his new friends. At least Trent was having a better time of the assignment than Reed. He hated his job and had nothing in common with any of his coworkers. It had been a long time since he'd been undercover in a role where he had a day job. Usually he worked as a collector trying to buy stolen property, as a fence, or occasionally as an art thief.

But the information the other agents had discovered led to Fort Sam, and Reed would work his way through the possibilities. One angle was to look for shipments that appeared out of place, items that didn't belong here or were coming from or heading to a base or division that didn't make sense. Reed's knowledge of Army practices was an asset here.

At least some of the shipments had to have happened years earlier, and it would be much trickier to access those without attracting attention. It would have been easier to investigate if he'd come on board as an auditor. Some department or other was always being audited for efficiency, spending, controlling losses, or just because the auditors needed to justify their existence. But no one would talk freely to an auditor or let their guard down. So while Reed was on the ground making friends, White had a forensic accounting team crunching stats to find anomalies or patterns in shipments at Fort Sam, then Reed could follow up with the soldiers involved.

But so far none of the rocket scientists at the Bureau had identified anything worth checking out. In the meantime Reed tried to make friends, with an eye toward spotting suspicious behavior.

So far the most suspicious behavior was anyone actually taking their job seriously. Back in Iraq, Reed hadn't dealt with logistics or supply. As long as his team had what they needed, when and where it was needed, his missions ran smoothly. Now he wondered how the Army had managed to achieve anything given how apathetic his colleagues were.

"You been back at Fort Sam long?" Reed had asked Staff Sergeant Gregson one day during lunch break.

"Almost a year. It beats the hell out of Kandahar and Fallujah. Nice and laid-back here."

"A little too laid-back, sometimes."

"You think so, Atwater? Wait till summer. You'll be glad you can take it easy. It gets fucking hot here in Texas," Sergeant Cray added.

"At least you've got a job." Gregson said. "They've cut back staff at most of the bases. Downsizing. We're lucky to be part of the medical unit because that's one area they won't cut back on right away. Too afraid to cut staff and let people get back to real jobs in the private sector, because they won't get them back if there's another deployment. Anyone who's not regular Army is exhausted after ten years of combat support."

"Hadn't thought of it that way."

"When's your enlistment up?" Cray sounded like he would be happy to leave at any time.

"Two more years," Reed said. "But I'm hoping to get my twenty. I don't want to get downsized. Got any advice for me here? I think I'd like to be able to stick around."

"You settling in okay, then?" Gregson asked.

"Yeah, so far, so good."

"You want to stick around, don't crap on the colonel."

"Whaddya mean?"

"Didn't see you at the Welcome Picnic yesterday, Atwater. Old Atkinson is a stickler for protocol," Gregson said.

"Is that so?" Reed could enlighten Gregson on old Atkinson, but he nodded and kept his thoughts to himself. "Is that going to hurt my chances here already?"

"Can't say. But he does tend to listen to his direct reports, so make sure you don't piss off anyone. At least look like you're doing your job, even if you aren't actually getting anything done. Appearances matter here. Plenty of guys trying to transfer in."

"Good advice. Thanks. Had a little misunderstanding about the plans yesterday."

"You married?" Gregson asked.

"Yeah. A few months now."

Gregson looked at his watch as a master sergeant strode across the room. "Lunch break's over."

"Sit down, men." The master sergeant returned their lazy salutes. "Take another five." He turned to Reed. "You Atwater?"

"Yes, Sergeant."

"I like to keep things relaxed unless one of the commissioned officers is watching. I'm Miller. My wife, Molly, told me she ran into you and your husband yesterday."

Gregson's eyes went wide, and Reed chose to ignore it.

"Yes, we had a nice chat in line at the Smokehouse."

"That's what she said. Anyway, just wanted to meet you and see if you like cards."

"Cards?"

"Poker?"

"I've been known to enjoy a few hands now and then."

"Well, if you can get away from the house on Thursday, we have a nice little game going. Or bring your husband along. Interested?"

"Yes, Sergeant."

"Good. Gregson, you'll be there too, right? And Cray?"

"Wouldn't miss it. It's at my house." Cray glared at the master sergeant, clearly not thrilled with how Miller had invited Reed over.

"Good. Gregson'll give you the details. Now, you can get back to work."

"Thanks, Sergeant." Reed saluted and Miller frowned, returned the salute, then strode back out the door.

"Got a husband, then?"

"Yeah." Reed tried to keep the challenge out of his voice.

"Good. Cray hates it when guys stare at his wife's tits." Gregson guffawed.

"I sure do." Cray didn't sound particularly amused with Gregson's comment.

"I couldn't be less interested in your wife."

"Glad to hear it," Gregson joked. "Less competition for me."

"Ha-fucking-ha," Cray said. He collected the trash from his lunch and wadded it up into a ball, which he hurled at the nearest trash can, knocking it over like a bowling pin.

Gregson laughed loudly as Cray walked out of the lunchroom.

"TROY, SWEETIE, we want to see your place! Why don't we have coffee there tomorrow?" Ronda Martinez squeezed Trent's arm and looked to Lynda Gregson for confirmation.

Trent tried not to grimace at her pincer-like grip or the suggestion. "We haven't got anything but a couch, a bed, and some plastic plates." It was the truth and rather embarrassing. "Why would you want to see that?"

"Hasn't your furniture arrived? It shouldn't take this long unless you're PCSing from overseas."

Fuck. Had he just said something that would give the game away? "Really? I'm new to all this. Rex and I haven't been married long, and I wasn't with him at the, uh—"

"Fort Bragg?"

"Right. Fort Bragg. I was living in LA, and we kind of met in the middle when we moved here."

"That's so romantic. You at least have some wedding photos with you, right?" Ronda wouldn't give up.

"Yeah. They're still in a box somewhere."

"Hasn't Rex helped you unpack?"

"No. It hasn't been a high priority."

"Rex doesn't care much about the house, does he?" Lynda shook her head and tsked.

Reed would kill Trent for making him sound like a lousy husband. "It's not that. We just have other ways to spend our time when he comes back from work."

"Aww, newlyweds." Ronda squeezed his arm again. "I can't remember that far back, but I'm pretty sure Bill and I were in love at one time about three kids and two deployments ago."

Trent gave a pained grin. "We don't want to stay in that awful condo if we can help it. I hope we can move into a house with a yard. I'd love a garden."

"Troy, honey, those awful condos are the nice base housing."

"Really?" He attempted to pull his foot out of his mouth again. He was lousy at this Army spouse thing. He gave up the thought of ever trying out for community theater either because he couldn't act his way out of a paper bag.

"There you are." Molly Miller walked up to their table, put down her Godzilla-sized coffee with whipped cream topping as big as any Texas hair and sat across from Trent. "This place is a zoo."

"Hey, Molly. We're trying to get Troy to invite us over to his house tomorrow. So much nicer than Starbucks."

"Now they just moved in not two weeks ago. Let the man settle in before you start snooping." She rubbed Trent's arm.

Why did all these women feel the need to touch him? He couldn't tell if it was a Texas thing, an Army thing, or if they were just horny and didn't get that he wasn't interested. Based on Ronda's comment, horny was at the top of the list.

"Oh, there's Katie." Lynda stood and practically bellowed. "Katie! Over here!"

Everyone in the entire Starbucks turned to look at Lynda except for Katie, who was wandering in the other direction. Finally Trent got tired of watching her and got up to bring her over to the table.

"Hi, everyone." Katie sat down. She pulled her thin sweater tight across her chest. It didn't fit very well because it was a couple of sizes too small. Ronda made an unpleasant expression, but the way Katie didn't meet their gazes told him a lot about how she got along with the others. "It's cold in here."

"That little sweater wouldn't fit my Chihuahua," Ronda said, twisting up her mouth.

"Take my jacket." Trent handed her the light jacket hanging over the back of his chair.

"Thanks." She took it with a shy smile and shrugged into it. The sleeves were twice as long as her pale, thin arms, and she reminded Trent of his little brother when he used to try on their dad's suits. Trent also liked wearing his mom's blouses and jewelry and had to fight Maggie for the best pieces.

"My mother-in-law will be gone tomorrow, so we can meet at my place next time. Thursday?" Lynda Gregson suggested.

"That works for me," Trent said. The others agreed, and they sipped at their coffees and gossiped. Trent decided then and there he better not miss any coffee dates or these women would turn on him, and he'd probably feel their claws in his back from ten miles away.

A COUPLE of days later, Trent was settled in enough to do some exploring off base. He glanced at his list of San Antonio sights. Right at the top was the Alamo, but he didn't want to go alone. He phoned a couple of the other spouses, and they decided to turn it into a full-day sightseeing excursion.

Sightseeing wasn't necessarily the best way to describe the day. Lynda and Ronda had jumped at the suggestion. Soon after they arrived and parked near the site, Trent discovered why they had been excited with the idea: the Alamo compound was about a block away from some prime downtown shopping and the Riverwalk.

They hurried him through the museum and grounds so they would have plenty of time for lunch and shopping before they had to get home to start cooking dinner.

That evening Reed asked about the "field trip."

"The Alamo's a lot smaller than I remember."

"You've been there before?"

"As a kid. Our family came down here for vacation at some point, but I can't remember much about it. We all wanted Davy Crockett hats with the tails, and my mom refused to let us wear dead animals on our heads." Trent laughed at the memory. "The fort seemed huge and exciting."

"You must have been really small, then."

"If you ask Mom, I was never really small."

Reed grinned. "Really young, then. So today was a disaster?"

"Not so much. Lynda is a world-class shopper. She'd be right at home in LA. She stopped at the most expensive boutiques and tried on fifty things." Trent paused to take a few bites of dinner. "Why do straight women think we're interested in helping them try on clothes?"

"I'd guess it's because their husbands wouldn't even be caught dead shopping with them. They're probably glad for a man's opinion."

"I hardly think my opinion of how their asses look in a skirt is going to do them any good figuring out what their husbands will like."

"So tell them that."

"I don't want to offend anyone." Trent finished his wine.

"Then don't ask my opinion." Reed pointed to the last piece of steak and helped himself to it when Trent waved it away. "However, if their questions or expectations upset you, then let them know you're offended. You're not doing gay men any favors by giving in to these misperceptions."

"Fine, Dear Abby. Thanks for the advice."

"You asked, remember?"

Trent nodded. "I did, and I appreciate your perspective. Are you doing any better with your coworkers than I am with the spouses?"

"Yeah. I got invited to a poker game later this week. Cigars, whiskey, and no wives."

"Can I come? I wouldn't mind some socializing that didn't include wives."

"That's funny. I was actually welcomed by one guy, Cray, because he thinks everyone is hitting on his wife."

"Oh, I know Katie Cray. She's a sweet little thing. Kind of reminds me of one of those Dogpatch cartoon characters. Doesn't own any clothing that covers everything it's supposed to cover."

That seemed to get Reed's attention. "What do you mean?"

"Tight shirts, short skirts. She's very voluptuous, kind of an innocent version of Marilyn Monroe. But the other wives look at her like she's a tramp." Trent looked over at Reed. "She looks so embarrassed that I don't think dressing that way is her choice."

"Her husband did come across as a real dick."

"I gave her my jacket at Starbucks and told her to keep it. I wish she'd come along for the shopping, because I would gladly have bought her some new clothes."

"Now I'm really curious about their relationship. Let me know if you think there's anything really wrong there, okay?"

"If he's forcing her into anything, then that's really wrong." Trent pushed his plate away. The discussion made his stomach hurt. Poor Katie looked like she'd jump out of her skin. "I'll let her know she can talk to me. That's one situation where I don't mind if she oversteps any boundaries. She might really need a friend, and some of the other spouses aren't exactly warm and fuzzy."

"I'm glad you'll watch out for her. And let me know if I need to deal with her husband, whether it's official or not."

"Okay. Thanks." Trent cleared the table and collected a few tiny scraps of food onto a saucer.

"What's that for?"

"Did you see the little black-and-white kitten outside?"

"No...."

"He's the scrawniest little thing. Black with a few white splotches and all-white front feet."

"Trent, we don't need a cat."

"I know. He can stay outside, but he looks hungry, so I'm going to put food and water out."

"We'll have every stray cat in the neighborhood, then."

"I'll put it out and wait for ten minutes. If he doesn't come, I'll bring it back in, okay?"

"Sure."

Trent collected the food and water and went out to the front step to wait for the tiny kitten.

ON THURSDAY he kissed Reed good-bye and closed the front door behind him when he left for work. That gave him two hours to write before he needed to leave for Lynda Gregson's house and the coffee club.

He hadn't planned on starting a new book, but the combination of utter boredom here on the base and being part of a new community gave him ideas and plenty of time to write. Even if he intended more sightseeing around San Antonio, he still had so many hours to fill while Reed was at work. Trent had called Katie and invited her to go with him to the nearby arboretum about ten miles north of the base. She hadn't taken him up on the invitation, but he hoped to have a chance to chat with her again today when he picked her up for coffee.

But when he got to Katie's house, he had to knock twice before she came to the door.

"Sorry, Troy, I'm not feeling up to coffee today." She opened the door about a centimeter so all he could see was one eye and a sliver of body. She was wearing a robe.

"Katie, are you okay? Do you need anything?" He had a bad feeling.

"I'm fine."

"You just said you're not up for coffee. Which is it?"

"Leave me alone." She sounded like she was about to cry and shoved the door shut. If it had been open more than a centimeter, it would have actually slammed.

"I'm sorry. Just let me know what you need. I'm here. Just call me, okay?"

"Give me your number again?" She opened the door a crack.

"I'll call your cell again, then you'll have my number."

"I—uh. Lost my phone."

That sounded suspicious, so he wrote his number on a piece of paper and handed it to her.

"Thanks."

"You sure you want me to leave?"

She shook her head, and he thought he saw a bruise on her cheek. He fought the urge to push the door open and make sure she was okay, but he waited. "I don't. But I'm afraid to ask you inside."

"Do you want to come out? Or would you like to meet me somewhere?"

"I don't want you to be late for Lynda's house."

"Don't worry about Lynda's coffee club. I'm not."

"Let me change, then I'll meet you at the park around the corner."

He nodded and walked toward the sidewalk. He didn't look back at the house as he headed for the small park and playground she had mentioned. About five minutes later, Katie arrived wearing jeans and Trent's jacket. She'd arranged her hair so it hung over her eyes, but Trent could see her eye and cheek were bruised.

She sat at the next bench rather than next to Trent.

"Troy, I can't hang out with you anymore. Or not in public. I don't know what to do."

"Will you tell me what happened?"

"Paul heard your message on the machine. He thinks you're... well, not just my friend."

"That's crazy."

"He's not crazy." Her voice rose and she got defensive, but her fear ratcheted up too.

"He's crazy to think I want to be more than friends. Doesn't he know I'm married and I'm gay?"

"No."

"Why not?"

"I didn't want to tell him that."

"Katie...." Trent paused before he let his frustration out. "Look, my husband Rex works with Paul. They're gonna play poker this week. I think they're friends. So there's no reason for him to worry about me and you."

"They're friends?" Her tone brightened. "Really?"

"Yes. If he says anything, tell him I'm Rex's husband." Trent glanced over at her. "And I'll start wearing more pink if it helps."

She laughed. The sound was like sunshine. Trent realized he'd hardly heard Katie laughing before, and now he just wanted to hold her in his arms and tell her jokes. "Pink might help."

"So now will you come for coffee?"

"I can't go looking like this."

"I'm from LA, honey. I'm sure I can do some makeup magic on you, and no one will ever have to know what's under there. What do you say?"

"Okay."

TWENTY MINUTES later they pulled up in front of Lynda Gregson's house in a different part of base housing. The lawn was perfectly groomed and flowering hedges lined the sidewalk. Trent squeezed Katie's hand, then rang the doorbell.

Lynda opened the door, laughing over her shoulder at someone behind her. Then she turned her attention to Trent and Katie. "Oh, I didn't think you two were going to show." She looked down her nose at Katie, then stepped aside to let them in.

"Just running a bit behind schedule." Trent held up a tray. "But I've got some cream cheese danish, almost fresh out of the oven."

"Did you make them, Troy?"

"Yes. An old family recipe."

"From LA?"

"From Oklahoma City." Trent grinned.

The others came into the hallway to greet him and Katie, who kept her gaze on the floor.

"Oh, Katie, you've done something different with your hair?" Molly Miller said. "I think that's what's different. It really suits you."

Katie flashed Trent a secret smile. She did look lovely after he'd worked on her makeup and hair. "Thanks. Troy showed me a new technique."

"Troy? So you're a hair stylist? I thought you were writing a book."

"I learned a few things from friends in the film business."

"Is that so? You get more fascinating every day."

Trent nodded and took the mug of coffee Ronda handed him. They probably wouldn't be particularly amused if they learned the source of the trick—one of his friend Mick's female porn star friends.

Everyone was gathered in the living room, an almost all-white expanse that made Trent's head ache. The Gregsons didn't have kids or the place would be filthy. Even the dog was snow white, a tiny purse-sized poodle.

"Wow, this place is incredible, Lynda."

"Thanks. We like collecting things on our travels. Let's try some of these pastries. Then I'll give you the grand tour."

"Can't wait."

"AND HOW did Katie do at the coffee club?" Reed asked when he got home.

"She came out of her shell after getting so many compliments. Only Lynda never really warmed up to her. That woman could learn a few things about hospitality from Martha Stewart. It's not just about serving good food. I couldn't care less what I eat as long as the company is good."

"Sorry it was such a bust."

"But it wasn't. That's what I wanted to tell you." Trent turned the water on in the sink, then sat down at the kitchen table, but he couldn't sit still and his eyes were practically glittering.

Reed appreciated Trent's diligence to make sure they weren't overheard. He checked his watch. Twenty minutes before he had to leave for Cray's house. He hoped Trent's story wasn't going to be his typical epic. "Can you wait till later to tell me?"

"After you've been smoking cigars and guzzling whiskey? I don't think so."

"You're welcome to join me."

"Pass. At least for now."

"Then summarize…."

"The Gregsons have a lot of stuff. A lot of expensive stuff. The kind of things our LA friends have and we don't notice. But here, for someone at Gregson's salary, it's a lot of expensive stuff. Some fancy china, real silverware, a huge closet full of clothes—his and hers. And she had a jewelry box that was locked."

"And how do you know it was locked?"

"I tried to open it when I pretended to use the upstairs bathroom. I couldn't find the key in any of the usual places."

"A woman who locks up her valuables when she has a bunch of nosy guests doesn't sound all that unusual."

"Fine. But they have two really nice cars, and there were a lot of photos of them in Europe."

"None of that is particular suspicious for military families. If you get stationed in Europe, it's cheap and easy to travel. The silver could be inherited. They might have huge car loans."

"Oh."

The way Trent's good mood crumbled made Reed feel guilty. "But that's great stuff to notice. I'll try to ask some pointed questions, and I'll get some details on Gregson's finances. Good work, Watson."

"I don't want to be Watson."

"You can't be Holmes."

"Then I'll be Irene Adler."

Reed burst into laughter. "Fine." He stood and kissed Trent on the top of the head, then turned the water off. "Gonna hit the shower and change before going over to Cray's. Care to join me?"

"I told you I'm not in the mood for cigars."

"I meant in the shower."

"Hmm. I thought you'd never ask."

THE SHOWER made Reed half an hour late to Cray's house. After hearing about Katie's bruises, Reed was inclined to cancel, but he needed to hang out with these men, and especially after Trent's sleuthing. Plus, it was an opportunity to see how Katie was doing and observe her husband's interactions with her.

"Glad to see you, Atwater. Oh, hey, you didn't need to bring beer."

"Sure, I did. I'm not supposed to drink whiskey."

"Why's that?"

"One of Troy's things. He also hates cigars, so I figured I had to choose my battles." Reed hated bad-mouthing Trent, but it was just BS to get the guys to trust him. Nothing helped men bond more than bitching about their spouses. He'd learned that technique long ago. An invaluable undercover trick.

Cray introduced his wife, Katie, and Reed agreed with Trent's assessment of her wardrobe. That crack Gregson had made about Katie's cleavage was spot-on. It made no sense that the jealous types wanted to parade their wives around in skimpy clothes and then beat the poor women when other men ogled them.

Katie was friendly to Reed, and thankfully, Cray didn't care. The gay card was a plus here, for Katie's sake, at least.

The evening went smoothly enough. Reed lost most of his money, purposefully trying to see if anyone was cheating and to encourage these men to underestimate him. If he'd won, they'd pay much closer attention to everything he did or said. Once they thought they were better than him at something, they'd keep inviting him along to card games and other events, never expecting him to notice anything.

One thing Reed spotted was top-of-the-line kitchen appliances like a fancy Kitchen Aid mixer, Cuisinart food processor, and Vitamix. He had to thank Trent because otherwise Reed would never have known how much those items cost. He peered into rooms and looked for other high-end items. At one point he went into the garage and spotted a wet-dream of a workshop with power tools Reed couldn't even name. Add in Cray's Tag Heuer watch and alarm bells started sounding.

The most telling item was a ceramic statue on a shelf in the living room.

"What's this? It looks really old," Reed said.

"Picked it up in Iraq during my tour there."

"Doesn't look like anything I ever saw in the market." Reed reached for the object, and Cray pulled his hand back before he made contact.

"It's a little nicer than the items they sell in the market. I paid more for that than Katie might like to know. Supposed to be a thousand years old. I suspect I got ripped off, so don't tell her it was expensive."

"Sure thing, man." Reed slapped Cray's shoulder in a gesture of manly solidarity. But his trained eye told him the item was genuine. Not as old or as valuable as the gold items, but it was museum quality. As soon as he got a chance, he'd look this one up on the list of missing artifacts.

Cray kept a closer eye on him after that, so Reed toned it down on the snooping and lost the rest of his cash by going all in when he knew Cray was bluffing. With the pressure off momentarily, Reed called it a night and headed home.

For Trent's sake, he stuffed his smoky clothes in a plastic bag and washed the residual odor from his hair and skin in the shower, then crawled under the sheets.

"Mmm. You're home early."

"I couldn't stay away any longer."

"I like it when you lie to me. I really feel like we're married." Trent was naked and warm, but when he pulled Reed in for a kiss, Reed couldn't help feeling a little insulted by Trent's remarks about marriage being based on lies.

When had Reed started caring so much about making their fake marriage a success?

24

THE NEXT morning Reed e-mailed Tom White with a status report on what he'd discovered so far. A Bureau forensic accountant had been assigned to go over finances from those individuals Reed suspected, and had also given him a list of soldiers at Fort Sam who had financial transactions that fit specific patterns.

Reed had to decide how best to make contact with those men who weren't part of the logistics team. So far they'd only identified one man with a different unit—Sergeant Bradshaw had worked with Cray and Gregson in Iraq, but when they had all returned stateside, Bradshaw headed up one of the medical supply units responsible for getting medical equipment back to the US. Medical equipment the Army no longer needed had been donated to local hospitals and clinics.

And what better way to smuggle items than in medical supplies. Who would question the contents of boxes marked for a hospital? But Bradshaw hadn't been at Cray's poker game the night before, and Reed hadn't managed to find a way to ask the supply team about him. Bradshaw wasn't in any of the photos Cray had displayed.

Until the next poker night, Reed resorted to the next best way to find out about Bradshaw: through his wife.

Trent was gnawing on some toast while Reed poured him another cup of coffee. He looked askance when Reed made the request. "You want me to accidentally run into her and suddenly become her best friend?"

"That's pretty much it. They don't have kids, so you won't have to hang out at the school trying to bump into her."

"Good. I don't need 'sexual predator' on my résumé." Trent shook his head. "What does she do? And what is her name?"

"Don't worry about her name. You haven't met her yet, so don't run the risk of actually using it."

"Good point."

"There is a reason the Bureau has us do four months of new agent training…. And they don't even teach everything there."

"Okay, so what does Mrs. Bradshaw like to do? I can't just stalk her."

"Nope." Reed pulled a printout from a folder he had set on one of the kitchen chairs. "Okay, she spends a lot of money at MAC. What's that?"

"Makeup store." Trent took another sip of coffee.

"Yeah, next on the list—"

"That's not a bad idea, Rex. Katie could use a makeover. That wouldn't be tough to arrange."

"She works out at the base gym, and she signed up for several cooking classes at somewhere called Cuisine-Art."

Trent groaned. "I guess I could take a cooking class."

"Bring Katie. She probably knows Bradshaw's wife, and that could help ease your way into a friendship."

"Fine. What are my other options?"

Reed read off a few other places Bradshaw's wife liked to shop off base. "She seems to use the credit card at Cuisine-Art on Fridays, and on Mondays she eats at an Italian place over at Riverwalk."

"Cuisine-Art it is, today."

"Thanks, Troy." Reed stood up and kissed Trent, then left for work.

Trent checked the Cuisine-Art website to see what classes they were running that day. Only two. Lunches of Love—"new techniques for making packed lunches a special treat for hubby and kids" and Noodlicious—"making your own pasta has never been easier or more fun!"

When they had to tell you something was fun and use an exclamation point, it usually wasn't. But Trent was prepared to take both classes, for Reed. At least he could bring Katie, and then it might actually be "fun!"

Lunches of Love started at eleven, so Trent called Katie at nine to invite her along. She sounded hesitant at first, but he offered to pay for her.

"It's not the price, but thanks for offering. I don't really like cooking. I used to, but lately I don't."

Trent remembered Reed's comment about all the expensive cooking equipment. Why had she stopped enjoying it? Was it because of her husband? He didn't exactly deserve any Lunches of Love. "Well, then, you're the perfect candidate. The classes sound like fun, and even if you never make anything, it will get you out of the house."

"That's true. Anything that isn't shopping or coffee. I've had enough of both."

Hallelujah. Trent usually loved shopping and coffee, but the women at Fort Sam had turned him off of both in the space of two short weeks. "So you're in?"

"Yeah. And Paul is doing something after work, so I don't have to cook for him. We can have a relaxing day, and I can still get home in time to finish cleaning up after last night's poker game before Paul gets home."

"Oh, damn. I forgot about that. Let me come over now and help."

Which is how Trent found himself with the perfect opportunity for more snooping. He felt a little guilty poking around in Katie's life, and rationalized it because Paul might be breaking a law, and if he went to jail, maybe Katie would divorce him. Reed had been right about all the fancy appliances and cookware. Katie even had a few items Trent didn't own back home.

"Hey, do you like this juicer?" Trent openly coveted the appliance he couldn't justify purchasing.

"It works great, but I hate cleaning it up." Katie's toneless reply made Trent's heart ache.

"And what's this?"

"Tea maker." She pointed to the buttons on the front. "You choose what kind of tea—green, herbal, etc.—and it knows what temperature to heat the water and how long to brew. It's actually my favorite appliance."

"You should have a tea party instead of coffee club." Trent eyed the machine. He wanted one of these in the worst way. "And then I'll get to use it!"

"You can use it whenever you want. Do we have time for tea now?"

"Sure." Trent was torn between watching her use the amazing appliance and getting more snoop time. The tea won out.

As much as Trent disliked Paul Cray, a part of him knew Katie's life would get even more complicated if her husband was implicated in the smuggling. He hoped they ran into the Bradshaw woman at Cuisine-Art so he could find out something to help Reed's investigation.

REED WAS at his desk in the supply depot inputting data from a shipment of weapons that had just arrived from another base. Between closing bases and bringing deployed soldiers home, the Army was moving a lot of items around, sometimes more than once, until the brass figured out who was going to do what where.

It was a game of Hot Potato, Army-style.

Thank God he'd been Ranger and special ops material. Probably no one out of West Point ended up in logistics, but maybe if someone had, the system would have been better designed. Well, he wasn't here to fix the Army.

The phone on his desk rang.

"Atwater."

"Sergeant, you've been scheduled for your annual physical exam. Report to San Antonio Military Medical Center, room 112, at fourteen hundred hours." The woman sounded pleasant, but her voice held an undertone Reed couldn't identify.

"Who is this?"

"Private Lincoln, records clerk. You'll be seeing Dr. Nicholls."

"Right. Fourteen hundred." He hung up. He shouldn't be scheduled for a physical. There could be some mistake, but he was grateful to get out of the office. By the time the exam was done, he would practically have the office to himself. Anyone who could knock off early did, especially on Friday. He'd have a chance to do some investigating.

He reported to the hospital ten minutes early and waited for his appointment. When the registration nurse didn't hand him a ream of forms to fill out, he got suspicious, but his curiosity was piqued, so he waited to see who Dr. Nicholls was and what he wanted.

"Sergeant Atwater, the doctor will see you now."

She led him to an office with an unmarked door, rather than an exam room, and asked him to have a seat. He wandered around to the other side of the desk hoping to find some identifying information but there was absolutely nothing personal on the desk or the walls. It could be a vacant office.

The door opened, and Reed pretended to be looking out the window when a man wearing a white lab coat entered.

"Atwater?"

"Yes, Doctor."

"Have a seat. You're probably wondering why you're here."

"Yes."

"Colonel Atkinson sent me to talk to you." Nicholls—if that was his name—sat behind the desk.

Reed didn't respond.

"I'm Lieutenant Colonel Nicholls, on the colonel's staff. He's given me a little background on your investigation, and since it wouldn't do for you to meet with him, I'll be your liaison."

"Fine."

Nicholls frowned. Or he frowned more deeply. He hadn't even been close to a smile before, but now he appeared positively unhappy. "The colonel would appreciate a status report."

"This isn't how we normally run an investigation. He should contact the—"

"He's asking *you*. Colonel Atkinson has his own way of running the show."

Reed wouldn't argue with that. And it sounded just like his father to get someone else in the middle. For personal things, it was Mom. For this, he sent his second-in-command. Why do a job yourself when you can delegate? That was what you learned in management classes in the Army.

"I'm still getting to know the soldiers we suspect of being involved, and I don't have any information to believe any of them is, nor do I have any evidence to eliminate any of them. It's going to take more than a couple of weeks, unfortunately."

"That's discouraging."

"Considering these men have been sitting on some of the items for several years, they aren't likely to make any major errors or suddenly change their MO. For us to barge in asking the wrong questions is only going to show our hand."

"Our?"

"My colleague is working from another angle."

"I didn't realize another investigator is on this assignment."

"Troy Atwater, who is here as my husband."

"You're married to him?"

These questions got Reed's spidey sense tingling. Wouldn't his father have briefed Nicholls? Maybe Dad didn't want to let on the personal connection. That was no surprise. "No. We're pretending to be married, and he's talking with the other spouses."

"And what has that avenue uncovered?"

"Nothing of note. Yet."

"I see." Nicholls stared at Reed with an expression indicating he was waiting for more information.

Reed would keep him waiting.

After a staring contest lasting a few tense moments, Nicholls let out an exasperated sigh. "I will pass this information on to the colonel. And here's my contact info." He pulled a card from his pocket and handed it to Reed. The phone number had been crossed out and its replacement written by hand. "Call me directly with regular updates, rather than disturbing the colonel."

"Yes, sir." Reed pocketed the card and tried to keep the annoyance from showing in his face. He wasn't in the Army and technically didn't owe this man or his father any official deference.

"Dismissed."

Reed got up and left. Nicholls came across too much like Reed's father for him to want to cooperate with the man. He'd be waiting a long time for those "regular updates."

The meeting left Reed tense, so he decided to go for a run instead of back to his office. No one would miss him for the rest of the afternoon. He hoped Trent had gotten some useful information about Bradshaw at Cuisine-Art. But if not, Reed at least hoped for something interesting for dinner.

25

ON MONDAY Reed received an encrypted file from Tom White. He wouldn't risk looking at it from his office computer, and he had a strange feeling he and Trent were being watched at home. They had to get out of the house to somewhere they couldn't be overheard.

"Hey honey, it's me." Reed phoned Trent during lunch.

"How's your day going? Do you miss me already?"

"Of course I do." Reed spotted Gregson coming toward him in the break room. He nodded while Gregson sat down. "How about dinner out tonight?"

"That sounds nice. What's the occasion?"

"Because I love you."

"Oh, that sounds really nice."

Gregson chuckled, and Reed wanted to deck him.

"Who's that laughing in the background, Rex?"

"Greg." Reed turned away from him while he wrapped up the discussion. "I'll be home by six. You mentioned someplace called White's? Or was it Whitman's?"

"White's. That's it. It's kind of a local secret."

"That's the one. See you later." Reed hung up.

"You can't really be that much in love."

"Because Troy's a guy?"

"No. I mean once you get married, the shine's off the apple. It gets a little boring. You'll see. Might be a little harder for you to find something on the side, but I bet you start looking before Easter."

Reed opened his lunch, deciding a comment like that didn't warrant a response. Trent had taken that class on the previous Friday, and Reed was wondering whether he'd actually made any of the recipes for lunch.

One plastic container was filled with sliced cucumbers and carrots—homemade pickles according to Trent. Another container had flatbread rolled up with turkey and Asian barbecue sauce. It smelled delicious. The third container had a cupcake with a heart drawn in icing. It was more interesting than a burger at one of the canteens.

"Is that cupcake homemade?" Gregson asked.

"No idea."

"What kind of sandwich is that?"

When Reed told him, Gregson pushed out his lower lip. "Well, he's really making an effort. That's actually kind of sweet. Wish Lynda would take some interest in cooking. She can't seem to take a break from shopping long enough."

It wouldn't be a good idea to point out that Gregson probably got what he deserved if he was cheating on Lynda. Reed stuffed food in his mouth so he wouldn't be expected to reply. The sandwich was delicious. If this kept up, he was going to gain a lot of weight on this assignment. Better start getting some exercise. Thankfully January was cool enough for outdoor workouts.

That evening he and Trent went across town to dinner at Pappy's Pizzeria, a casual spot where no one cared Reed had his laptop out.

"What did you hear from White?" Trent asked after chomping through two pieces of delicious pizza.

"Nothing good. He can't find any significant anomalies in anyone's finances. They all have something out of the ordinary, but nothing large enough to indicate they are involved in items like the goblets or the items that showed up at US museums during the past two years."

"Maybe it isn't *one* of them." Trent popped a disc of crispy pepperoni into his mouth.

"They *could* be working together. But they get along awfully well. Gregson outranks the others, but they're all pretty friendly with each other. I can't see Cray staying friends with Gregson if they worked together on the smuggling. Not over this many years. Most criminal enterprises break down because the members get greedy, don't agree on when and how to sell the goods or how to split the cash."

"It's also strange that they do so much socializing within that department. I think it's kind of odd they see each other outside work several times a week."

"They were deployed together. It creates bonds and it can also separate you from guys who weren't there. You know they can't understand what you went through. I don't find it particularly odd."

"Wouldn't they also be worried people would connect their unit to the smuggling?"

Reed put his fork down. Trent was right. It would raise eyebrows if several guys from the same unit suddenly had a bunch of extra cash, which is why Reed suspected all of them. "I see circumstantial evidence they are working together, but there's not enough actual proof to arrest anyone. I think I'm going to have to try another tactic."

"Like what?"

"I'll let you know when I figure it out. How's Operation Petticoat coming along?"

"What?"

"Gossip with the spouses?"

"Oh." Trent frowned. "That's kind of a sexist remark."

"Don't you start on me."

"What's that mean?"

"Gregson. He told me I'd start cheating on you by Easter."

Trent blinked and bit his lower lip. "Why'd he say that? Is there some guy paying you too much attention? Or is Greg interested in you? Is he bi-curious? Or just a dick?"

"He's a dick. A big dick, and not in the good way." Reed took Trent's hand. "And no one is paying me any attention who shouldn't. You have nothing to worry about."

"I hope not. I don't want to have to explain to Katie or Molly why we're having marital troubles if they hear you're cheating."

"We won't still be here at Easter. At least not if I can help it. *I'll* confess to smuggling the gold if I have to stick around the supply unit office for another three months."

"It can't be that bad. You should try taking a class at Cuisine-Art."

"Really? My lunch was delicious."

"I didn't use any of the new 'techniques' on you." Trent made quotey fingers, giving Reed his clear opinion on the class. "Today's lunch was all me."

Reed chuckled. "Why don't you make me lunch back in LA?"

"Because you can make your own damn lunch." He slammed his hand down on the table.

"With an attitude like that you're going to be single the rest of your life, buster."

"You can make your lunch tomorrow too. And dinner for the rest of your life." Trent crossed his arms over his chest and turned his face away from Reed, then burst out laughing. "Is this our first fight as newlyweds?"

"Just don't call your mother and complain about me, whatever you do."

"I'll call *your* mother and complain. How's that?" Trent grinned, but Reed didn't find the comment even remotely amusing.

26

REED'S WEEK crawled at a pace a snail would find boring. All he had to look forward to was another poker night on Friday. This one was at Gregson's house.

"Why don't they invite the spouses?" Trent asked Thursday at breakfast.

"Do you want to go?"

"I didn't say that. Just curious."

"Because they want to drink and smoke cigars and bet money, and they don't want their wives bitching at them about it."

Trent frowned. "I see hanging out with these guys has had a negative effect on you."

"What makes you say that?" Trent was making french toast for breakfast. He stood at the stove watching it cook.

"Why do you assume the women 'bitch' about those things? And you don't usually lump all of a group together. You hate when people do that to us." He flipped some french toast onto a plate and put it in front of Reed. "Butter and syrup."

Reed slathered butter on the delicious-smelling slices, then poured syrup. "Oh, I love when you make it with cinnamon bread."

"I made the bread yesterday."

"Still hanging out at Cuisine-Art?"

"Don't change the subject. Poker. Wives. Bitching...." Trent waved the spatula at Reed, then served himself some breakfast and sat down.

Reed chewed for a minute. Trent's comments weren't off base. Reed had tried to get into the mindset of his supply unit coworkers. He didn't usually bring home that kind of attitude. Then again, he still suspected someone might be listening.

Trent put syrup on his toast and stared at Reed, not satisfied with the silence.

Reed nodded, then pointed to his ear, then to the ceiling. Hopefully Trent would get the idea. He did because he nodded.

"So do you want to come along on Friday?"

"Why would I be invited if the other spouses aren't? That doesn't seem fair."

"Considering the way you're bitching at me this morning, I'm not sure I want you monitoring my every move." He made sure to smile and blow a kiss at Trent so he'd know it was a joke. Sometimes Trent got far too literal.

"I won't bitch. I'm kind of interested in meeting these guys."

"And woman. Corporal Bell will be there. They pretty much treat her like one of the guys. I hope that remark didn't offend you."

"Not as long as you do the dishes."

During the rest of the meal, they confined the discussion to boring topics like dry cleaning and grocery shopping. Then Trent got up and put his plate in the sink. "Dishes?" Then he walked out of the room.

Reed shook his head and smiled as he cleared the table and started filling the sink with water. He really missed their dishwasher at home. When he turned the water off in the sink, he heard Trent's voice. Reed listened and realized Trent was on the phone. He couldn't hear many specific words but made out something about lunch plans.

When he finished the dishes, he found Trent in the living room reading a book.

"Heading out to work. See you later."

"Have a nice day," Trent said with an exaggerated Stepford wife intonation.

"You too. Got any big plans?"

Trent shook his head and reached up to bring Reed's face down for a kiss.

As Reed walked to his car, he wondered whether Trent had been telling the truth. Whatever reason Trent had for not telling Reed about his lunch plans, Reed wasn't worried.

Okay, maybe just a little.

TRENT LEFT the condo at eleven thirty and walked to the park two blocks away. A pearl-green Prius stopped at the curb and honked. The driver waved, and he sprang up and strode toward the car. He glanced around, then opened the door and slid inside, as best he could since the seat wasn't pushed very far back.

"Oh, dear, let me just help—"

"I'm fine. Used to it." He adjusted the seat and stretched his legs out a few inches more.

"Oh, I'm so glad you could meet me."

Before he knew it, Trent was engulfed in a tight hug. He waited for it to pass. "I'm as excited about this as you are."

"Do you have any place in particular you'd like to go?"

He glanced out the window wondering whether anyone had seen him. "Anywhere off base."

"Of course. There's a lovely little hotel downtown. I think you'd like it."

"Anywhere is fine." Trent gazed out the window, wishing the base weren't so huge. Every time they passed a blue car, he thought it might be Reed. How could he explain what he was doing? Reed would be furious.

Please drive faster.

After ten minutes of awkward chitchat about the base, they parked outside Mokara Hotel and went through the front door. Two minutes later they were sitting at a small table near the window in the elegant restaurant. The hostess left menus and served water.

Then they were alone.

"Oh, Trent, I'm so thrilled for a chance to get to know you."

"Me too, Mrs.—Maya."

Reed's mother put her menu down and reached for his hand across the table. He felt really awkward, as if everyone else in the place were looking at them, wondering why this elegant silver-haired woman was here with him.

"I hardly know where to begin. There are so many things I want to know. About you, about Reed, about your lives together." She glanced down at the table and blinked a few times. "I'm sorry. It's been so difficult…." She fumbled in her purse and pulled out an old-fashioned cloth handkerchief, pale pink embroidered with a delicate dark pink edging.

Just then the waiter returned. "Ready to order?"

"A few more minutes, please," Trent said. He focused on his menu to give Maya a moment to compose herself. She hadn't seemed the type to cry. She seemed the type to send *you* crying, a tough, no-nonsense woman who could handle herself around soldiers and stand up to her husband.

Nothing on the menu particularly appealed. The food was probably good here. At least it smelled fantastic—fresh bread and spices from various cuisines from Tex-Mex to Thai—but he didn't have much appetite. Whether it was not telling Reed the truth or what he might learn today, he couldn't say. But he knew everything between him and Reed could change forever.

After they ordered Maya stared at him for a few uncomfortable moments. "I'm sorry, Trent. I've never met any of Reed's boyfriends. God, I hate that word. Partner sounds kind of clinical…. Well, I just want to see what kind of man Reed has chosen to spend his life with."

"It's only been about three years."

"Why do you say only? Three years is a long time for someone who's never had a romantic relationship before."

He was about to correct her when he realized she was talking about Reed. Had Reed never been in a relationship before him? He hadn't shared many details, only a little about Peter Isett and a nameless guy who'd been in his special ops unit. "Romantic" wasn't the first word that came to mind from what little Trent knew.

"I hope I meet your expectations."

"Of course you do. I haven't been close with Reed for many years, but he's a good man who makes good decisions. I don't question his integrity or that he expects as much from others as he expects from himself. You must measure up to some pretty high expectations."

"I never thought about it like that. You're right about Reed. He does have high expectations. But since we've been together, I think he's learned to relax a little."

She nodded. "It takes some time to adjust after combat. It's very hard to trust others enough to relax. I'm glad you've been there for him."

The food arrived, cutting off Trent's opportunity to ask the question that had gnawed at him nonstop since that afternoon in Colonel Atkinson's office. Instead they made light conversation about his life with Reed in LA and some of their travels.

When they'd moved on to coffee, Maya added lots of cream to hers. "Blair doesn't care for cream, and he isn't afraid to let me know when he sees me adding it. He'll never know!" She stirred her cup and took a sip, letting out a little moan of pleasure. "Real cream. You can't beat it!"

Trent stirred his coffee, also with cream and raw sugar. He was glad she had relaxed around him enough to admit her fondness for cream, and her annoyance at Blair's reaction.

"You've indulged my curiosity enough today, Trent. Let's get to the reason you're here."

He sipped more coffee, prolonging the moment. Maybe he didn't want to know. Was it even his business? Did he have the right to poke into Reed's life without at least telling him?

"You're quiet all of a sudden. I'm such a chatty Cathy."

Trent chuckled. Usually he was the one described as chatty. From Reed, "chatty" was a mild description. "Okay, tell me."

"What did Reed tell you so far?"

"Almost nothing. He barely mentioned you or Blair before the day of the picnic, and then he gave me a little background. How his dad acted almost as if he didn't exist after he came out to you. Reed did sports, went to West Point, joined the Rangers, all hoping to win back his father's approval, and he never could. He seems to have just swept that part of his life under a rug."

"Yes. It was awful. There were a lot of ups and downs over the years. I can't possibly say there was any way to avoid it, but Reed refused to even consider that his father might have had a good reason."

Trent started to stand up. There was no *good* reason for how Reed's father had acted. Lunch and their conversation were going so well until that moment. How could he have ever believed this woman had Reed's best interests at heart? He'd been a fool to come, a fool to think he and Maya could get Reed and his father speaking again.

"Thank you for lunch but I can't listen to this anymore." His mother had taught him more manners than to walk away, even though he wanted to do just that. Then he stopped. "Never mind about lunch." He put some cash on the table and turned away.

Maya reached out and grabbed for his elbow. "Wait, Trent. Don't go just yet."

"I'm not sure there's anything you can say now to change my opinion of you."

"Then I won't try. I'll clarify."

Trent wouldn't change his mind.

She looked at him then took her hand off his arm. "I'm pleased that you didn't stand on ceremony when it comes to sticking up for Reed. That just confirms my belief he's found himself a very good man." She took a nervous sip of water. "Let me tell you Blair's reasoning and you can decide for yourself."

"It will have to be spectacular."

"It's rather simple, though it's quite unfortunate. You see, Blair knew Reed planned to enter the Army. From the time he could walk and talk, he would imitate his father. Saluting, marching, that sort of thing. Reed thrived on moving around the world, going from base to base. It was his dream to follow in Blair's footsteps, especially as his father moved up the ranks. And Blair wanted nothing more than for Reed to have that chance. But the situation for gay service members was terrible. Blair never agreed with the regs, but he had to uphold them. He went out of his way not to find out information he might have to report. Even before DADT, he made sure not to ask or see anything. He's never cared less for Reed because he's gay. He's been terrified for him that he wouldn't get the opportunity to achieve his dreams in the Army. It was a very difficult choice for Blair. He takes Army rules—for good or bad—seriously. He chose not to resign because he thinks he can make the Army a better place for the soldiers under his command. He had to give up his son to do it. Because he didn't want to have to turn Reed in."

When she finished speaking, Trent let the words sink in. It wasn't how he would have done it, or how his father would have, but he saw how a career Army man might think that was the way to accomplish his own goals and not ruin Reed's chances too.

"Why didn't Blair just tell him this?"

"At first he didn't know how to handle the situation. Then he realized that even talking about Reed being gay would put him in a terrible position."

"You could have explained it long before now." Trent couldn't keep disdain from his voice.

"If you've spent three years with my son you know why not."

Trent nodded and a smile broke out of its own accord. "He just won't listen to some things. If my dad were in that situation, I think he would have quit. He's made some sacrifices for me. My whole family has."

"Blair's a good man and a good leader. Not everyone who gets promoted is a good man who cares about the soldiers serving under him. Some do it for their own reasons, not to make the Army better or to help others achieve goals. The Army needs more good leaders to provide role models. This was so incredibly important once boys started getting deployed to combat again. A lot of bad decisions are made during war, and boys die. I think Blair knows how to get the job done with less risk to his soldiers. I can't expect you to understand all the decisions involved over the years. But I wouldn't have stuck with Blair if he wasn't the kind of man Reed has grown up to be."

Trent fiddled with the napkin draped over his coffee cup. "You could have led with that line." He gave a weak smile. All this new information made his head spin, and he didn't know how to process everything he'd learned today.

"Well, I'm not a writer. Never been much good with organizing my thoughts. I've usually let my heart do that for me."

He put his hand over hers. "I understand what you've told me. I'm not sure whether or not to tell Reed any of it."

"I'll follow your lead on that, Trent. But I would like him to know. If he can understand, they may be able to salvage something of their relationship before it's too late. If not, well, I don't suppose we'll be any worse off than we are right now."

But Reed might never forgive me. The thought sent shudders through Trent's entire body.

27

"DON'T FORGET I'm going to the card game at Gregson's house tonight," Reed said as he checked his uniform in the hall mirror the following morning. "You coming along?"

"Maybe. I don't know yet." Trent came in from the kitchen. His hair was messy and he had dark circles under his eyes.

Reed noticed his own eyes were a little bloodshot. Trent had tossed and turned most of the night and kept Reed up.

"I'll tell them you're a maybe. But I'll be home first, and we can go over there together."

"Okay." Trent's voice was listless.

"Are you coming down with something?"

"Like what?"

"Like a cold. You haven't been yourself for a couple of days." Reed pushed hair from Trent's temples. He didn't feel warm. Something was up, though.

"Then maybe I shouldn't go tonight."

"I'll cancel. I should stay home and take care of you." Reed leaned in to give him a gentle kiss. "I'll check in later."

"Don't change your plans for me."

As Reed walked to his car, he wondered what was going on. The Trent he knew would have been in seventh heaven at the idea of Reed staying home to make sure he was okay. He would have made a big deal about Reed even offering. Was this Trent's cover personality or was something really wrong here?

It could have something to do with the secret lunch. Reed had asked Cray in a roundabout way whether Katie and Trent were hanging out together the day before, and Cray said something about the dentist. So whoever Trent had met was a big secret.

Trent didn't keep secrets from Reed. He hated when Reed kept secrets, and now the shoe was on Reed's foot. He didn't like it one bit.

Why wouldn't Trent trust him? If he was still acting strange and looking miserable on Saturday, Reed would ask directly what was going on.

TRENT WAS still under the weather when Reed was ready to leave for poker night. "Call me if you need anything."

"Right. Then the guys will tease you if you come running home to me."

"I didn't say I would come running home." Reed let out a soft chuckle.

Trent didn't find the joke amusing. "Have fun, or get some info, or whatever." Then he shut his mouth quickly. "Crap."

"Don't worry about that now."

At Gregson's Reed was preoccupied with Trent's strange mood. He lost the first two hands and not even on purpose. He had to get his head in the game—and not just the cards. This wasn't a social visit; it was work, and he had intel to gather.

They took a break after about an hour, and Reed explored Gregson's house for incriminating evidence of big spending. Cray spotted him looking at the home-theater system in the den.

"Gregson must really be into music with a system like this," Reed said, trying not to let Cray get in the first word.

"I guess. I think he uses it more for gaming, and maybe his wife watches movies. That's not really my thing."

"Gaming or movies?"

"Movies and music. Gaming I like. What about you?"

"Never really got into it. But if I had a setup like this, it might be another story. Wonder how much something like this would set me back."

"Ask Gregson. I've got no idea. Three, four thousand, maybe?"

A system like this cost much more, far more than Sgt. Rex Atwater could afford on his salary. "Wonder how Gregson found the green for toys like this? We know what he earns."

Cray looked around and nodded. "That's a good question. I never thought about it before."

Reed watched for any sign of deceit, but Cray seemed to be telling the truth. Or at least he believed what he was saying. Too risky to pursue the discussion any further without raising alarms. Just then Gregson came into the room.

"Hey, how much this setup cost you?" Cray asked. Again, he looked sincere, and the blatant question took Reed by surprise.

"A lot." Gregson gave a nervous laugh. "Good thing the wife's uncle croaked and we got a little chunk of change. Let's start another round. Might be your only chance to buy something like this, Cray. Assuming you win." Gregson laughed again, this time more convincingly.

"Count me in for that," Reed said and followed them out of the room.

Later in the evening, he found an opportunity to get each of the others alone and put similar questions to them about Gregson's possessions or those of his wife. Each soldier had a similar response. No one knew how Gregson could fund his and his wife's expensive tastes. Both the suspects and the guys who weren't under suspicion displayed the same emotions and bewilderment. All Reed's training and experience in interrogation told him that no one here knew the source of Gregson's disposable income. No one mentioned the wife's inheritance. Trent might be able to ask Lynda Gregson directly.

Or he could if he was acting normal again. If not, White could have someone check into it.

THE CHANCE came sooner than expected. On Sunday Cray invited his unit and their spouses over for the Super Bowl. Everyone would be there, and Reed would have a perfect opportunity to see them all interacting. He couldn't risk asking more pointed questions about Cray's spending habits after grilling everyone—however subtly—on Friday about Gregson. But Trent could query their spouses, including about Lynda Gregson's dead uncle.

Reed and Trent went out for breakfast to discuss what and how to ask questions. Trent was still distracted.

"You up for this today? Let me know if you can't do it."

"I can do it." Trent's tone sounded defensive. "I haven't fucked anything up yet, have I?"

"That's not what I meant. I know you can do it. You're good at this. You've gotten good information for me. But are you up for it today? We have to be careful—"

"I said I can. Don't you trust me?" He knocked his coffee cup over, and it spilled onto the seat, forcing Reed to shift out of the way of the hot liquid.

Reed almost said "No." It wouldn't be a good idea to upset Trent any more. If only he knew what was eating him. "Of course I trust you. If I didn't, we wouldn't be having this discussion. You wouldn't even be here. You'd be home in LA wondering when I'd be done with this investigation."

"Are you saying I complain about your job?"

Reed bit his lip and counted to three. A server came by with towels to clean up the spilled coffee, and the distraction defused the volatile situation.

"Trent, what is going on? I'm really worried about you. Please talk to me."

To Reed's surprise, Trent looked like he might cry. When he finally answered, he sounded like it too.

"Reed, I'm so sorry for snapping at you." He put both hands on the table and reached for Reed's hands. Then he held them tight. "I wanted to help you, and I don't know whether I've made things worse or not. It's just because I love you."

"You're not making things worse. You're helping me a lot. I'm grateful for your help. Now, cheer up and don't worry. Everything's going to be fine."

"That's what you think." Trent said the words under his breath, but Reed caught them and he started worrying even more.

"Trent?"

"I'll explain everything tomorrow. Now let's go do this Super Bowl thing."

28

THE SUPER Bowl party was more about drinking beer and eating than football, since none of the Texas teams had made it. When Trent cheered for the 49ers, one guy made some homophobic comment related to San Francisco, and Reed stood up, ready to deck him, but Gregson settled him down, then told the loudmouthed guy to leave if he was going to talk like that.

Trent was impressed with Reed coming to his defense and even more so that Gregson told the guy off in front of everyone. Then some other guys in Reed's unit backed Gregson up, and the guy shut up and didn't say much for the rest of the party. He was probably pretty scared when Trent stood up and the guy noticed that he was tall and worked out. Luckily he'd worn a shirt that showed off his muscles in a not-too-gay way. Reed called them Trent's I-might-be-gay-but-don't-fuck-with-me muscles.

It wasn't late when they left the party, so they walked around the neighborhood to exchange information they'd collected.

"What did you find out?" Trent asked. "Anything good?"

"I tried to talk to a couple of the guys from the unit who weren't at the card games. Two were in Iraq with Gregson and Cray. One of them joined the unit after they came back to the States. Neither of them gave me anything useful."

"That's too bad. I'm not sure I have much to add."

"You never know."

They crossed to the next block and a black-and-white flash approached them from someone's yard. Trent stopped and bent down to pick up the tiny cat. "Domino! I haven't seen you for a couple of days. Maybe you've got a girlfriend?" He scratched behind Domino's ears and the kitten's whole body vibrated with silent purrs. Godiva preferred not to be picked up—*she* chose when she'd interact with the food providers—so Domino's sweet, outgoing personality lifted Trent's spirits. He brushed the soft fur against his cheek, then put the kitten down.

"I hope he doesn't have fleas," Reed said.

"Well if he does, you'll find out soon enough." Trent grinned. "Always the animal lover, eh?"

"That's not what I meant. He's wild, and he might give you something."

"I can protect myself against a kitten." Trent flexed a muscle and Reed tugged at his arm and kissed his biceps.

"So what did you find out from Katie?"

"Not as much as I'd hoped. Cray came into the kitchen while we were chatting about some cruise they took. She doesn't know much about the finances because he handles everything. As long as she stays to her allowance, they never talk about money. He decides about cars and those kinds of big expenses. She doesn't even know what bank their account is at."

"That sounds positively Victorian."

"I know." Trent didn't say anything for a few minutes. "Do you think a lot of marriages are like that? Straight marriages?"

"Probably some of every kind of relationship has one partner who's very controlling. Gay couples too, I would think."

"I don't know any gay couples like that. Most of our friends have separate finances, not just because of all the legislation and tax issues. They just never pooled their resources."

"Does a joint checking account doom a relationship?" Reed's tone was teasing.

"I'm serious."

"Me too. We don't have our money pooled, but we share expenses because we have two incomes. If there's only one income…."

"But Katie deserves to know what's going on with their money."

"Katie deserves a lot more than that, Trent. But that's her decision to make."

"I know." Katie brought out all of Trent's protector instincts. If Reed closed this case, they'd leave, and Trent worried about her.

"Let's get home. I want to get up early and send Tom a status report before work."

"Why don't you do that tonight?"

"I have other plans for tonight." Reed wrapped an arm around Trent and kissed him right there under the streetlight where anyone could see.

Trent couldn't wait to get home.

THE NEXT morning Trent was staring at his laptop hoping for some inspiration when he heard a noise at the front door.

"Hang on, Domino, let me grab your bowl!" Trent stopped in the kitchen, and the scratching at the door turned into soft pounding. Not Domino.

"Troy?" Katie.

Trent dropped the bag of cat food and raced for the door. When he flung it open, Katie crumpled onto the hall floor.

"What happened? Are you okay?"

"I'm sorry… I just…."

He slammed the door and knelt beside her. Purplish bruises blotched her face, and her lip was split and bleeding. He pulled her into his arms. "Sweetie, it's okay. You stay here with me and Reed."

"No, I can't."

"You can't go back."

"It was my fault, Troy."

"Come sit on the couch." With an arm around her waist, he helped her sit down. In the brighter room, he saw more bruising. "Let me make some tea and clean you up."

"Tea sounds good." She was trying so hard not to cry that Trent wanted to.

He put the water on and then went into the bathroom. "I don't have a lot of first-aid stuff." He gently washed her face, then brought back the tea.

"Thanks." She reached for the mug, and as soon as he let go, it crashed to the floor, splashing hot tea on the couch and carpet. "I'm sorry. I'm so clumsy." She cowered as she spoke, as if Trent might hit her for spilling tea.

"Let me see your hand." Without anything more than first-aid training, Trent thought the wrist might be sprained. "It's not bruised, so I don't think it's broken, but you should get it X-rayed."

"No hospital."

"Katie, you're going to the hospital if I have to carry you there."

Now she did start crying. "You sound like him."

"Oh God, I am sorry. I'm just worried for you." He calmed her down and stroked her hair, but he was afraid he'd hurt her just by touching her. "I'll feel better if I know you're not seriously hurt, okay? So let's go to the hospital—off base, okay?"

She nodded, probably too tired to resist, and Trent took advantage of that.

TWO HOURS later she was bandaged and had her arm in a sling. It was only sprained, the doctor had said. "Only" being so far off the mark that Trent nearly laughed.

As they drove back to base, he got lost, postponing the moment when he'd have to either take her home or figure out how to get her to stay with him. He pulled over to the side of the road to check the map app on his phone.

"Katie, I don't feel comfortable sending you home. Why do you want to go back? If you can explain it to me...." He hoped she'd realize how ridiculous her excuses would sound after she'd just been to the hospital.

"I don't know where I'd go. Or how I'd live without Paul. We've been together since high school."

"And Texas was part of the Confederacy during the Civil War, but that didn't mean it was a good idea."

"I don't get it."

"It just means that change can be good, and maybe you'd be better off alone than with this kind of thing happening all the time."

"It doesn't happen all the time."

He wanted to believe her. But then it meant that his friendship with her might contribute to Paul's behavior. *Please, don't let this be because of me.* "What do you mean? Was it because of something yesterday at the party?"

She nodded. "After everyone left, he asked me what I was talking to you about. You know, the money stuff. About the cruise and the nice appliances."

"Why did that get him upset?"

"I'm not sure."

Trent thought he knew the answer. "What did he say?"

"That our money stuff wasn't anyone else's business and not to keep talking about our private stuff." Tears dripped down her cheeks. "He probably thinks I told you about him... you know, this kind of thing."

"Of course I know." Just one more reason to hate Paul Cray. "I don't know what you see in him, but I'll stop trying to change your mind."

"Okay. Thanks."

"I just want you to promise me one thing. If this happens one more time, will you let me take you to a shelter for a night or two? The base probably has a good support group, and I know you don't want that. But at least let someone besides me talk to you."

"Okay. I promise."

He put his hand across the space between the seats and gently squeezed her hand.

They drove back to the base in silence, and he dropped her off around the corner from her house. As she was about to get out of the car, he held her hand and looked her directly in the eye.

"Remember what you promised?"

"I remember." She walked away.

Trent sat in the car for a few minutes in case she changed her mind and came back. Her promise didn't mean much. She probably wouldn't tell him the next time Paul hurt her.

REED WAS at his desk when Trent called to describe how he'd spent the day with Katie at the hospital. He took his cell outside so no one would overhear the conversation, especially Paul Cray.

"Troy, calm down please." It was hard to keep calling him Troy when he was so upset. Reed hated having to keep up pretenses when something was wrong.

"I can't. You didn't see her. And you didn't have to watch her walk right back to that house. What if he kills her?"

Reed's stomach knotted. There was no good solution here. "What about the military spouses—"

"She won't talk to anyone in the Army. She's afraid it will hurt his career."

"He should be locked up, not pursuing a career. This is exactly what the Army doesn't want."

"So, what do we do?"

Trent always thought in terms of "we." It still had the power to give Reed pause. Trent trusted him and relied on him. It was a lot of responsibility after being on his own for so long, but Reed found more comfort in this every day. Except for that one secret Trent still hadn't confessed about his mysterious lunch. That could wait.

"Let me look into it. The law is so tricky with domestic issues. In civilian cases, charges need to be filed by the spouse. You can't report it. And I know that doesn't help. I'm on your side. Katie's side. Either stay home, or go over to her house and wait with her. But when he comes home and finds you, it could make things worse."

"That's not very helpful." Trent's tone wasn't accusing. He sounded exhausted and hopeless. "Okay, I'll wait here. I don't want to risk anything else. Or I could wait around the corner.... What do you think?"

"Sure. Stay out of sight, but close enough so you'll see when he comes home. Just please don't go in there on your own. I'll get there as soon as I can."

"Okay." Trent sounded relieved to have some course of action.

As Reed hung up, he took a deep breath. This was not going to end well. Someone was going to get hurt, physically or emotionally. Probably both. Chances were it would be Trent and Katie who suffered.

At quitting time, as Reed prepared to leave, he noticed Paul Cray was still at his desk. If Reed could get to Cray's house before he did, then he and Trent could make sure nothing happened to Katie, at least that night.

His e-mail dinged with a new message.

From T. Watkins. An encrypted message from Tom White. Just what he needed right now. Unfortunately he did need the information, but he didn't need the delay. He opened it and bit his lip when he spotted a photo—probably from a gay-porn web site—of a guy in tiny blue trunks bending over.

An arrow pointed to the guy's ass with the words "Wish you were here."

Reed couldn't help laughing. Last time it had been a photo of adorable puppies. Clearly Tom was getting bored. But it was a safe way to send messages, encrypted into the image.

"Should you be looking at that on the Army's time, Atwater?" Paul Cray hovered behind Reed.

He closed the e-mail. "No one says anything about the porn you look at." The words were out before he could stop them. Bright move.

"Well, my porn is normal, faggot."

"Paul, did you finish that report?" Gregson stood in the doorway, and he didn't look happy.

Paul chuckled like he'd been joking and clapped a hand on Reed's shoulder. "Just e-mailing it to you now."

"Good."

It was just the break Reed needed. He grabbed his jacket and cover and headed out the door. He raced toward the Crays' house and found Trent parked around the corner. Reed pulled up behind and waved to Trent before getting out of the car and into Trent's passenger side.

"I left a few minutes before Paul. He's in a bad mood today. Let's talk about how to handle this."

They came up with a plan in the event of a problem. After Paul arrived home, Trent moved the car closer, where they could see in the front windows. Once they knew he wasn't coming out right away, they walked toward the house to listen for sounds of raised voices or violence.

"It looks okay," Trent said.

"From the street, it usually does." Reed waited as long as Trent wanted, then they went home.

AT HOME Reed showed Trent Tom's porny e-mail, and they had a laugh. After running the decryption software, Reed read the financial report while Trent ordered pizza. Neither was very hungry.

Trent ran water in the sink and sat at the kitchen table.

"Looks like Lynda Gregson's uncle did leave her some money a few years ago. Sixteen thousand dollars. Not a fortune, but it would cover quite a lot of the purchases we spotted. Gregson owes a chunk on credit cards. If he's involved, he's covering his ill-gotten gains very well."

"How much does he pay on the credit cards?" Trent asked.

"Why?"

"He could be faking the credit card debt to disguise the spending. If he only pays close to the minimum, he's probably not. Even a crook wouldn't like paying all that interest to the credit card companies if he doesn't have to."

Reed grinned. Trent was picking up some good investigative skills. It made Reed proud to see how much his self-confidence had grown from when they'd met. "Pretty close to the minimum payment. We should dig deeper, but I'm tempted to rule him out." Reed paused. Now *he* was saying "we."

"Next?"

Reed summarized the reports on two other men, including Bradshaw. Both had suspicious spending patterns, wildly fluctuating bank balances over the past four years, but minimal debt. Cars were paid off, and they didn't generally run credit card balances.

"Whoever is paying them isn't doing it directly into their main bank accounts. I see several transfers from other accounts in their name, so I'll need to send another request to Tom."

Trent chomped two inches from Reed's ear. "What about Cray?" he asked, mouth full of pizza.

"He's not in this report. Maybe we'll get that data tomorrow."

Trent stood up. "Tomorrow, tomorrow," he sang and broke into a full version of the song from *Annie* as he danced around the kitchen.

"What did you get on that pizza?"

29

REED HAD parked near the supply unit office the following morning and was just getting out of his car when someone jumped him from behind and got him in a chokehold. His Special Forces training kicked in, and he dislodged his attacker using elbows and feet and had the guy on the ground in about three seconds as something metal crashed onto the asphalt.

"Cray? What the fuck was that for?"

Cray scrambled to his feet, picking up a golf club and brandishing it in Reed's direction. "Don't play dumb with me."

Reed grabbed for the club, but Cray swung out of his way. Instead of hitting Reed, he smashed the club—a heavy wood that would have crushed a skull like a pumpkin—through Reed's windshield. Grinning, Cray must have thought he'd won, because he let his guard down, allowing Reed to snatch the club out of his hands.

"That's very mature, Cray. Just tell me what your problem is."

"You. You and your nosy fucking faggot husband. You two keep out of my business and stop filling Katie's head with faggot nonsense. I'm warning you. Next time it won't be a fist or a golf club."

Just then Gregson drove up and parked in his assigned spot. Cray was rearranging his tie when Gregson walked over.

"What's going on, gentlemen?"

"Just some swing practice. I haven't got the hang of it yet," Reed said.

Gregson's gaze went from Reed to Cray and back again. The smashed windshield was out of his range of vision. "This isn't the place for golf practice."

"No, Sergeant," Cray said with a shit-eating grin Reed would gladly punch off his face.

The good news was one way or another, Paul Cray was probably going to jail. Reed hoped he had the proof he needed before Katie or anyone else got hurt.

As Gregson walked into the building, Cray grabbed Reed's shoulder. "Stop asking so damn many questions. You'll be sorry about that too. One thing I like to buy is weapons. Not just firearms. You don't want to find out what all's in my collection."

"I agree with you there." Reed broke the golf club over his knee and slammed the pieces down against the asphalt. Then he stepped away and waited for Cray to walk back into the building, rather than turn his back to Cray. Even with Reed's experience, Cray might get the drop on him next time or find another weapon to use on Reed.

Rex Atwater was supposed to be a slightly-below-average solider. Using Special Forces techniques to teach Paul Cray a lesson could blow Reed's cover. Thankfully he was close enough to the end of this investigation that it might almost be worth it.

WHEN CRAY left for lunch, Gregson called Reed into his office.

"What's going on with the two of you?"

"Nothing, Sergeant."

Gregson frowned. He looked a lot like Tom White right then, and Reed had to suppress a smile.

"I want to hear about it if there is something, Atwater. You aren't doing yourself any favors by letting him get away with anything."

Reed simply nodded. Time enough to deal with Cray later, if he wasn't part of the smuggling ring. If he was, then everything else would take care of itself.

REED ARRIVED home later than usual. He had waited for Cray to leave, then added another forty-five minutes, just in case Cray intended another parking-lot ambush. The coast was clear when Reed left the building, though he remained hyperalert to his surroundings.

Trent was in the kitchen when Reed got home, and the house smelled amazing.

"Lasagna for dinner."

"Mmm." Reed paused and sniffed the air. "Please tell me it's not vegetarian? I need some meat."

"In that case, we could postpone dinner." Trent turned off the oven. Then he grabbed Reed's belt and pulled him in for a kiss.

Reed kissed back, not caring what was for dinner. He maneuvered Trent against one wall, and before he knew it, his shirt was off, his pants were around his knees, and Trent had most of Reed's cock down his throat. He watched Trent working away, licking and sucking. When Trent trailed his fingertips down the back of Reed's knees, Reed leaned back and laughed.

"You're tickling me. Not fair since I can't get away."

Trent pulled off just far enough to speak. "You can, you just don't want to." He punctuated the sentence with an intense suck while looking up with big, innocent hazel-green eyes.

"I was the one who wanted some meat…." He fluffed Trent's hair.

"When you're done, I'd be happy to put you across the table and give you some." He flashed another wicked grin up at Reed.

"That might be nice."

"Might?" Trent raised an eyebrow. He reached for the nearby bottle of olive oil and drizzled some on one hand. Then he pushed a long, slick finger inside of Reed. "Might?"

Reed shuddered at the pleasurable sensations coursing through his body, and every muscle and nerve ending zinged. "Oh, definitely."

Trent licked away as he homed in on the magical little spot inside of Reed.

Reed's knees went weak, and he leaned against the wall, balls aching and nipples tingling. Then orgasm slammed into him so suddenly he lost complete control and shot pearly strands all over Trent's chin and chest.

But Trent just kept massaging him through the waves of pleasure until Reed was pumped dry. As soon as Trent pulled his hand away, Reed slid down the wall into a helpless puddle of happiness.

Reed had to close his eyes and catch his breath. "Wow, that certainly made up for the beast of a day I had." He kissed Trent so he wouldn't have to explain anything. Not yet. Now, all Reed wanted was to feel Trent's tongue against his, Trent's skin against his, and Trent's cock in him.

The wall phone rang.

Reed ignored it and pulled Trent closer, but Trent moved away. "I'm sorry, but it might be Katie…."

It might, Reed thought. After Cray's foiled attack, he might be home taking it out on Katie in a far different manner than Reed and Trent.

Trent flashed him an apology and sprang up to get the phone. "Hello? … Hello? … Who is this? … Katie?" Then he put the phone down and turned to Reed, who was still on the floor. "No one was there. Or no one said anything. I think I heard breathing. And since you're *here*, it wasn't phone sex."

Reed closed his eyes and exhaled. All thoughts of a nice predinner fuck disappeared.

"Tre-Troy, we should talk about—" Reed hoisted himself up and took Trent's hand. "Come into the living room."

"Why?"

"That call kind of ruined the mood. I'll make it up to you later."

They sat on the couch, Trent's jeans still unzipped and white streaks drying on his chest.

"The phone call. I think it might be Paul Cray." He held up a hand to deflect Trent's questions. "He threatened me this morning, and said a lot of nasty stuff. We need to be careful dealing with him."

"I'm not afraid of Paul Cray."

"You should be wary of him. He seems to be having a meltdown. Whether it's because of the investigation sniffing around him or what, I don't know. But he's getting unpredictable." Reed steeled himself, then dove right in. "Trent, I'd feel better if you went home to LA while I finish this up." He didn't care if someone was listening anymore. Fuck 'em. He was close to collecting the evidence he needed. But nothing was worth risking Trent's safety.

"I'm not running home with my tail between my legs because of some bully."

"Then be careful where you go. And please let me know if you leave the house. I can't deal with you running around with God-knows-who and not telling me the truth about it." Reed stopped. He hadn't intended to phrase it that way, but the thought of something happening to Trent got the better of him.

"I'm supposed to report all my activities to you? Maybe you should put a GPS tracker on me? And you're criticizing the way Cray treats Katie?" Trent glared.

"It's not the same thing. I'm concerned for your safety. Otherwise I— Crap, I didn't mean to sound like that." He took Trent's hand. "I'm sorry." He kissed Trent's hand.

"I'm sorry too. I've got reasons for what you think I'm lying about."

A car went past and Trent glanced toward the street. It was dark, and Reed couldn't see anything suspicious through the front window.

"Forget it for now. But Cray's likely going to get more violent."

"What's he going to do to me?"

As much as he hated to, Reed had to tell Trent about that morning. "I'm not talking about you—"

"Katie...." Barely suppressed anger seethed from Trent's body. "She could—"

Noise on the front step interrupted him. Trent zipped his pants and turned toward the door.

"Trent, don't. Just come back here and we can—"

"Maybe that call *was* Katie. You've got me really worried for her." He went to the door and reached for the knob.

Reed nodded. He was worried for Katie too.

Trent opened the door

"It's just Domino. Hey, little boy, I haven't seen you since yesterday morning. Let's turn the light on so.... Domino?" Trent's tone got Reed's heart racing. "Domino?" It was almost a shriek.

Reed ran onto the front step and found Trent staring at a black-and-white lump covered with red. In the bright porch light, the colors were nightmarish and stark. He grabbed for Trent and tried to get him back in the house. The sight was too much even for Reed. But Trent wouldn't move, his eyes fixed on the horrible image. He stood like a giant statue until Reed gently took his hand. "I can't leave him like that."

"Come inside and I'll take care of him, okay?"

Trent nodded. He broke down once they were inside. Reed steered him to the couch and held on while Trent sobbed for a few minutes. Then he pulled himself together and pushed Reed away.

"I'm fine. I'll be okay." He wiped at his eyes with a shirttail.

"Stay here. I'll bring him in, okay?"

Trent nodded, lips pressed together as if it took everything he had not to cry.

Reed found a small cardboard box in the closet, then went outside and put the small, broken body in it and secured the flaps. Even he wanted to cry after seeing how the poor loving little kitten had been hurt. Whoever did this should pay. *Would* pay. Once Reed knew Trent was okay, it was time to call the MPs.

Trent was on the couch with tissues and red-rimmed eyes. Reed sat close to him and kissed his cheek, then buttoned up his shirt and brushed hair out of his eyes.

"I'm going to call the MPs now. They'll want a statement. Are you okay to deal with that?"

Trent nodded, then shook his head. "Give me a few more minutes."

Reed put an arm around Trent and held him. Trent was a big guy, muscular, and he'd gotten a lot tougher since he'd met Reed. But inside he was soft and sweet and all heart. He was a set of contradictions, complicated, and that was why Reed loved him so much. And why right now Reed was hurting too.

"Are we going to tell them who we are?" Trent asked.

Good question. "Not if we can help it. I don't think they'll check into your background, and I'm pretty solid as far as Army history goes."

"Why did he do that? Domino was just a poor, defenseless animal." Trent's mouth trembled when he said "Domino" and Reed's heart ripped in two.

"I didn't get a chance to tell you about this morning. I should because the MPs will want to know why I didn't report it or mention it to you."

"What happened?" Trent's anxiety escalated visibly and his voice wavered.

"Cray tried to attack me in the parking lot this morning."

"What?" Trent's eyes went wide. "Tried?"

Reed swallowed and rubbed his palms on his thighs, wishing he could delay this discussion. "He jumped me, but I got away from him easily." He'd explain about the windshield later.

"What did he say?"

"He told me to mind my own business, and then he called us... names."

"Reed, maybe that wasn't about us. It could be he's feeling heat about the investigation. You're getting close, and he's using homophobia so you won't realize he's in on it. Throw you off the scent."

Reed stared at Trent for a few moments. "I don't know. It feels really personal now."

"Did Cray make homophobic comments before today?"

"No. He even looked a little surprised when that guy said something during the game."

"So?"

"Are you saying you don't want me calling the MPs?"

"I don't know what I'm saying. I think he belongs in jail even if he's not in on the smuggling. But do what you think is right."

Reed stood and walked into the kitchen. It was still warm from the lasagna. Good thing they'd turned off the oven. He glanced at the wall, where half an hour earlier they'd been having a great time. As he reached for the phone, someone knocked on the door.

"Don't answer the door!" he shouted to Trent. "Let me go."

When Reed peeked through the eyehole, he saw Katie Cray. He yanked open the door.

"You're okay." She let out a soft sigh. "How is Troy?" She spun around. Her hair was damp against her temples, and her face shone with perspiration. She clutched a purse to her chest and was wearing sweats and pink terrycloth slippers.

"Katie?" Trent came into the hallway, and Katie threw herself into his arms.

"You're both okay." Her voice was low and faraway. "I don't know what...."

"Come sit down." Reed herded them into the living room. She sat next to Trent on the couch, and Reed stood in front of them. "Katie, what happened?"

"I thought he hurt you, Troy! I thought he... killed you." She gulped in air and sounded on the verge of hyperventilating. "He was in such a bad mood when he came in from work. Then he went out without saying anything. He came back a little while ago, and I heard him in the garage, but he didn't come inside. When I went to look, I saw the hedge clippers had something dark on them. I thought it was blood and that he'd come here and stabbed you. So I ran out the back door like this." She looked down at her slippers, which seemed even more incongruous after what Reed had seen. "But you're okay. Thank, God."

"He... hurt Domino," Reed said.

"Where is Domino? He'll be okay, though, won't he?"

Trent shook his head. Katie hugged him and started crying.

"Oh, God, I'm so sorry. Sweet little thing. I was showing Paul photos of him a few days ago and—" She stopped and pressed a hand to her mouth. "Oh, this is my fault!"

"No, it's not," Trent said. "Shhh." He tried to comfort her, even through his own pain.

To Reed's surprise, Katie pulled herself together in a short time. She pushed hair out of her eyes and looked at Trent.

"I'm ready to listen to you and leave him, Troy. Tell me what to do now."

Trent looked up at Reed. "What about the MPs?"

Reed made a split-second decision. "I'll deal with them. You take Katie somewhere safe. There should be a number in the base directory for the domestic abuse hotline. They'll put you somewhere safe, and we won't be able to talk to you for a while. But we'll figure out how the MPs can get a statement from you later on about Domino."

Katie shook her head. "No. Let me make a statement about that first. Then Troy can call the hotline."

"You don't want him coming over here in the meantime, Katie." Reed tried to juggle protecting two people and keeping his cover.

Trent sat up and looked at Reed. "I know who can help with this. She'll take you somewhere safe where you can make a statement, and then help with the other arrangements."

"Not Lynda or Molly. None of the other wives from the unit."

Trent smiled. "No. Someone better."

Trent had Reed's attention now. "Who?"

Trent glanced up and stopped just as he was about to speak. He had that deer-in-the-headlights look. "Mrs. Atkinson."

"The colonel's wife? I can't just call her. I've only met her a couple of times, at tea parties and a couple of barbecues."

Trent looked at Reed again, then back at Katie. "I'm friends with her."

"What?" Reed tried not to bellow. God, he hoped he didn't sound like Paul Cray. "Since when?"

"I'll tell you later. It's not the most important thing to deal with tonight."

"Agreed. But we *will* discuss it."

FOR EVERYONE'S safety, Reed drove Katie and Trent to the colonel's house after Trent called to make sure Maya could help. She was horrified with the developments but welcomed Katie into their home.

"Trent, stay here until I come get you when I'm done with the MPs."

"Why is he calling you Trent?" Katie asked.

"Long story," Trent replied.

Reed left them in the living room as his mother walked him to the door.

"Be careful, Reed."

Reed glanced down the hall toward his father's office, then back to his mother's pale, drawn face. She reached for his hand as he opened the door. "He's not here. Away for some meeting in Austin, then off to DC. Maybe you could come for dinner while he's away?"

This was the last thing he needed right now. With Trent, Katie, Cray, and the investigation, his brain didn't have room for family drama.

When he didn't reply, she squeezed his hand. "I understand, dear. But I hope we'll have a chance to talk a little when this is all cleared up." She kissed his cheek.

She wore the same scent she had since he was a boy. Roses and some other flower, sophisticated and not cloyingly sweet. It transported him back to happier days with a suddenness that left him dizzy. He leaned in close for a hug. Her arms around him felt so much frailer than his memories. She'd gotten old when he hadn't been looking, and now it came to him how much he'd missed her elegant strength.

"Yes, Mom. I will. I promise." He inhaled again, wondering how with that simple embrace she'd eased his anxiety.

She let go and stood in the doorway as he walked to the car, and waited for him to drive away safely, just as she had so many times in the past.

30

REED MADE a report to the MPs, a team of a male and female officer, about Domino, the incident that morning outside their office, and his suspicions of Cray harming his wife. Once he was satisfied they took the domestic abuse issue seriously, he told them that Katie was staying with the Atkinsons.

A little after 0200, they called to say Cray was in the stockade. He wouldn't be released to the company commander due to the nature of the allegations. Reed felt only mild relief. Too much had already happened, but at least there wouldn't be any more violence. He'd call White in the morning to discuss how to proceed.

He texted Trent to see if he wanted to come home, but Trent wouldn't leave Katie alone in the middle of the night. Reed showered, then realized he was ravenous. They'd never gotten around to dinner. The pan of lasagna was in the oven, still slightly warm. He cut a corner piece, the cheese still perfectly crispy, and ate.

In bed alone he missed Trent more than he expected. This was the first time Trent had come with him on most of an investigation, so it had been a while since they'd spent more than one night apart. Trent was busy taking care of someone else while Reed lay alone wondering what he was doing.

The change in perspective was eye-opening. Is this what Trent went through while Reed was away, immersed in a case, for weeks at a time? Reed couldn't bear the thought of spending more than one night on his own here.

Before 0700, the phone rang.

"Trent?" Reed realized too late he'd slipped up on the name.

"Atwater, it's Gregson. I've been briefed about what happened last night. I hope you and Troy are okay."

"Yes, Sergeant. We'll be okay. Katie will too."

"I'm sorry to hear what happened. I wish you'd come to me yesterday and told me about Cray's attack on you, and on Katie."

Me too. Would that have prevented Domino's death? He'd thought he was protecting Katie, but someone else got hurt instead, including Trent.

"I was concerned speaking with you might set him off, but he was much more dangerous than I thought."

"That's why we have regs for these things."

"Yes, Sergeant."

"I'm shocked and upset about it, and so is Lynda. She's been crying since last night. Look, I don't want to rehash the events. Take today off, then tomorrow I'd like to discuss how to move forward."

"Thanks. I'll see you tomorrow."

Reed hung up and collected Trent from his parents' house. Reed waited in the circular driveway so he wouldn't have to deal with an invitation to breakfast. He wasn't ready for that yet.

"Morning." Trent kissed him as he pulled the door shut. He tasted minty. Leave it to Reed's mom to have extra toothbrushes for even unexpected guests.

"Let's go home. There's a lot to talk about."

Trent nodded. "Your mom wants Katie to stay there for a few days instead of going to a shelter. It will depend on whether Paul gets bailed out."

"He won't."

Back in their condo, Reed made breakfast, just toast and scrambled eggs. They sipped coffee but neither was hungry.

"Reed, where's… the box?"

"At the MP Station. I'll collect him later and we can bury him or—"

"Let's worry about that later."

Reed nodded. He didn't trust his own voice.

Trent drew circles with his fork on the plate. "I owe you some explanations, Reed." He looked up. "About your mom."

"That can wait too. I'm not ready to discuss it yet. I want to put Paul Cray behind us first. White's going to call me when he gets into the office, but I'll be questioning Cray today or tomorrow. There's just some jurisdictional BS to deal with."

"Okay."

TRENT SPENT the day watching old movies. It had been a long time since he'd done that, but it was all he could manage. Reed had been sweet enough to put Domino's food and water bowls away out of sight before he left for the MP Station and his session questioning Paul Cray.

None of the movies kept Trent's attention, so he walked around the neighborhood. When he went past the spot where Domino used to run out to him, Trent had to turn for home. He spent the rest of the day baking cookies and cupcakes he didn't want to eat, then drove the treats down to the hospital, where they would be distributed to patients.

He visited Katie for a while. Maya was out of the house at some luncheon, talking to high-school girls about studying science. Trent didn't want to be alone at home, so he stayed until Reed called to say he was on the way home.

"Reed?" Trent walked into the hallway. He'd taken his time so Reed would get home first.

"Kitchen."

Reed was chopping vegetables for a salad. The table had been set, and there was a bottle of nice wine on the table. Bordeaux, already opened.

"Wow, you've been busy. What prompted this?" Trent asked as he brushed up close to give Reed a kiss.

"Yeah. I needed to keep busy. How are you doing?"

"I baked a hundred cupcakes today and took them to the children's ward at the hospital."

"Did you save some for me?"

"No."

"Then I won't share my wine or dinner." Reed flashed a smile, but it did nothing to lighten Trent's mood.

"I can bake more tomorrow."

They couldn't keep up the pretense of everything being fine during dinner, so they ate mostly in silence.

"Did you interrogate Cray?"

"I questioned him."

"What's the difference?"

"National security. I wouldn't have minded interrogating him." Reed sipped wine. "The session went better than expected. I had an agent from the local field office in the room with him while I fed him questions from the observation room. I knew Cray wouldn't talk to me. When he didn't give up anything of use to the agent, I decided I had nothing to lose by speaking to him directly."

"And did you have ways of making him talk?"

"Yes. I call it bending the truth."

Reed broke into a grin and Trent's mood lifted enough to join him. "Tell me."

"I told Cray who I really was and what I wanted to know about the smuggling ring. He played dumb until I told him he was in a lot of trouble already for the assault on me, the damage to government property, domestic abuse, and other charges. I *might* have given him the impression we could discuss pleading those down if he told me what I wanted about the smuggling."

"You wouldn't reduce those charges." Trent put his hand down on the table with more than enough force to get his point across.

"I didn't say the charges *would* be reduced, just that we could discuss it."

Trent grinned again and finished his glass of wine. "And what did he tell you?"

"He's definitely involved, but he doesn't know who else is part of the ring. He won't roll on the ringleader, which makes me suspect it's an officer. White's getting subpoenas for military records. A lot of what we need is still classified for national security."

"I know someone who could help."

Reed's smile ebbed away. "Is this about my mother?"

"No. Your dad. I'm sure he could cut through the red-white-and-blue tape for you. Or he could access the information and—"

"Trent, I've been doing my job just fine without asking my daddy for help."

"But in this case, he's got special qualifications that make him the only person who can help."

"Thank you, Dr. Phil. Now send my boyfriend back from the body snatchers."

"I'm back to being your boyfriend? Aren't we Rex and Troy, the happily married gay couple who throw the best parties?"

"We haven't thrown any parties. And I don't want to go to another one and talk about the same boring shit with the same boring people."

"I take it our Army days are numbered?"

"Dwindling, though I don't know when we'll be done here for certain." Reed speared the last cucumber slice in his salad bowl and ate it. "But till then we're still Troy and Rex, and we're still blissful newlyweds."

"Good. I'd hate to think our marriage didn't last three weeks."

"You're a good husband, Trent."

"Troy."

"No, Trent. I like being married to you."

Trent felt all warm inside. Reed was getting oddly sentimental. Probably just the events of the past day, and it wouldn't be a good idea to read too much into it.

"It's been fun, for the most part."

Reed brought Trent's hand to his lips and kissed it. Trent felt even warmer.

"Speaking of marriage, Rex, I think you owe me some conjugal duties."

"I thought you'd never ask." Reed stood and pulled Trent up.

31

"I DON'T want to be having this discussion right now." Reed put the mug to his lips and drank, scalding his mouth and tongue, then spilling coffee on his shirt and crotch. "Sonofafuckingbitch." He stood and glared at the coffee stains as the pain subsided.

"Let me help." Trent grabbed a handful of napkins and rubbed at Reed's crotch. He looked up and gave a winsome smile. "Better yet?"

Reed glared at Trent.

Trent countered with the I'm-sure-a-blowjob-would-make-things-all-better grin.

Reed couldn't stay mad at Trent when he used that one, but he tried. "No. It's not. And a blowjob isn't going to fix what's really wrong."

"Take your pants off."

"This isn't the time." But it could be. No, it couldn't. Shouldn't. *Focus*!

"Not for *that*, so I can treat the coffee stains." He watched as Reed slipped the pants off. "We can get back to *that*, when I'm done here. Oh, shirt too."

Reed sat back down in his Army-issue boxers. For some reason Trent liked them and wanted Reed to wear them. There was still a warm, damp spot where the coffee had spilled, and a red blotch on his thigh. Probably more coffee on Reed's clothes than in his cup. He refilled the cup as Trent put some stain treatment on.

It was a miracle that even though Reed was angry, Trent still offered a BJ and then cleaned up the coffee stains. Damn, he was lucky. Really fucking lucky that Trent hadn't given up on him. Though, given how'd they met in Bangkok with Reed needing to steal Trent's backpack, spilled coffee was nothing.

But it hadn't been the coffee that troubled Reed.

Trent came back from the bathroom and leaned down to kiss the back of Reed's neck before taking his seat at the table.

"Thanks, Trent. I'm sorry for getting upset."

"I knew you'd be upset, which is why I didn't say anything about seeing your mother at first."

"So, why did you go behind my back?"

"Because I wanted to find out why things are so messed up in your family."

"If I wanted you to know, I would have told you." Reed blew on his coffee this time and took a tentative sip. "I didn't think it mattered to you. You never asked."

"Didn't I?" Trent buttered his toast and took a bite. "Cold." He frowned and got up to put more bread in the toaster. "It does matter. And the reason I never asked outright is because whenever the subject of your family came up, you'd practically rip my head off."

"That bad?" In retrospect, Reed acknowledged he had reacted badly when the topic of family arose—even Trent's family. And just how did Trent manage to get Reed listening to him now? So much for Reed avoiding it.

Trent nodded. "And after the day of the picnic, I had to know. I wanted to know, because I could tell there was something under the surface that no one talked about and—"

"And if you found out and made everyone sit around holding hands and singing 'Kum Ba Yah,' we'd all be one happy family?"

The toast popped, and Trent took his time retrieving it and buttering before responding. "So I called your mother, and we went to lunch one day."

Reed watched as he finished the first piece of toast and sipped coffee. "And?"

"So you do want to know?"

"Jesus, Trent, if this was one of your novels we'd be on page one thousand before you even get to the damn story." Reed smiled because he was used to this by now. Good thing he didn't have to meet with Gregson for another ninety minutes.

"Okay. Your mom told me why your dad wouldn't talk to you. End of story."

"There's a middle ground between a long story and the massively abridged version, you know?" Reed took the last piece of toast. "But it's not rocket science. I told you, he couldn't accept my being gay. That's the beginning of the story and the end of the story. There *is* no story."

"So now you want to hear what she told me?" Trent looked Reed in the eye for a long, searching moment. Without waiting for a response, he continued, "That's not true. Your dad has no problem with your being gay. He just wanted to protect you from his obligation to report gay soldiers. He loves you, but he didn't want to have to choose between you and the Army, so he—"

"So he picked the Army?" Reed shook his head. He'd put this topic and the associated pain away on a shelf where it couldn't hurt anymore. It had been bad enough seeing his parents a few weeks earlier and telling Trent. But Reed could not open that door again. For almost twenty years, it had been better to keep his parents on the other side of it.

"I'm not explaining it very well. But your mother changed my mind, and trust me, I wasn't buying it either at first. My interpretation is that he thought this was the best way for you to get what he thought *you* wanted, a career in the Army. One man wasn't going to change the rules, but he thought both of you could do some good staying in the Army and working on change from inside."

"I left before any changes happened."

"But that was your choice."

Reed reached for the coffee and found it had gone cold. His stomach was sour after this discussion. "So, are you and the colonel buddies now too?"

"No. I haven't seen your dad except for that Sunday. I wouldn't because that would be a betrayal."

"And hanging out with my mother isn't?"

"Reed, I know you still talk with her sometimes, so I didn't consider meeting her off-limits."

As much as Reed didn't want to admit it, Trent was on his side and had only wanted to help. No one was worse off now, unless he refused to forgive Trent. "I'm not happy that you went behind my back. I wish you had told me. I might not have applauded the idea, but I would not have stopped you. It's the secrecy that hurts more than what you did."

Trent got up and stood behind Reed, wrapped his arms across Reed's shoulders, and kissed his ear. "I should have told you. I felt awful keeping the secret. Physically and emotionally."

"Is that why you were sick last week?"

"Yeah." Another soft brush of lips against Reed's cheek. "It turned out well, though, since your mom's been able to help with Katie."

"It could just as easily not have turned out well, Trent."

"I know." Trent straightened up. "Will you forgive me?"

"Of course." Reed wouldn't dream of saying no, especially because Trent had been upset at his own deceit, and he sounded so contrite. "Forgive me too?"

"I will if you do something special for me."

Reed suspected from Trent's expression that the something might not be what he expected, but he nodded anyway. "Name it."

"Can we go to dinner at your parents' house? Your mom said he's out of town till the weekend. At least talk to her."

Reed paused. *One, two, three, four, five.* Only then did he reply. "Yes, but only because you want this so badly. Once. Then this topic is closed for discussion. Agreed?"

Trent wagged his head, then agreed.

"I have to see Gregson this morning, so I need to find another clean uniform."

"What time's your appointment?"

Reed checked his watch. "Ten thirty."

"Seeing as how you're already undressed, let's put those forty-five minutes to good use."

Reed was convinced something about this kitchen turned Trent on. "Is that an order?"

A deliciously wicked grin spread across Trent's face. "Yes. It most definitely is. Stand up."

Reed did. Trent pulled him in for a deep, electrifying kiss. His cock hardened against Reed's body, lined up along Reed's erection.

"You know a man in uniform gets me hot?" Trent's voice was husky.

"I'm not in uniform…."

"That gets me even hotter." Trent stepped back a pace. "That's an order too."

Reed slid his fingers into the elastic waistband of his boxers and slid them past his hips, and they fell the rest of the way on their own. His erection sprang forward.

"Very nice." Trent wrapped warm fingers around Reed, and he went from hard to let's get this show on the road. "You know how to use that weapon, soldier?"

"Yes, sir."

"Show me what you can do with it."

32

"RUN THAT past me again, Atwater." Gregson leaned back in his chair and stared at Reed as if he had just done a strip tease.

"It's Acton. I'm here following the trail of a number of items taken from the museum in Baghdad that have surfaced recently."

"Acton. With CID?"

The Army Criminal Investigative Division ran the majority of these cases. Reed shook his head. "FBI."

"You don't say. You had me fooled, but I knew there was something off about you. Just couldn't put my finger on it. You ex-Army?"

"Ranger."

Gregson slammed a palm on the arm of the chair. "That's it. That's what did it."

The reaction intrigued Reed. He never got made. "What?"

"You were too—I don't know, hardworking. Like you actually wanted to do a decent job. And the walk, you got the walk, not the slouchy look."

"I *was* trying to be a slouchy slacker," Reed said with a chuckle.

"Naw. These guys are counting their days or years to separation or retirement. Even the ones who do a decent job don't have their hearts in it. The supply unit isn't the place for winners. Winners who come through here get transferred or promoted out pretty quickly."

"I'll keep that in mind."

"So where's your investigation? I see Cray's a suspect, but I haven't been able to talk to him. Is he part of it?"

"He is. We're working on rounding up the rest." Reed interlaced his fingers in his lap. "For a little while there, you were on the list of suspects."

Gregson leaned forward and peered at Reed. "Those questions about my home theater? That part of it?"

"Among other things. If you didn't owe on your cars, I would have looked a lot more closely."

Gregson shrugged. "Anything I can do to help?"

Reed glanced toward the door. It was shut but not locked. "I could use some information about who was in the unit in Iraq and where they are now. Whoever's running the show keeps the men isolated, so no one knows who else is involved. Tell me about the commissioned officers."

"I was there, but just a sergeant. You asking about NCOs too?"

"Anyone smart enough to organize the men, then keep everything quiet for so long and pace the flow of items onto the market. We only hit on the Army connection because a couple of unlikely events were discovered, almost by chance. There are no coincidences."

"There was Major Collins, who ran the unit at Fallujah. He's a lieutenant colonel now and part of the staff at Fort Sam. He's one of those career officers who's been climbing the ladder, but slowly. Atkinson took him out of this unit a few years ago."

Reed took notes. "How does he get along with the men? Do they respect him? Much contact as far as you know?"

"He's about average. No better or worse." Gregson paused.

Reed translated that to mean Collins was a career officer moving up the ranks but not attracting notice from anyone, not excelling at any leadership skills that the Army loves. It didn't bode well for him to make it to the next level.

"Oh, Collins' wife is lovely. She used to have a cookout every month or so. I haven't seen her around lately, but then again, she's probably hosting the more senior officers now."

"Next?" He paused. "Tell me about the other staff here who were in Iraq." Something nagged at him deep in the recesses of his brain. Pieces of the puzzle were connecting, but a few were too hazy to see where they fit.

"Lieutenant Colonel Nicholls and Major Contreras."

Nicholls. A piece snicked into one of those empty spots. "What do you think of them?"

"Nicholls is Colonel Atkinson's right-hand man. He runs the place when the colonel's away, and he's extremely competent. He was in Iraq, but not with this unit. I think he served under Atkinson at another base. He wouldn't dream of stealing anything."

Reed nodded so as not to stem the flow of information.

"Contreras just transferred out to Walter Reed. He's got more medical training and experience, and a spot opened up with more upward mobility. He was with this command in Iraq and wasn't particularly popular, but he was respected."

"Noted. Now back to who's still here."

"Major Palma. He was at another base right out of Iraq, then came here after Collins moved up. The men seem to like him. He's younger than Collins, and that seems to make a difference. He's taken leave recently. I think his wife or daughter needed some special medical treatment."

Reed scribbled and hoped he would be able to read his writing later. "That's too bad." But it might be good for him. A financial setback coupled with an emotional drain on the family might have led him to get careless.

"The master sergeant, Martinez. He was staff sergeant for the battalion in Iraq. Lot of guys looked up to him back there, and more now. Got wounded early on and moved to a noncombat role. He pisses green, though, so I can't see him being involved. But of those three, I think he would command the type of respect that would lead a soldier to go to jail rather than rat on him."

"This is great stuff. It should help me focus the investigation. We haven't brought in any of the others yet, so I still need to keep my cover here."

"Who are the others?" Gregson dropped his voice to a whisper, but his eyes flashed with curiosity.

"I'm not at liberty to share that."

"Fuck you, Atwater." Gregson slapped the desk and chuckled. He really was an easy-going guy. Reed might actually miss him when this got wrapped up.

"Thank you, Sergeant." Reed stood and gave an overly formal salute, holding until Gregson returned it.

REED WENT back to his desk and pretended to care that a truckload of something didn't show up where it was expected and had fucked up some training exercise or another. He felt guilty for not trying to find it, but the staff sergeant who berated him for five minutes got what he deserved. It was scary how good it felt to wield the little bit of power Rex Atwater had. The power not to fix something that was wrong.

His cell phone chirped. Trent. "Atwater."

"Hi, Rex, sweetie." Trent made loud kissing noises and Reed covered the phone with his hand so no one would hear it.

"Are you having an emergency at home?"

"No."

"Too bad."

"Bored? I *could* have an emergency."

"Is there a reason you called?" One of his coworkers was staring, so Reed tried to sound annoyed.

"Some guy called and said Dr. Coals wants to see you. He sounded kind of sexy, though. I'm already a little jealous because I don't get calls from doctors at home."

Mysterious phone calls at the house were not good, especially as they were a few days from completing this investigation. "What's the number?"

Trent read it off, and Reed wrote it on a pad. "Thanks. I'll see you later."

"Okay. And we're going to dinner at your parents' tomorrow. I arranged it with your mom when I called to see how Katie is."

"That discussion will have to wait for later." Reed hung up and smiled politely at the glare he got from the guy two desks away. The single guy who never got personal phone calls. In Reed's temporarily petty mood, he reflected on the satisfying sex he and Trent had had that morning. Corporal Nosypants probably couldn't dream of sex that good.

What the hell is wrong with me?

He short-circuited that mental tangent by staring at the phone number for Dr. Coals. Then it hit him. Dr. "Coals" was Dr. *Nicholls*. Lt. Col. Nicholls, his father's über-competent right-hand man, calling to check up on the state of affairs.

He dialed the number Trent had given him.

"Nicholls."

"Colonel Nicholls, Rex Atwater. You called my house."

"I figured with everything going on lately, you would be at home."

"I've got plenty to do here. How can I help you?"

"Let's meet. Same office, fourteen hundred."

"Can't we just meet at *your* office? I hate hospitals. Plus, the parking sucks."

"The hospital at two." He hung up.

Reed stared at the phone for a moment. There was efficient, and then there was rude. But he should probably keep the colonel informed now they'd made one arrest and another was imminent.

He left the building at lunchtime and drove off base where he could talk to White. He relayed the information Gregson had given him and asked for background checks and phone records, financials, Facebook. The whole nine yards.

"And check property deeds, including family members, especially spouses and kids," Reed added. "For all the suspects. I'll need some hard evidence to get them to turn on the officer."

"Already done for the men in your unit. Check your e-mail when you get home." White guffawed.

"Wish you were here too," Reed replied sardonically, shaking his head. "I could have used a not-safe-for-work warning on that last one."

"You opened it at work?" White's laughter reached new heights. Reed heard a crash and wondered whether Tom had fallen off his chair. Served him right. Reed hung up.

AT FIVE minutes past two, Reed informed the nurse at "Dr." Nicholls' office that he had arrived. He was ushered in immediately. Nicholls sat behind the desk, again wearing the doctor's lab coat.

Reed remembered to salute before sitting down.

"Sergeant, please update me."

Reed moved to sit down and noticed Nicholls compress his lips.

"Have a seat."

With a nod, Reed settled into the chair. "We've made one arrest and have identified several others involved. Warrants are being drawn up and will be carried out within the next twenty-four hours."

"Who else will you be bringing in?"

"I'm not authorized to release that information at this time. I believe the MPs and US Marshals will be working together to gather the suspects."

"I'd like to be able to brief Colonel Atkinson with some specific progress. I'm going to need a list."

"If you contact my Bureau supervisor, I'm sure he would be happy to relay whatever information you need."

"This isn't a request now. It's an order." Nicholls deepened his voice and looked Reed right in the eye.

"I'm sorry, sir, but with all due respect, I don't report to you where this investigation is concerned. You understand chain of command, and I'm simply following orders I was given." Anyone who knew Reed— including Tom White—would understand how much bullshit he'd just heaped on the desk, but Nicholls was starting to annoy him. Even if Reed knew the names of everyone in the ring, he wouldn't tell this guy.

"I'll do that. At least tell me what you've got pointing to the ringleader. That's Colonel Atkinson's chief concern right now, that a senior officer might be involved. He'd like the courtesy of knowing in advance of any arrest who it is, so he can contain the fallout before anything goes public."

"The colonel can contact me directly if he wants any more specific information." Reed couldn't help breaking into a smile. He'd see whether Trent was right that Reed's father had changed. Would his father actually call to find out who was about to get arrested? "I've got to get back to work gathering nails for this guy's coffin. I'm sure you'll agree that's the most important thing right now."

"So you know who it is?"

"Yes." Reed stood and walked out of the office. Even though he'd left the Army years before, his training made it difficult to lie directly to a superior officer, even one who was more hindrance than help. At least once he got home, Reed expected to have the last few pieces of information that should help him nail the bastard.

33

BY LUNCHTIME on Friday, arrest warrants had been processed for all the soldiers with suspicious spending patterns. Tom White had flown into San Antonio, and Reed met him at his off-base hotel to pore over financial statements, posting history, and other specific evidence the forensic accountants had collected for them.

"We're still not being granted access to the military performance reports—"

"NCOERs for the enlisted men, OERs—"

"Typical Army alphabet soup, not that the Bureau is immune to that shit. Those are going to be our best resource before questioning any of these men," White said, putting a thick stack of printouts down on the table with a thwack.

"Men and *woman*. One woman."

White shook his head and rubbed his eyes. "Soldiers."

"Even the Army has gender-neutral terms." Reed grabbed his cup of coffee and discovered it was empty. "Room service, or you want to move to a coffee shop instead?"

"We've been over this information three times. I don't know what else we're going to find. I need those NCOERs before I start talking to those soldiers."

Reed agreed. The DoD was holding up the paperwork because they wanted to run the investigation, and shutting out the Bureau until the jurisdictional dispute was resolved. Vibrations from Reed's pocket interrupted his thoughts. He grabbed the phone and answered. "Atwater."

"Hi, Rex." Trent's smile came through loud and clear, and Reed couldn't help smiling back. He turned away from White.

"Troy."

"How's your project going? Because your mom is expe—"

"That's tonight? I can't go." Work was such a convenient excuse.

"You should take a break," Tom said, drowning out Trent's reply.

"What? Hang on, Troy." Reed turned to Tom. "It's just dinner. With the colonel's wife." He didn't need to say more. Tom knew the situation.

"That's not the worst way to spend a Friday evening."

"You didn't fly out here so I could hang out with my mother."

"No. But maybe your mother could help persuade the colonel to grant us access to those reports. Unless you want to ask him yourself."

"Thankfully he's out of town, or there would have been no discussion of dinner."

"Reed, this isn't about you and your father anymore. This is about the investigation. Can you just be prof—"

"I am being professional!" As soon as the words were out, the irony practically hit Reed over the head. He gave a self-deprecating chuckle. "Point taken."

"Rex? Reed? Hello… I'm still here." Trent's voice came over the speaker.

"Sorry, Trent." Reed glanced up at Tom, who was nodding. "Sure. I'm on my way home now."

As REED and Trent drove along the curved driveway, Reed slowed the car to a crawl. The mass forming in his stomach got larger and heavier, and the last thing he wanted to do was to eat. Trent reached across the gap between the seats and put a reassuring hand on Reed's thigh.

"This is going to be fun," Reed said with as much enthusiasm as he could muster.

"In case you were thinking of trying out for a play, don't." Trent squeezed Reed's thigh and winked. "You're worse than the actors in Mick's pornos."

"Gee, thanks." He parked, then smoothed his slacks as they moved up the walkway toward the front door.

The door opened before Reed even knocked. His mother stood there wearing a pale green sweater and a tweedy knee-length skirt.

"Trick or treat?" he said.

"Come on in." She had a huge smile on her face as he stepped inside. Behind Reed, Trent entered and shut the door. "Let me look at you!" She pulled him into a tight hug, and when he inhaled her familiar perfume, the years dropped away. He slid his arms around her waist and returned the hug.

"Hey, Mom. It's really good to see you. Really."

"I'll go entertain myself...." Trent squeezed Reed's shoulder and disappeared down the hall.

Reed wanted to grab his collar and keep him from leaving, but Trent dashed out of reach as if sensing Reed's intention.

Now he was alone with his mother in the high-ceilinged hallway. They hugged for several minutes, and Reed wasn't the one to let go first.

"Let me get a proper look at you, honey. You look so good. I see life with Trent really agrees with you. I'm so glad to see you looking happy and healthy."

"You look great too."

She smoothed a hand along her hair. "Well, a lot grayer than last time."

"It was only a week ago. You've barely aged since then."

She gave him a playful smack on the arm. "Such a charmer. Come, let's have a seat in the library." She waved a hand in the opposite direction from the one Trent had taken. Odd that he knew his way around this house while Reed had only spent a few minutes here so far.

"I'd like that." He followed his mother, grateful now that Trent had given them some time on their own. Trent had such good instincts when it came to understanding people. At least people's emotions. Reed seemed only to understand how people reacted when money was involved, which made him a good agent.

"I don't even know where to start," his mother said as they settled onto the low couch. Around them, built-in bookcases went nearly to the ceiling. They were full.

"Are these your books, or just for show?"

"Ours. Your father hates to give books away."

Mention of his dad broke the mood for a moment, but Reed shrugged it off. "I guess it's just books he feels that way about." A chill settled over the room as soon as the words were out.

His mother's smile melted away. "That's not fair."

"I know. It's a difficult subject. I'm working up to discussing it."

"Good. I know I can't expect everything to change right away either. Let's take this one step at a time."

"Okay."

A door shut loudly somewhere down the hall.

"Maya! I made it back early."

Reed's mother turned her head toward the voice, then back to Reed. "Oh. I didn't expect...." She put a hand to her mouth and her eyes went wide.

"I believe you," Reed said. But that didn't solve the problem. He wasn't ready to talk to his father just yet. Not until he and his mother had a chance to discuss things.

"Maya?" Familiar footsteps came down the hall toward the library.

Reed's heartbeat accelerated. How many times had he heard them coming toward him as a kid? Then later, as a teenager, wondering whether his father would open the door and find him doing, or even thinking about, something he shouldn't? Too many. How could those footsteps still strike fear into him, more fear than gunfire or the sound of IEDs? Blair Atkinson, the US Army's secret weapon!

"Honey?" Colonel Atkinson stood in the doorway. "Oh. Reed. I wondered whose car that was."

"Colonel." Reed was surprised at the pain in his father's eyes at being addressed by the rank, but couldn't bring himself to say Dad.

"It's nice to see you, Son." His father shifted his weight from foot to foot. "I'll go change and…."

Reed swallowed so loudly he heard it echo around the room twice. "Uh, sir, Trent and I are here for dinner."

"Right. I'll eat something in the kitchen." The pain was back. Why did it hurt Reed, too, when he saw it?

"I'm sure there's plenty," Reed said.

His mother reached out and squeezed his hand, and a smile brightened her face. Little red splotches on her cheeks faded away.

"That will be nice," she said. "Really nice."

"Yes. I'd like that, Son. I want to change out of my uniform first." His father nodded, and Reed noticed his father's small smile as he nodded to Maya and left the room.

"I'm so proud of you, dear."

Reed shrugged. "I need to talk to him about the investigation anyway. I guess it's convenient he's back."

She shook her head. "Fine. Even if that's all you want to talk about, it's a start."

"Rome wasn't built in a day."

FIFTEEN MINUTES later, after some pleasant catching up, his mother stood. "Let me go check on dinner and on Trent. I feel awful for leaving him alone! I'm a terrible hostess." She stopped in the doorway. "I'll be back in a minute."

"Trent can take care of himself," Reed said, but she rushed out of the library anyway. He stood and wandered over to a wall covered with photographs and framed newspaper clippings. To his surprise, he discovered most of them were stories about him from military newspapers. He ran a hand over his hair as he spotted an old West Point photo, where he sported a cadet's buzz cut. He did not miss the Army hairstyles.

The photos and stories were in roughly chronological order and continued through missions where national security and safety prevented names and photographs from being included. Only his father could have known the stories were about missions in which Reed had participated.

"You've got an impressive record there, Reed."

He turned at the sound of his father's voice. So much for his Ranger and Special Forces training if his dad had sneaked up on him. He didn't respond.

"I'm very proud of what you've accomplished."

Reed stepped away from the wall and stared at his father. He bit back the bitter words that sprang to his lips.

Blair Atkinson continued anyway. "I am proud. It's my fault I never told you myself. I don't blame you for hating me. I earned that. I accept responsibility."

Reed glanced down at his feet. God, he felt like he was thirteen again. Hot anger boiled up in his throat.

His father let out a bitter laugh. "I see you're not going to disagree with me. That makes for a nice change." The second laugh held more regret than bitterness. "I know apologizing won't make up for the years we lost. I lost. The decisions I made. I won't make excuses. There are no excuses, just consequences."

This wasn't how Reed pictured their reunion. He'd expected to hurl blame and accusations at his father and watch the man brush them away like crisp autumn leaves. Who was this man standing across the room from him? Reed suspected it was simply an act, to assuage the old man's guilt. Well, Reed wasn't falling for any of it.

"I know you hate lectures. I hoped we'd have a conversation."

"I don't know how to respond. You barely resemble my father."

"Is that good or bad?" His father gave a soft smile.

Reed didn't laugh. "I'm not sure. I guess it's an improvement. I didn't like the bastard much."

"Me neither."

Neither seemed to know what to say or do next.

"At least we agree on one thing." Reed gave a wry smile.

"Let's call that a win. Maybe we should eat now, before things have a chance to go pear-shaped."

Reed was still wary. Did his father think a few clippings on a wall and some long-overdue praise would sweep away twenty years of pain and self-hatred? "I am hungry. Mom disappeared." At least keeping the discussion to food would be neutral territory.

"She's with Trent in the living room. I'm looking forward to meeting him. She's had nothing but praise for him. Sounds like you have good taste."

"I think it was luck more than anything. At least at first." Reed paused. "You don't want to hear about that."

"I do. I'd like to. It'll be more entertaining to hear how you met when I can get both sides of the story."

"I—uh." Reed stopped. "I did not expect you to want to hear anything about Trent, or about my relationship with him. Or that you'd be smiling about him."

"I'm not who you think I am, Son. I hope we'll have the chance for you to discover that yourself. Telling you isn't going to change your mind, or erase anything that happened in the past. But I'd like to be able to show you. If you'll let me." He put up a hand. "I know it's not going to happen tonight. One step at a time."

Reed hadn't expected this sudden rapprochement. "Look, this is all a little hard to swallow here. Until I have proof your new attitude is more than empty words, I'm really not comfortable talking about my personal life, including Trent. I don't believe you've suddenly had a PFLAG epiphany."

The smile faded from his father's face. "I deserve that. And I won't push you. I know your mother would like to spend some time with you, even if you don't choose to see me. Do you have any idea how much longer you'll be at Fort Sam?" His dad sat on the couch, and Reed took a seat at the other end. "Are you allowed to discuss the investigation at all?"

"I thought you—" Reed stopped and analyzed his father's face. "Didn't Nicholls tell you?"

"Tell me what?"

"The status update."

"Nicholls? No. I didn't know you'd been working with him. I guess that's the beauty of delegation. Need to know goes both ways. I guess I didn't need to know." He grinned.

That didn't make sense. Nicholls had said the *colonel* had requested information. Reed's gut ached again.

"I could use some help from you, actually...." Reed still couldn't quite say "Dad," though now "Colonel" felt too awkward. Maybe he'd just call him Blair. If he ever talked to him again.

"What do you need?"

"DoD has been giving the Bureau pushback on obtaining reports on the officers we believe might be involved. We can't get much beyond postings. But I'd like to take a look at disciplinary actions, NCOERs, that kind of thing. Can you help at all?"

"How many soldiers are we talking about? Commissioned, noncommissioned?"

"Some of both. I think five names all together."

The doorbell rang, and his mother's heels clip-clopped to the front door.

"I don't feel comfortable handing over everything." He steepled his hands and touched his fingertips under his chin. "How about if you give me a list and the kind of thing you're looking for. I'll skim through, and if I spot any red flags, we can—"

Commotion from the hallway caused them both to turn toward the door. Raised voices echoed, then subsided.

"—we can discuss the situation."

"That seems fair. I'm up against a time constraint. When do you think you could take a look?"

His mother spoke again. He pulled the list of names from his pocket and handed it to his dad.

"Sounds like it might be dinnertime. I'd be happy to check after we eat." His dad glanced at the list. "Hmm. Well, I can save you some time right away. You can definitely cross—"

"Sorry to interrupt." Reed's mom poked her head into the library. "Sergeant, is that your car out front? The MPs are saying it's been reported stolen."

"Yes, it's mine." He stood. "I'll talk to them."

One of the MPs hovered in the hallway. He saluted the colonel. "Sorry, sir, but we need to follow up on all reports."

"Not a problem, Corporal."

"If the sergeant is in a meeting with you, perhaps we could just get the keys...."

"Sure." Reed stood and fished the keys out of his pocket. He showed his military ID. Thankfully nothing in the car had anything with Reed or Trent's real names on it. All the documents pertaining to the investigation were at the hotel with White. Reed had a flash drive in his pocket, but the MPs would hardly ask for that.

"So, based on this list, you can definitely take Nicholls out of the running. I trust him with my life. I'd vouch for Collins too. However, I will still take a look at everyone when we have more time and you tell me what I should be looking for in their records."

"Thanks, Colonel." Reed used the rank in case either of the MPs was in earshot. He hadn't expected his father to respect his request even after stating categorically that neither Nicholls nor Collins could be involved.

Five minutes later the MP returned the keys to Reed and apologized with a formal salute.

"Dinner will be in about five minutes," Reed's mother said. She didn't remark on the fact he and his father were having a quiet conversation.

"Sounds good. We're just finishing up in here," Reed's father said.

The doorbell rang again.

"I had no idea this place would be so busy on a Friday," Reed said.

"Usually it isn't."

Reed's mother spoke to the new arrival in the doorway. She didn't raise her voice this time. Probably someone she knew.

"Let me just wash up," Reed said. He got up and left his father staring at the list in his hand.

He was coming out of the downstairs bathroom when he spotted his mother setting platters on the table in the dining room. "Wow, dinner smells fantastic. Do you need some help, Mom?"

"No, I've got it." She straightened up and smiled. "I see you and your dad—"

"What on earth is going on here?"

Reed's father raised his voice at the other end of the house, startling Reed and his mom. "What's that about?" he asked.

"Oh, one of your dad's staff stopped by about some emergency."

"Let's just talk about this." The colonel's voice was louder this time.

Another voice spoke, and Reed's senses went to high alert. "Trent!" He ran down the hallway, his mother trailing behind.

When he got halfway to the living room, his dad was standing in the doorway, posture alert but stiff. Reed stopped dead in his tracks and put a finger to his lips as his mother started to speak.

"Rob, let's discuss this on our own. Leave him out of it. He's a civilian."

"It's too late to discuss anything," Lieutenant Colonel Nicholls said, his voice cracking with emotion.

"No. It's not too late. But if you harm him, then it will be too late."

"He's an undercover agent. I know he's been investigating me. I know they're about to make an arrest."

"Put the gun down, Rob. That won't solve anything."

Reed's mother dug her fingers into his shoulder. "Reed? Do something." She made a motion. "Go around to the side door."

"Let him go, Rob. He doesn't have any evidence against you."

When Reed got to the side door, Nicholls was pointing a gun at Trent's head.

Reed's heart stopped again at the way Nicholls' hand trembled. The gun could go off. From this angle he couldn't see Trent's face. Like Reed's dad, Trent stood stiffly, hands at his sides. An empty martini glass sat on the table, and Reed knew Trent had been caught off guard. Even so, Trent had no experience dealing with this sort of situation.

"Let him go, Rob. Take me if you feel the need for a hostage. The authorities will definitely listen to you if you have me to make sure they negotiate instead of just shooting you."

Nicholls turned toward the colonel. "No one is going to listen to me." He practically sobbed. "They're already on to me. Ask him." He waved the gun at Trent again.

"Sure they will. I will. I'll listen. And they'll listen to me." The colonel took a tentative step into the room.

Nicholls swung the gun away from Trent for a moment.

"Trent, come here," Reed's father said.

As soon as Trent moved so much as his head, Nicholls swung the gun back toward him, and Reed's gut twisted. He glanced at his father's face, but his dad didn't seem to notice Reed was there.

The colonel put his hands up. "I'm giving up, Rob. I'm your bargaining chip. But only if you let Trent go. I'm far more valuable to you."

"I'm keeping the gun, Blair."

"Sure. Keep the gun." Reed's dad took another step into the room. "Definitely keep the gun. If you feel like shooting, shoot me. Who doesn't want to shoot the CO?" He laughed.

Reed couldn't breathe, but this time it wasn't fear for Trent. It was the way his father was moving closer, moving between Nicholls and Trent.

"What's it been? Three years? Three?"

"What?" Nicholls seemed confused. Reed was confused too. If only he hadn't left his weapon at their house. He could move fast, but not faster than a bullet between Nicholls and Trent or his dad.

Reed saw Trent's fingers wiggle. Then his father pointed toward the floor—with two fingers. Then one. Then Trent dropped and Reed's father rushed Nicholls. Darkness fell on the room as glass shattered and a gunshot echoed around the room.

Reed's mom screamed.

In the dark, Reed heard sounds of a struggle and more breaking glass. Staying low, he rushed toward the sound, remembering the position of the couch so he could avoid it.

"I got him," Reed's dad said. "Lights, Maya." No one else said anything. "Maya?"

The ceiling lights went on.

Reed's dad was sitting on top of Nicholls. Trent was still face down on the floor, and Reed ran to him and helped him up. "You okay?" He ran his hands up and down Trent's body. Only when he was certain Trent was fine did he glance up at his ghost-pale face. "Trent?"

"Yeah. I'm… I'm not hurt. I wouldn't say I'm okay, though. More scared than anything." Trent's voice was shaky, barely more than a whisper.

"Thank, God." Then Reed glanced at his dad and noticed the blood staining his sleeve. "Dad! Dad!"

"It's barely a scratch. Maya, call the MPs and an ambulance."

Nicholls was unconscious on the floor, with the colonel still sitting on him, dripping blood onto the green uniform.

"Dad, I can't believe you did that. You could have been killed."

"But I wasn't."

"That sounds like something you'd say, Reed." Trent finally spoke. "Thank you. Both."

"Dad, you said you trusted Nicholls with your life."

"I do."

"But after this?" Reed gestured toward the unconscious man.

Reed's dad stared at him, brows knit. "This?" He glanced down. "This isn't Nicholls. It's Collins. What makes you think this is Nicholls?"

A few more puzzle pieces snapped together for Reed.

"I'll explain that at the hospital." Just then the sound of sirens rang through the silence.

34

REED AND Trent drove to the hospital while Maya went in the ambulance with Blair.

Thankfully it wasn't far. Reed parked in the lot near the emergency room and took a moment to collect himself, running his hand down the back of his head and neck, the skin clammy with sweat.

"Reed, what are you waiting for?" Trent asked as he popped open the passenger door.

"I just need a minute. Come sit back down here."

Trent turned toward Reed. "What's wrong?"

Reed's heart thudded like timpani, and his vision clouded for a moment. He closed his eyes, but that didn't help. When he opened them, Trent was staring at him. Reed leaned forward and pulled Trent into his arms and held him tight. He needed to feel Trent's body against him, Trent's heart beating, and that stubbly cheek against his own. Trent was here with him, alive. It could have turned out so differently tonight. Reed hadn't put the pieces together quickly enough, hadn't realized how close he'd gotten, hadn't understood the signals right in front of him.

"Trent."

Trent put his arms around Reed and brushed his lips to Reed's ear. "Your dad's going to be fine. Don't worry."

"I'm not worried about him. I'm scared because I almost lost *you*."

Trent leaned back and peered into Reed's eyes. "You okay?"

"No. I'm not okay. I'm—" He swept his hand along his head again, forgetting his hair was about two millimeters long. "You know how much I love you?"

Trent shrugged. How could he be so damn calm right now? Usually this was where Trent would be gasping for air and hanging on to Reed. "I guess so." He gave a shy smile as if he didn't think Reed could love him enough to be so worried.

"Well, at least twice as much as that. Probably more."

"Really?"

Reed pulled Trent close and kissed him hard on the mouth. Could he express the intensity of his feelings through a kiss? If he tried, he'd probably hurt them both. It would have to wait. Right now, Trent was safe. But Reed's mother needed him.

"Really." He gave Trent a less intense kiss and got out of the car. On the asphalt Reed's knees gave way slightly, and he paused to let the dizziness pass and gulp the cool night air. The bright lights outside the ER blazed into his retinas, and he took Trent's hand as they walked into the hospital.

The waiting room was half-full. Probably normal for a Friday night on an Army base in Texas. By midnight it would be standing room only. Maya wasn't anywhere in sight. Reed went up to the registration desk.

"I'm here to see Colonel Atkinson. He should have arrived in the past ten minutes."

"Have a seat. I'll let you know if there's news. You're not allowed back."

"I'm… his son. I need to see him. My mother needs me."

She looked Reed up and down, taking in his civilian clothes and buzz cut. "I'll need some ID."

Reed pulled out his wallet. "I've got a different last name," he said as he pulled out his FBI credentials.

"Let me talk to my supervisor." She looked at Trent. "Are you family?"

"He's my husband," Reed said. He stared at her, expecting some kind of judgment.

"Will you both please wait a few moments? I should be able to let you in. You can have a seat if you like." She gave a soft smile, not too cheerful given that they were in the ER.

"Let's sit," Trent said.

Reed nodded and took Trent's hand and they sat, thighs touching, squeezing each other's hand.

The nurse returned and waved them along the hall toward the double doors marked Authorized Persons Only.

Reed tugged Trent to his feet, and they rushed through the doors and to the end of the hall, where Reed's mom sat, tears streaking her face, even paler in the unforgiving fluorescent lights.

"Oh, sweetheart, I'm so glad you're here." She put her arms around Reed, and he pulled her in tight.

"What did they tell you so far? How's Dad doing?"

"He's in surgery. A piece of the bullet hit a bone." She ran her hand along her upper arm. "It's fractured, and they don't know how difficult it will be to repair." She sobbed once she'd gotten all the words out.

"I'm so sorry, Maya," Trent said. He took both her hands in his and squeezed them. "It's my fault."

"Nonsense."

"No, it's my fault," Reed said. "Mom, it is. I almost got Dad and Trent hurt. And you could have been hurt too."

"But everyone's alive, honey. Your dad's arm will take a while to mend, but it's—"

"That's only because we were all lucky. It shouldn't have come down to luck. I'm trained better than that."

"Reed, we were at your parents' for dinner. It wasn't a special ops combat mission. No one could know…."

Reed spun on his heel. "But Trent, that's the point of training, so that when something happens, you move without needing to think or prepare. I completely underestimated the situation." He looked down at his hands, traces of his father's blood dried along his fingers. "Thank God Dad and Trent were able to think more quickly."

She smiled. "Yes, they did, didn't they?"

"I learned a lot from Reed," Trent said with the glimmer of a smile that made Reed's heart swell with pride. "Who wants coffee or something else? I'll go find a vending machine." Trent glanced to Maya. "Coffee?"

She shook her head. "I don't need the caffeine. Water would be fine. Something cold. Thank you, Trent."

"Coffee sounds good. Thanks." Reed gave Trent a peck on the cheek, then sat down on one of the hard plastic seats next to his mother.

"I made a nice roast for dinner. You would have enjoyed it."

Her ability to make small talk impressed Reed. He was still a bundle of nerves. How could she not be more worried about his father? "I forgot about dinner!"

"I asked our housekeeper if she could clean up. Maybe we can try again after…." She looked toward the closed doors marked "OR 2."

He wasn't ready to discuss that just yet. "Yeah. That sounds good. I'll have to see what happens when we start questioning Nicholls."

"You mean Collins."

"Collins. Right." Images of the evening's events flashed through his brain like a clip from the eleven o'clock news. "Collins. I'll have to go and talk to him later on."

"Of course. Even without what happened tonight, I'm in shock that he was involved with this at all." She bit her lower lip as if recalling something. "I heard a few things—things your dad said—but I didn't believe everything. Now, a lot of it makes sense."

"What do you mean?"

"You should ask your dad. It's Army business and maybe not something he was supposed to tell me."

"We were going to discuss my suspects after dinner."

"So did you get to—"

A woman wearing surgical scrubs came into the hallway, pulling her cap off and interrupting Reed's mother. "Mrs. Atkinson?"

"Yes?"

"I'm Dr. Lessing. Your husband's fine. We were able to repair the bone, ligaments, and blood vessels. He should have no serious complications, except for his golf game."

"He's okay? Really?"

For the first time since Reed had arrived at the hospital, he noticed strong emotion flooding his mother's expression. She'd held it in—the perfect Army spouse putting on a brave face—until now.

"Yes, ma'am. He's in the recovery room, and you can go see him in about twenty minutes. Then he'll be taken to his room and stay here for a day or two."

"Thank you, Doctor."

Lessing nodded to Reed's mom and then to him before disappearing back into the ER.

Trent arrived about five minutes later, carrying bottles of water. He handed them out. Before Reed even said anything, Trent said, "The coffee was awful. Stick with water." He turned to Maya. "Any news?"

"Yes, Trent, he's out of surgery. We can see him in the recovery room shortly."

"And?" Trent glanced toward Reed warily.

"The surgeon said he's fine, except for being shot. He'll be fine."

Trent curled his lip into a half smile. "Thank God. I'm still feeling so guilty."

A man in scrubs came up to them. "Mrs. Atkinson, your husband is in recovery now."

"Mom, you go see Dad. I don't think they want all of us in there."

She stood up and nodded. "You'll come by to see him later, Reed? In the room?" Her eyes looked sad again. This time it wasn't because she was worried about her husband.

"Yes, Mom. I will. I promise."

She squeezed Trent's hand and followed the hospital worker.

Trent sat down. "That's good news."

Reed leaned back against the wall and covered his eyes with his hand for a moment. "Yes. It is." In his pocket, his phone buzzed. He pulled it out—Tom White. "Yeah, Tom?"

"I'm just getting the news now. How's your dad? And you and Trent?"

"My father is out of surgery. Trent and I are here at the hospital. Did you talk to Collins yet?"

"No. I'm waiting for you. Will you be able to come in to question him tomorrow?"

"I can come now if you like."

"Stay with your family."

"Everyone's fine. Besides, I'd rather we start nailing his ass ASAP."

"Okay. The MPs are going to need a statement from everyone. How about if they start with you and Trent tonight, then get to your parents tomorrow?"

"Sounds good. We'll be there soon."

35

REED DIDN'T sleep at all. Trent slept on a couch in the temporary office the MPs assigned Reed and Tom White while they took turns interrogating Collins. By dawn they'd gotten the whole story out of him. The rest would be a matter of jurisdictional horse trading. Once Collins had signed his confession, White sent Reed and Trent home.

Trent drove while Reed dozed in the passenger seat.

"We're home." Trent shook Reed awake in front of their house.

"Already?" He barely remembered leaving the MP Station.

"I'll make breakfast and some good coffee for you while you're in the shower."

"I'm not even hungry."

"You should eat. Then have a nap. I can call your mom if you want to know how your dad is doing."

"Shower first. Then I'll see if I have enough energy to eat or talk." He leaned in toward Trent and missed when he tried to kiss him. "Or kiss." He barely had enough energy to smile.

The shower felt great. Reed scrubbed away the events of the past twenty-four hours. He wrapped himself in a towel and sat down on the bed for a minute before dressing again.

The next thing he knew, it was past noon and the sun was high in the sky outside the bedroom window. He sat up and rubbed his eyes.

"Trent, why'd you let me fall asleep?"

"Because that was my fault?" Trent was frowning as he entered the room carrying a tray.

"No. Just a question. You didn't have to bring me breakfast. But thank you."

"I know how you get horny in the kitchen, so I thought you might be hungry in the bedroom." He set the tray down on the bedside table.

Reed laughed and pulled Trent into bed with him. The movement dislodged his towel and Trent leaned over and grinned. "Nope, still horny."

"I'm hungry too."

"Which do you want?"

"Do I have to choose one or the other?" Reed slid a hand under Trent's shirt and up the firm planes of his chest until he felt a nipple harden under his palm.

"The breakfast is hot right now."

"So am I." Reed lay next to Trent and kissed him. He tasted like coffee, and he smelled like cinnamon, and the heat of his skin against Reed's made Reed dizzy. "I need to kiss you more than I need food right now."

"And I need to take my shirt off for this kissing?"

"And your pants."

"That's the kind of kissing I like." Trent pulled his shirt off and slid out of his sweats, then wrapped himself around Reed.

They kissed for a long time, at first tenderly exploring each other, then with increasingly insistent hands. Reed closed his eyes and let his fingers reacquaint themselves with Trent's body. The soft spots, the firm ass, smooth back, and velvet-soft skin covering his rock-hard cock. They took turns kissing and caressing each other, licking and sucking nipples, cocks, navels.

"What would you like?" Trent asked after another long kissing session.

"I kind of like this." Reed looked into Trent's eyes as they lay face-to-face. In this position he could see Trent, kiss him, or stroke his cock—or all at once. He leaned closer and sucked on Trent's lower lip for a moment. With eyes closed, Reed concentrated on the taste and textures his tongue encountered, while he wrapped a hand firmly around Trent's cock and varied the speed and angle of his movements to get Trent to make different noises. Each little moan or grunt got Reed closer to his own orgasm, which Trent coaxed from him.

"Let me know when you want me to finish you," Trent whispered against Reed's cheek.

"Whenever you get tired of this."

"In that case we'll be here forever. I love this." Trent put a hand behind Reed's neck and pulled him in tight for another slow, sweet, lazy kiss.

The only sounds were their soft moans, heavy breathing, hands on flesh, and the scrape of stubble against skin. After they'd both come, they licked each other clean and then traded more kisses under the warm shower.

Wrapped in towels, they stood staring at each other in the bedroom. Drops of water dripped off Trent's light brown hair and ran down his chest. Reed flicked the tip of his tongue to catch one fat drop clinging to a nipple.

"That's where we started a few hours ago," Trent said.

"Has it been that long?"

"I don't know. I wasn't paying any attention to the time. I was enjoying myself too much. And I was enjoying you." He nibbled at Reed's ear.

"Glad to hear it." Reed was ready for another round of slow lovemaking. Unfortunately his phone rang and ruined the plan. "Atwater." The name still tripped off his lips.

"Reed, honey?"

It was his mother. He immediately let go of Trent's cock. "Mom? How's Dad?"

"He's fine. I'm at the hospital with him. He's asking about you and Trent."

Reed stepped back and he spotted the guilty grin on Trent's face. "We're just catching up on sleep after last night. Is it visiting hours?"

"Honey, your dad's the CO. If he wants visitors, it's visiting hours."

"Nothing like throwing his weight around." He added a laugh so it wouldn't sound like an insult. In the past it was exactly the kind of insult he'd hurled at his father.

"He's looking forward to seeing you." She hung up.

IN THE car on the way to the hospital, Trent turned to Reed.

"How do Collins and his smuggling ring fit in with the goblets in Turkey?"

"They don't. At least not directly."

"What does that mean?"

"Someone else sold the goblets to Matthews. But he definitely did purchase items from Collins in the US. Items brought in through the supply unit. We only discovered Collins' activities once we began to dig into Matthews' illegal art purchases. If that plane hadn't crashed, we might not have found Collins for quite a while. It would have happened eventually, though." Reed turned into the hospital parking lot and stopped the car.

Trent reached to unclip his seat belt, then stopped. "Why's that?"

Reed smiled. He'd enjoyed having Trent in on the investigation. He'd offered some valuable assistance, and it was a pleasure for Reed to discuss his work with someone who was truly interested. "There's been a new influx of looted items coming from Iraq and now Syria. ISIS has been orchestrating looting and grave robbing in order to sell antiquities to raise money. One of Collins' suppliers in Iraq or Turkey has been using Collins' people to smuggle the smaller items into the States. They've been cropping up in a few smaller museums and reports via insurance companies."

"How will you catch them?"

"Collins will give up names to reduce his charges."

Trent's body stiffened and he balled his hands into fists, but he didn't reply.

"Don't worry." Reed leaned over to give him a kiss. "He's still in plenty of trouble for the attack at my parents' house. The question is who will punish him? The feds, the Army?"

"Hopefully, all of the above."

Reed nodded. "Cliff and her team will work on those leads with the local agencies." He stopped. "And just to put your mind at ease, Deniz is still working with her, and doing just fine. I forgot to update you on that, but you just reminded me."

"That's good to hear. Maybe we could go back to Turkey for a real vacation someday."

"We should. I'd love to be a real tourist for a change."

Trent looked surprised at Reed's answer, but his smile made Reed decide they would definitely return, so he could give Trent a real—and safe—vacation.

36

OUTSIDE HIS father's hospital room, Reed felt the all-too-familiar doubts creeping up again. What was he doing here?

"You okay?" Trent asked.

"I don't know what to say to him now."

"Why not?"

"I don't know." But Reed did. He saw concern in Trent's eyes. Concern and support. And he remembered the way telling Trent about the problems with his father had made Reed feel better. And it had led to everyone being here in the hospital. More guilt gnawed at Reed's stomach lining.

"Let's sit for a minute first." Trent led Reed back to the waiting area near the elevator. "Now tell me what's wrong. I know when you're lying."

Reed frowned. Not telling Trent the whole truth had ceased to be an option recently. Reed wasn't sure how he felt about that. "I might have been wrong about him. About a few things anyway." He twisted his fingers. "I'm starting to believe what you were telling me, about his reasons for pushing me away. And I wasn't very nice to him last night when we were talking in the library. He was nice to me. He was understanding, and complimentary, and proud of me—and of you—and I acted like an ass."

"Considering your past, that seems natural."

"But then he put his own life at risk for you. There were other ways to handle it. But he chose to do it that way. He proved to me that he wasn't just bullshitting me. He really meant what he'd said."

"That's a good thing, isn't it?"

"But then I'm the ass for not believing him. He's the better man here."

"Why does one of you have to be the better man?"

"I don't understand." Reed pressed his lips together.

"He was wrong for a long time in the way he treated you, regardless of the truth of the situation. Right? And yesterday, you didn't treat him well, regardless of the reality. Right?"

"So, what, it balances out?"

"I think it does. And you can't blame yourself for the way you acted up until a guy pointed a gun at me, Reed. You only did what was common sense, given the series of interactions you and he have had over the years."

"You lost me again, Trent."

"You know game theory? Where people have to make deci—"

"Yes, I know what game theory is. How do you know about game theory?"

"I'm not just a pretty face, you know."

Reed reached up to stroke Trent's cheek. "No, you are certainly not just that. And I didn't mean to insult you. Only that it didn't seem to be a topic you would come into contact with."

"I learned some back in that class at Quantico, so I studied some more. I have a lot of free time."

"I get what you're saying. It makes sense from that perspective. But that's math and logic, Trent. You're usually reminding me about emotions."

"There's an emotional aspect to the relationship with your dad as well. That's why you can't see the patterns very well."

"You convinced me. I'm not the only one to blame. And nothing will change if we don't both try."

"That's just what I meant."

Reed rewarded Trent with another kiss. "And I don't know what I'd do without you."

"I know."

Reed peered around the doorway into his father's hospital room. Blair Atkinson had one arm in a blue canvas sling and was sitting up in bed. Reed's mom turned around. "Oh, you're here. Let me—"

"Reed, Trent, come in." Blair's voice was surprisingly robust considering he'd been shot and had surgery the night before. "Well, Trent, it's nice to finally meet you in a truce zone." He held out his good hand to shake Trent's.

"Nice to meet you officially, Colonel."

"Call me Blair." He turned to Reed. "Good to see you, Rex."

"I'm Reed again."

"Good. Glad that's over. Hell of a result. I can't wait to hear what Collins told you."

"Blair, why don't we save that for another time, when you're home again?"

"Nonsense. This has disrupted my base, my life, almost got Trent here killed. I want to know what the hell that man was thinking."

"Why did he come to your parents' house? I don't understand why he suddenly lost it like that," Trent said.

"I think that's my fault." Reed frowned. "When he was pretending to be Nicholls and asking for status updates, he fished around for information about whether we'd discovered who the ringleader was. I said we were close to making an arrest, just to get him off my back. But it must have made him think we were on to him." Reed sighed. "And he thought you were another agent, Trent, which is why he targeted you."

"I was helping the investigation, but I didn't think anyone would see me as a threat." Trent let out a nervous laugh. "I suppose it's a compliment."

"That's just so odd that the MPs came by right before." Maya knitted her brows.

Reed nodded. "The only explanation I can think of is that he sent them to make sure Trent and I were there." He turned to his father. "I could use some more specific information from you, if you're up to it."

"Of course. Anything to make sure he gets what he deserves," Blair responded gruffly, not bothering to hide his anger at Collins.

"Why don't we come back in a little while, then." Trent turned to Maya. "Let's grab a coffee or something."

Blair waved them good-bye and turned to Reed. "Start talking. And don't leave anything out."

37

REED SCOOTED the horrible bright green plastic chair closer to his father's bed, and the scraping sound set his teeth on edge.

"Collins should be signing his confession right now."

"With four witnesses to what happened at my house, how did he expect to get away with it?"

"I don't think he did. I think he wanted someone to stop him. Permanently. Otherwise he would have just run."

His father nodded. "You have more experience with law enforcement, so I'll take your word for that. But how on earth did he get involved in smuggling the artifacts in the first place? I told you—before he pulled a gun last night—I would never have suspected him."

"He hasn't wanted to discuss that yet. We'll probably find the answers in his military records. Tom White, my supervisor at the Bureau, is still trying to get access. JAG is stonewalling."

"Typical." Reed's father frowned. "I'll give you my password. You can log in from my home office and check into whatever you need to."

"Won't you get in trouble for that?"

"Who cares? What are they going to do, arrest me too?"

"They could."

"Screw the DoD and Homeland Security. If you find nothing, no harm done. If you find what you need, then they'll make more fuss coming after me."

Reed stared at his father for a moment. Who was this man? He resembled the man Reed remembered from his youth in appearance only. "You might lose your chance at making general."

"If that's how they decide, then I don't want the promotion. Just more paperwork and bullshit." He paused and glanced toward the door. "But your mom might not agree. Just don't tell her."

"Sure."

"Why did you call Collins 'Nicholls'?"

"That's how he introduced himself to me. He summoned me to the hospital for a checkup and called himself Dr. Nicholls, said he was your right-hand man and that I was to provide him with regular status reports, which he would relay to you."

"Interesting." Reed's father rubbed a thumb across his chin, apparently lost in thought. "He was lucky you and I weren't in communication."

"Did anyone on your staff know I'm your son before now?"

"No. And no one knows except the hospital staff, unless you've told them."

"No." Reed pulled a small notebook out of his shirt pocket. "What do you know of Collins' service in Iraq?"

"I've been going over that this morning. He was a solid officer, good leader, in charge of an infantry company in the early days of OIF1. I didn't know him at that point, but something went wrong with one of the missions, leading to an unacceptable friendly-fire incident on his watch. Back then a lot of inexperienced officers were put into combat with even less experienced soldiers, so we had a lot more casualties than we should have. But the brass came down exceptionally hard on Collins and shipped him behind the lines to the supply unit where he couldn't get anyone killed. He didn't manage to move up until I gave him an opportunity when I got to Fort Sam."

"*You* did?" Reed remembered Trent mentioning how his father had tried to give people second chances. One of those justifications for his decision to remain in the Army despite the anti-gay regs.

"Yes. He was one of the oldest men in his rank, and since our unit wasn't in the rotation for deployment again, it seemed that whatever had happened wouldn't recur." He glanced at a spot past Reed's shoulder. "Another thing that caught my attention at the time was that Collins had been given some small commendation for working with the Iraqi nationals, including turning in items being sold by locals on base. It impressed me that he'd built a close relationship with locals."

"He turned stolen items in?" Reed glanced up from his notepad. "What else do you remember about that, specifically about Collins?"

"That's it. Now you see why I never suspected his involvement."

Reed sat back in the chair, going over the pieces of information he had now. "Something made him stop turning items in. Or he used that as cover so he could keep some of them for himself."

"What did the other men say?"

"I haven't spoken to them since he's been taken into custody. But his arrest might loosen their tongues." Reed checked his watch. He'd been talking with his father for nearly an hour, and he hadn't yet felt the desire to strangle the man.

"You need to leave?" The tremor in his father's voice surprised Reed.

"I'd like to wrap this up quickly but—"

"Let everyone stew for the rest of the weekend. They might be a little chattier in a day or two."

"Under normal circumstances, I'd agree. But I don't want to give JAG a chance to freeze the Bureau out." Laughter echoed in the hallway. Trent and his mother appeared in the doorway a moment later. "You two seem to be having a good time," Reed said.

"We are," Trent replied. "What about you two?"

"We've been going over the case," Reed's father replied.

"Blair, is that all you're interested in?" His mother let out a disapproving sigh. "Maybe Reed doesn't want to talk about work all the time."

"Sorry. You're right."

"You're kidding, right?" Trent said, laughing. "He loves talking about work."

Maya's stare shut him up more quickly than anything Reed had ever seen before. He'd have to learn how his mother did that. "Trent, I could use your help with something else…." She grabbed Trent's elbow and propelled him toward the door as he glanced helplessly back at Reed.

"Your mom is as subtle as ever." Reed's father chuckled.

"She hasn't changed much at all." Reed pressed his lips together and a weight formed just below his diaphragm, making breathing difficult. "I-uh. Look, Dad, I—"

"Yeah. Me too."

That had been easy. But it wasn't right. Leaving things unsaid was why they'd spent the past fifteen years without speaking to each other. "No, Dad. I'm sorry I didn't listen to Mom when she tried to explain things to me. I can't say I completely understand, even now, but I didn't even try to understand."

If Reed had expected his father to respond with the typical bluster and justification, he'd been wrong. For once, his father was speechless. Tears trailing down his cheeks said more than any words ever could.

His father shook his head and started to speak, then stopped and pressed his fingers against his eyelids. "You have nothing to apologize for. I let you down. I had my reasons for what I did and how I treated you back when I might have made a difference in our family, in our relationship. Your mother was just as angry about my behavior as you were. Perhaps more."

"She was?"

"She was. I didn't do anything to help you work through the questions you had about sex and growing up. That was my job as a parent."

Heat pooled in Reed's gut. "And what, you would have been able to change how I turned out?" He spat out the words. The butterflies he'd felt now resembled attack helicopters circling around in his stomach.

"Of course not. You are who you are, and you always will be. I didn't stop loving you when I understood you're gay. But I did start worrying about you in more ways than you can imagine."

"A lot of parents go through that, and support their kids anyway."

"Yes, that's where I fucked up. I could have supported you without hurting anyone's career. I just didn't want to listen to your mother's suggestions. Being a parent isn't something we get much chance to learn. Hell, I had more instruction in leading soldiers than in how to raise a son to be a good man." He smiled, but his eyes were still sad. "You turned out really well without me. I am very proud of you."

Reed had waited so long to hear these words, but he still fought the urge to question his veracity. The sorrow weighing down his father's voice made the decision for him.

"Thanks, Dad." Reed tried to smile, but it hurt. A lump had formed in his throat, and his eyes stung. He couldn't think of anything else to say, so instead he moved to the edge of the bed and put his arms around his father for the first time in nearly twenty years.

They held each other awkwardly for a moment, Reed trying not to hurt his father's injured arm and his father holding on too tightly with his one good arm. But it felt good. And the helicopters subsided into tiny butterflies again.

They had let go, wiped their eyes, and started talking about basketball when Trent and Reed's mom returned.

"Well, at least you're not still talking about work." She walked to the edge of the bed, reached out to the back of Reed's neck, and squeezed as she slid her hand down to his shoulder. "And you're both wrong. Celtics, all the way this year!"

They both protested her ridiculous comment, and even Trent joined in the laughter.

"I NEED to meet with Tom for a while." Reed started the car in the hospital parking lot. "I'll just drop you off at home."

Trent nodded, but his widening eyes told Reed that Trent didn't want to be home alone right now. If there were any other way, Reed wouldn't have left him on his own. But today he needed to take care of some urgent matters.

Events over the past few days had made an unexpectedly huge impact on Reed. When he'd seen Trent in the living room with Collins and the gun, it altered the way Reed perceived him. For the first time Reed really saw Trent, saw who he was, and just how much he meant to Reed.

That wasn't the only thing that shifted.

Despite the potential danger, Reed loved his job, maybe even because of it. He'd loved being a Ranger and working special ops.

He'd taken risks all his life, never considering the consequences. Since meeting Trent, he'd been more aware of the dangers, but it hadn't made him change who he was, and how he worked.

Then, witnessing his mother's relief that his father wasn't seriously injured, a new reality came crashing down on Reed.

Reed loved his job, but suddenly, reliving that moment of fear, it came to him that he loved something else even more.

Some*one* else: Trent.

And Reed knew exactly what he had to do.

38

THREE DAYS later they sat around the table in the Atkinsons' dining room.

"We've got signed statements from everyone at this point," Reed said as he heaped roasted potatoes on his plate. There wasn't much room for them, considering how much roast beef he'd taken. But he hadn't eaten his mother's cooking in years, and he wasn't going to pass up the chance to enjoy some of his favorite dishes.

"Does this mean you'll be leaving soon?" his mother asked.

Reed glanced at Trent, who caught his eye and smiled. "No. We're going to stay an extra week or so. Maybe drive up to Oklahoma City to visit Trent's family, then fly back from there."

"I'll be glad to get out of that house," Trent said. He put his fork down and stared at his plate for a moment. Reed knew he'd been thinking about the kitten again. "We're getting a room at the Mokara. It'll be a nice change."

"Oh, it's lovely." She turned to Reed's dad. "It's where Trent and I met for our secret lunch."

"A hotel?" Reed's father slammed his hand on the table. "What's wrong with staying here?"

"We didn't want to put you out. Last time we came for dinner, someone got shot...." Reed grinned. "Besides, Trent really likes hotels." Reed caught the flush that crept up Trent's cheeks.

"Don't blame it on me." He turned to Maya. "I'd be happy to stay here. I want to say good-bye to some people on base."

"You sure settled in here, didn't you, Trent?" Maya asked. "You like living on base?"

"Not really. No offense, Blair. I did meet some really nice people, but I didn't like a lot of things I saw here."

"None taken," Blair said. "Most Army families are wonderful. Because of Reed's investigation, you've been mixing with a subset that probably doesn't represent the average soldier. And things have been more difficult in general lately, with a lot of soldiers not getting the support and treatment they need. I—"

"Blair, I'm sure Trent doesn't need your Army lecture." Maya cut a piece of meat with extra vigor as she admonished him.

"I wasn't lecturing."

"Now your family is starting to sound perfectly normal," Trent whispered to Reed.

"Is that a good thing?"

"Reed, fill us in on what you learned when you were able to talk with all the soldiers involved—" Blair said.

"That can wait," Maya interrupted. "I have one little surprise first. Is anyone ready for dessert?"

Three noes seemed to surprise her. "Well, let me just show you what we have for dessert." She stood and knocked softly on the door to the kitchen, then sat back down again.

A moment later the door swung open, and a woman came out carrying two platters.

"Katie!" Trent practically leapt from his chair, knocking it over. "You look amazing!" He hugged her, then stepped back to take in her new appearance. She had cut her hair, wore only light makeup, and had on an apron over a tasteful, loose-fitting dress. "Wow. With everything going on the past couple of days, I didn't get to ask Maya how you were."

"Have a seat, Katie," Reed said. "Did you eat?"

"Yes. Thank you." She turned to Trent. "I got a job at Cuisine-Art!"

Everyone cheered, and she blushed to the roots of her hair and looked down at her lap for a moment. She wiped tears away and then went on. "With Paul in jail, I could move back into base housing, at least for a while. I guess once we're divorced, the Army won't let me stay here, but by then I should be earning enough."

"You've got a place on base as long as you need it," Maya said, patting Katie's hand. "Don't you worry."

"Maya's been kind enough to hire me to bake desserts for some of the base events." She beamed at Trent. "I get to use all that fancy equipment Paul bought me."

Reed opened his mouth, then decided not to mention that it might be seized as evidence at some point in the future, but her husband was in enough trouble with the domestic violence and assault charges, the Army didn't need to go after him for the smuggling too.

"That's fantastic, Katie," Reed said instead. He felt as if he were meeting an entirely different person than the one he'd known before. "I am sorry about ev—"

"Oh, no Rex, don't you be sorry at all for me. I'm lucky I met Troy—Trent. And I never would have if you weren't here looking into the other trouble with Paul. I have you to thank for bringing Trent with you here."

Reed nodded because he didn't know how to respond. He looked at Trent and felt proud and lucky to be part of Trent's life. Somehow, Trent touched so many others in positive ways Reed couldn't have imagined.

"I should stop talking y'all's ears off!" She turned to Maya. "I promised Rhoda I'd help her put together a menu for the next poker night on Friday. Trent, here's my new phone numbers and e-mail. I hope you'll say good-bye before you leave." She pulled a slip of paper out of her apron pocket and handed it to Trent. Then she waved shyly and slipped back into the kitchen.

"Wow, that's great news," Trent said. "Thank you for taking care of her, Maya."

"My pleasure."

"Reed, let's get back to the case," Blair said now that the touchy-feely portion of the evening appeared to be over.

Reed looked to his mother for permission before responding. She nodded.

"Dad mentioned that Collins had been given a commendation for turning in artifacts following the initial looting of the museum, but that was before the friendly-fire incident. It seems once he got sidelined out of combat, he continued to collect illicit items but didn't turn them all over to the authorities. He might have intended to at some point, but in fact he turned over only about two-thirds of what he had found. He kept the best pieces—the gold, jewels, some undamaged items. He even had soldiers turning items in to him, but no one made any connection between what he collected and what he turned over." Reed sipped water, then continued. "Two of the men involved said he'd given them reward money over the years, and in return they promised not to mention the items. A few others signed statements that he effectively blackmailed them with threats to reveal that they had purchased the items from locals in the first place. That was how he dealt with the more honest soldiers. The less honest ones got paid for their silence."

"Sounds like the honest men lost out simply for being honest in the first place," Maya said.

"Yes, that's often the way it works out in these situations," Reed replied. "I see similar situations all the time in my work. But the men who were threatened may in the end receive some of the reward money offered by Iraq and an archeological society."

"How can you tell who's being honest about that?" Trent asked.

"The honest guys don't have fancy stereos and cars, for the most part. They feel guilty about taking the money Collins offered. I'll be heading up some additional investigations and retrievals later on. Some of the pieces are in museums, private collections… there's a lot of cleaning up to do." He turned to his father. "And we wouldn't have gotten the most important information without your help accessing their military records. Thanks for trusting me with that."

"Any time."

It felt good to hear his father put such trust in him. He'd been waiting for that kind of approval for a very long time.

IN THE car after dinner, Reed turned to Trent. "I have something I want you to see." He pulled away from the house and headed for the MP Station.

"I hope I don't have to see Collins, or Paul Cray." Trent's voice was tight.

"Nothing like that."

Trent followed Reed into the building. At the door, Reed flashed his FBI credentials and the soldier on duty waved him and Trent through. They went down a few more hallways to a room guarded by another MP, who also checked Reed's ID before opening the door.

Reed flipped the light on and waited to see Trent's reaction.

"Where…? Is this from Collins' place?" Trent stepped to the shelf loaded down with small sculptures, cuneiform tablets, and several shining gold pieces. Each item sported a small tag identifying it.

"It's awaiting transfer to the San Antonio Field Office. Nothing as impressive as those goblets, but I thought you should see what we turned up so far. There's likely to be more. He'll hold out on us for a deal."

"This is pretty impressive." Trent reached a hand toward a set of small cups fashioned from gold, gleaming even in the low light, but stopped before touching it.

"Go on. I won't tell."

Trent shot Reed an impish grin and picked up one of the gold pieces and practically caressed it. His obvious pleasure, and his reverence for the delicate item, touched Reed. He'd made the right decision bringing Trent here to savor the result of their investigation.

"WHAT DO you want to do about the hotel?" Reed asked when they were back inside the car in the parking lot.

"It's up to you. If you want to stay with your parents for a few days, that's fine with me. That's what you were asking?"

"Yeah. You decide. I know you really wanted to stay at the Mokara."

"I do like hotels. Especially the one in Istanbul. I can't believe that was only a few weeks ago. It feels like another lifetime."

"That's the job."

"I don't know how you can go back and forth between stories and names and personalities like that."

"Sometimes it is tough. But my favorite part is coming home to you." Reed took Trent's hand and planted a kiss on the back. Then another, then he pulled Trent close and kissed him so much he almost didn't want to let go, but they were parked in front of the MP Station.

"That's sweet. But let's not sit here all night...."

Reed made a split-second decision. He started the car and headed for the base exit.

"Hotel, then?"

"Yeah. At least for tonight. I want one last night alone with you."

"I really like the way that sounds."

TRENT SAT in one of the plush chairs in the lobby with the suitcases while Reed checked in. He felt self-conscious with the shabby luggage that worked perfectly for Rex and Troy, but looked out of place for Trent and Reed in one of San Antonio's prettiest boutique hotels. Reed seemed to be smiling even more when he came back with the key. They held hands all the way up in the elevator. A man in an exquisite Italian suit looked down his nose at Reed's buzz cut, and Trent wanted to say something, but Reed kissed his cheek and distracted him.

The room was lovely, making Trent hate their suitcases even more. They were barely inside five minutes when a knock sounded at the door and a bellman wheeled in a room-service trolley. Reed tipped him, and he saluted and left.

"What's this?"

"A surprise."

"I'm over surprises for a while." Trent's stomach churned. He pulled the dome off the cart and found a bottle of champagne chilling on ice. "This one is okay. But after this, no more?"

Reed nodded. "Sure. I understand. Should I open this now?"

"If you want. I kind of want to get to bed soon."

"Oh. Are you tired?"

"No, which is why I want to get to bed soon." Trent peered at Reed. Had he only imagined the heat building between them in the car? Now Reed looked ready to hang out and chitchat all night. Trent put an arm around his waist and slid his hand along the curve of Reed's ass. "Soon." He kissed Reed, pushing his tongue inside Reed's mouth, but Reed didn't return the ardor.

"Let's have some champagne first, okay?"

Reed was acting strange. He never postponed sex. Then again, the case had just wrapped up, and he'd been going through some big emotional things with his dad. Of course he wasn't going to be himself. Trent chastised himself for expecting too much.

"I'd love some." Trent took the flute Reed offered him and was about to take a sip.

"Hey, let's have a toast."

"To what?"

"To the end of one thing and the start of something new."

"What does that mean?"

"I don't know. I heard it somewhere, and it kind of fit the situation."

"Your parents? I'm glad you and your dad are talking." They weren't back to normal, and they would never forget the past, but they'd arrived at a significant place of détente.

Trent sat in the wingback chair watching Reed pace around the room. "Come over and kiss me or something. You're making me nervous."

Reed took a sip of champagne and nodded. "Sorry." He stumbled two feet from Trent and dropped something. "Hang on." He put his flute down and dropped to his knees to look under Trent's chair.

He straightened up and started to stand again, but stopped. "Trent."

"What?" He looked down at Reed half-kneeling on the floor. "What did you drop?"

"Nothing." Reed turned to Trent and looked distressed. "Trent, something has been worrying me lately."

"What?"

"With that guy nearly killing you—"

"He didn't even come close—"

"—and my dad getting shot, and well, everything else… I was really scared. At the hospital the other night, I didn't want to let go of you."

"I remember. I remember that tonight too. It seems a long time ago."

"I felt something I couldn't describe. Not passion or physical attraction—not only that. But I knew if something happened to you, I would lose part of myself—far more than half. I'd lose my entire heart and my will to get through every day." He looked up at Trent.

Then Trent realized Reed wasn't getting up, he was on one knee, and he was still there. The room started spinning, and Trent couldn't breathe. It felt like a dream, but not the kind of dream he could ever have imagined.

"Reed?"

"Shhh. Let me finish." Finally Reed smiled. "You asked me something in Istanbul, and that discussion has stayed with me ever since." He took Trent's left hand. "You took Troy's wedding band off. I hadn't realized how used I'd gotten to seeing it until you did. Or how used I'd gotten to saying 'my husband' and introducing you that way. I hadn't realized how natural it would feel to say that. And now seeing the empty space—" Reed touched the pale skin where the wedding band had been for more than a month. "—it looks like something's missing. Not just on your finger, but here." He touched his chest and then Trent couldn't see Reed's face, only a blur.

"Reed?"

"Trent, will you marry me?"

Trent squeezed his eyes shut and sniffled. Probably not very romantic or attractive. He nodded because he knew he wouldn't be able to speak.

"Can you say yes? Because I really want to hear you say yes."

"Yes." It was a kind of squeaky whisper. Then the tears took over, and it was like driving in a downpour with no windshield wipers. He felt Reed slip a ring onto his finger, and after a minute and some tissues, he could almost see again.

"Reed? What's this?" Trent wiggled his fingers and saw a green flash surrounded by blinding white sparks.

"It's the ring from Istanbul."

"But…." Trent peered at it, heart thudding. "I don't remember these diamonds."

"I had those added. Is it too much?"

Who says no to diamonds? Reed clearly did not know him very well at all. "It's even more beautiful. I don't know what to say."

"You could say yes again."

"Yes. Yes to anything."

"Anything?"

Trent nodded.

"In that case, let's get to bed."

"I thought you'd never ask!"

Reed slid his arms around Trent's waist and kissed him so hard it almost made Trent cry again.

"There's one thing we'll need to figure out," Trent said.

"Only one?"

"For starters." Trent grinned. "Who's going to change his last name? Since Acton isn't your real name, there's no reason you couldn't become a Copeland."

"I haven't given much thought to my name for years, glad not to wear my father's name around on a uniform anymore. It's why I have no trouble changing identities for the job. But I hadn't considered that option." Reed started to unbutton Trent's shirt. "But you've got the perfect opportunity to convince me right now why I should."

"Can I change my answer? Maybe you need to convince me why I should marry you."

Reed unzipped Trent's pants and wrapped a hand around his erection, sending shivers up and down Trent's entire body. He flicked his tongue along the head of Trent's cock till it was so hard it might break off.

"Never mind."

AUTHOR'S NOTE

LIKE THE three Precious Gems books before this, *24-Karat Conspiracy* draws on experiences of my own visit to Turkey. I'm a huge history geek, and it was such a thrill to land in Istanbul and have the chance to explore a city that has so many layers to its history. Even though I had previously visited Morocco, nothing prepared me for the delights of Istanbul, a sprawling city that spans both sides of the Bosporus River. New colors, sounds, smells, and sights bombarded me, drawing me in.

Istanbul is a microcosm of Turkey. You can visit the old harems of the Sultan's palace just a short walk from some of the most impressive mosques in the world. You can take a ferry ride from Europe to Asia, still inside the city limits of Istanbul. You can visit the beach, swim in the chilly Mediterranean, or visit the strange, almost lunar landscapes of Central Turkey in Cappadocia and Pamukkale.

And you can eat a dizzying array of amazing food. If you haven't tried Turkish food, make sure to give it a try. And there's nothing like a Turkish breakfast. The huge spread Trent and Reed enjoy at their hotel: yogurt, olives, bread, honey, fresh white cheese, and strong coffee, is an everyday custom for Turks.

Making my visit to Turkey even more special was the chance to stay in the homes of Turks I met while traveling. People I met in one city would arrange for me to stay with a friend in a different city. Everyone was incredibly gracious and welcoming. I honestly can't wait to go back!

This book also deals with items looted during wartime. It's an age-old problem, and the fall of Baghdad and subsequent looting of Iraq's national museum led to the loss of thousands of artifacts, priceless in both value and history. Interpol, Europol, and the FBI continue to look for the items, and surprisingly, they continue to recover and repatriate items.

Over 15,000 items went missing. Currently half of them are still missing.

Most recently, it appears ISIS is digging up archaeological sites of historical importance and selling artifacts to fund their operations. I learned of this while I was writing this book, and it gave the work of Reed and others who investigate stolen artifacts another layer of reality.

Many of the recovered items were found in private collections in the United States and Europe, some in museums, in ways similar to how Reed and the FBI discovered the illegal antiquities in this book.

Don't miss how the story began

Rarer Than Rubies

Precious Gems: Book One

By EM Lynley

When Trent Copeland runs into Reed Acton at a Bangkok airport, he thinks the handsome American is too good to be true. Why would someone like Reed be interested in a quiet, introverted gay-romance writer? After all, even an obvious tourist like Trent can see that there is more to Reed's constant unexplained appearances in his path than meets the eye.

Reed Acton has one mission and one mission only—he needs to get the map that was accidentally slipped into Trent's bag and keep the mobsters who want the priceless artifact from taking deadly revenge. Trent Copeland is a delicious and damned near irresistible diversion, but Reed can't afford distractions right now, especially if he wants to keep Trent safe.

From Bangkok's seediest back alleys to the sacred north, the two men will fight to stay one step ahead of the bad guys and learn that the only treasure worth finding is... each other.

http://www.dreamspinnerpress.com

Italian Ice

Precious Gems: Book Two

By EM Lynley

In this exciting sequel to *Rarer Than Rubies*, gay romance author Trent Copeland and former FBI agent Reed Action head to Italy for a Roman holiday. What should be a relaxing and romantic vacation is interrupted when Reed's not-so-former boss asks for his help with a case. Trent's shocked to discover in the six months they've been living together in LA, Reed hasn't been completely honest about his "retirement."

Reed heads for Sicily on the trail of a suspected antiquities-smuggling ring and to find Peter Isett—a former FBI partner he also hasn't been completely truthful about. Stung by Reed's dishonesty, Trent questions what else Reed might be hiding. But when he overhears something that tells him Reed's life is in danger, Trent follows Reed to a remote chain of ancient volcanic islands off Sicily's northern coast. Soon Trent is caught up in the smugglers' web, and Reed must decide between his heart and his mission—a decision complicated by his past with Peter. Reed's position is perilous: unless he can learn to put the past behind him, he risks destroying everything he's built with Trent.

http://www.dreamspinnerpress.com

Jaded

Precious Gems: Book Three

By EM Lynley

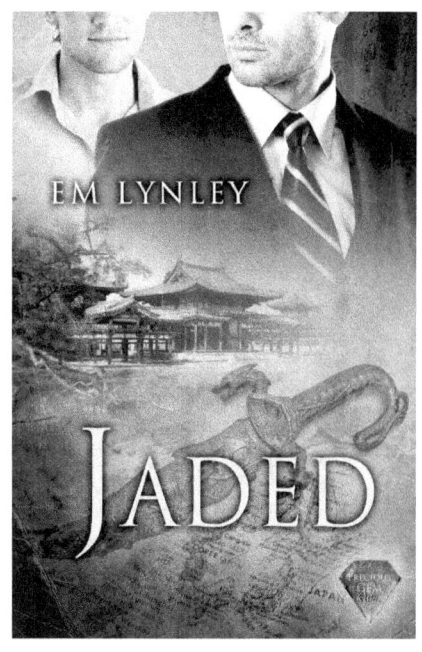

Gay-romance writer Trent Copeland finds his life in a rut while his boyfriend, Special Agent Reed Acton, is away on an undercover mission. After attending a special course at FBI headquarters in Quantico, Trent's eager for another challenge. He jumps at the opportunity for a trip to Japan to oversee appraisals of two art collections to be sold at the gallery he co-owns. But the trip isn't all cherry blossoms and Hello Kitty. When one of the collectors he meets—rumored to be the head of a Yakuza gang—turns up dead, Trent is accused of the murder and thrown in jail.

Reed drops everything to help find out who really committed the crime. He's in unknown territory in Japan, forced to navigate Tokyo's sex underworld to unravel the truth and save Trent. He poses as a "host" at a seedy late-night club. When Reed's undercover activities place him at a ruthless Yakuza leader's sex party, he must be willing to go to any lengths to secure Trent's safety and freedom. But trusting the wrong people brings both Reed and Trent to the Yakuza leader's attention. If they're ever to have a happy ever after, they'll first have to call on every skill just to stay alive.

http://www.dreamspinnerpress.com

EM LYNLEY has worked in finance, the wine industry, and high-tech, though she'd rather be writing hot man-on-man romance. She spent ten years as an economist and financial analyst, including a year as a White House Staff Economist, but only because all the intern positions were filled. Tired of boring herself and others with dry business reports and articles, her creative muse is back and naughtier than ever. She has lived and worked in London, Tokyo and Washington, D.C., but the San Francisco Bay Area is home for now.

Contact EM:
Website: http://www.emlynley.com
Blog: http://emlynley.livejournal.com
Twitter: @emlynley
Facebook: http://www.facebook.com/emlynley

Bound for Trouble

By EM Lynley

BOUND FOR **TROUBLE**

EM Lynley

"You'll fall for Ryan Griffiths. The more danger he's in, the hotter BOUND FOR TROUBLE gets."
-Cecilia Tan, author of *Slow Surrender*

Daniel "Deke" Kane is a broken man, facing the end of his career in the FBI. He's on desk duty after a botched drug raid left the suspects and two children dead. He's got one chance to prove himself, or the only thing he'll be investigating is the Help Wanted ads.

Ryan Griffiths has been on the run for ten years. Forced onto the streets when his father kicked him out, Ryan earns his living in other men's beds. Finding his john dead in a hotel room drives him under the radar until a favorite client gives him a chance at a safe, clean life. But Ryan's relatively stable new world shatters when Deke Kane catches up with him.

When Deke's tasked to take down a drug dealer with terrorist ties and a taste for the dark side of BDSM, his only chance to get close is the suspect's interest in Ryan, and he convinces Ryan to become a confidential informant. In return, Deke offers Ryan immunity from his past. As Ryan falls under the drug lord's domination, Deke finds himself falling for Ryan.

Now Deke has to choose between Ryan's safety and his own future.

http://www.dreamspinnerpress.com

Dirty Dining

By EM Lynley

Jeremy Linden's a PhD student researching an HIV vaccine. He's always short of money, and when biotech startup PharmaTek reduces funding for his fellowship, he's tempted to take a job at a men's dining club as a serving boy. The uniforms are skimpy, and he's expected to remove an item of clothing after each course. He can handle that, but he soon discovers there's more on the menu here than fine cuisine. How far will he go to pay his tuition, and will money get in the way when he realizes he's interested in more from one of his gentlemen?

Brice Martin is an attorney for a Silicon Valley venture capital firm. When he's asked to take a client to the infamous Dinner Club, he finds himself unexpectedly turned on by the atmosphere and especially by his server, Remy. He senses there's more to the sexy young man than meets the eye. The paradox fascinates him, and he can't get enough of Remy.

Their relationship quickly extends beyond the club and sex. But the trust and affection they've worked to achieve may crumble when Jeremy discovers Brice's VC firm is the one that pulled the plug on PharmaTek— and Jeremy's research grant.

http://www.dreamspinnerpress.com

http://www.dreamspinnerpress.com

The Delectable Series

http://www.dreamspinnerpress.com

The Delectable Series

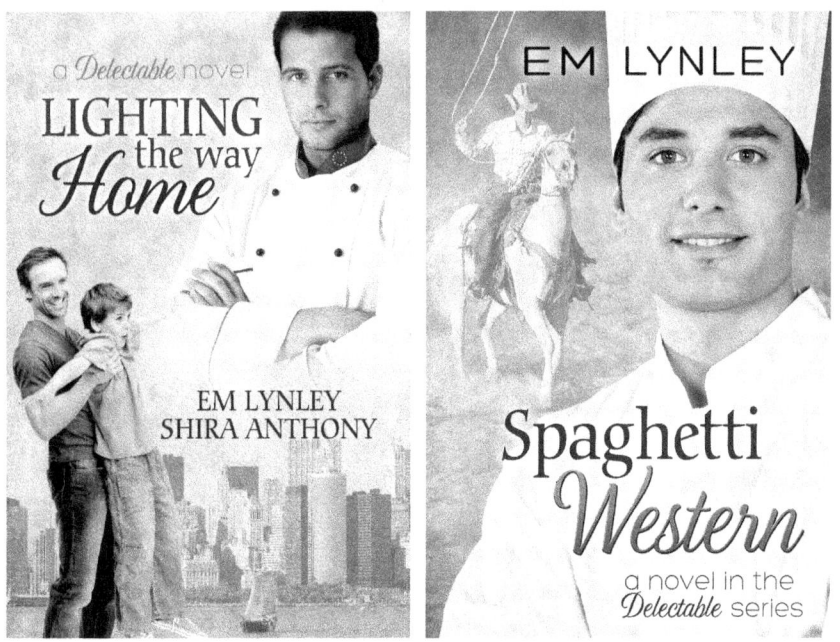